DEADLY DEALS

K. L. GODWIN

authorHOUSE®

AuthorHouse™ UK Ltd.
1663 Liberty Drive
Bloomington, IN 47403 USA
www.authorhouse.co.uk
Phone: 0800.197.4150

Published by AuthorHouse   08/13/2015

ISBN: 978-1-5049-8895-7 (sc)
ISBN: 978-1-5049-8894-0 (hc)
ISBN: 978-1-5049-8896-4 (e)

Print information available on the last page.

CONTENTS

CHAPTER 1

LORD EDWARD HAMSTON

ERVES, CURIOSITY, AND DISPLEASURE. Not the best mixture of emotions, to make the perfect concoction for a clear thinking mind. My head was swimming around with thoughts, doubts and wonders, as I marched through the main entrance to a very old, but stunning manor. I strode with confidence, in an attempt to conceal my feelings of discomfort. As soon as I arrived inside the wonderful, grand main entrance, I couldn't help but take a sudden intake of breath, because of the sheer beauty of the place. The manor never failed to amaze me.

I strolled away from the enormous, glittering chandelier that hung effortlessly above the centre of the main entrance hall. Each little delicate diamond shone like stars in a night sky. I cruised past the dark oak staircase that had fine, gold gilded swirls and patterns on the baluster, with a thick blood-red slice of velvety carpet, casually laid down the centre of the steps. The staircase itself looked wide enough to easily fit a grand piano in the middle of it. It was surrounded by dark oil paintings, which were in very good taste, and matched the dark décor. What a sight! It was such a shame I couldn't admire it for long.

I slowly found myself not focusing on the gorgeous surroundings, but more on myself. Each step I took was with determination, and the strength of my steps echoed down long, vast corridors. My steps slightly quietened down eventually, as the marble flooring turned into thick, heavy, wooden planks beneath my feet. I knew I was very close to the west wing, which made me shudder slightly inside, but I still retained a brave exterior. I knew this manor like the back of my hand, but what unnerved me was, I wasn't sure what was about to happen next.

Before I knew it, I had finally reached the west wing of the manor, and was about to enter a large drawing room, in which I had been instructed via a mysterious email that was sent to me, to go to this very room at a specific time. I stretched out my hand which was slightly shaky, and grasped the rounded brass doorknob. My anxiety suddenly exploded within me, to the point were it felt as if the doorknob was mocking me. I hesitated to open the door in fear. The thought of what could have been waiting for me within this room was a scary aspect, and there was a good reason for my uneasy, and irrational ways, too.

I then decided to hover my free hand close above my pistol which was strapped tightly to my upper thigh, for quick and easy access. I had a deep seated feeling that there was a good possibility I was going to need it. I took a deep, calming breath and pushed the door open, still trying to keep a steady state of mind and body. When the door was fully opened, I took a small yet sturdy step into the old fashioned room.

All was quiet, and peaceful, just like the rest of the manor. I removed my hand away from my pistol and relaxed, but only a little.

"No need to use your gun Sweet, Cheeks!" A rough voice filled my ears, nearly causing me to have a heart attack! As I quickly came to terms with the fact that someone else in this room, my mind processed the voice that sounded so familiar. Then I realised I knew exactly who it was. I peered to my right and saw Ricky Hollow, A.K.A Quick-Shot. His tall, slim body was lingering over the glass alcohol cabinet. "I doubt any trouble will kick off today," he pronounced whilst swiftly plucking a crystal decanter, which appeared to be half full of whisky, out of the cabinet.

I slowly pulled my hand away from my gun, and made my way towards him, but I still didn't feel at ease. Ricky was called Quick-Shot for one very good, and clean reason. He could draw his gun and fire it quicker than you could blink, and his victims were guaranteed to be ripped apart by his bullets. His lightning fast reactions and moves, and his reputation for never missing a target was what made him an exceptional killer, and also a big threat.

"You honestly think I can relax, when soon enough there will be another three world-class assassins joining us? How can you be so chilled?" I was puzzled as to how Ricky was able to keep his cool attitude about himself, unless it was all a front. Ricky grinned at me cheekily, whilst brushing his muscular right hand through his thick, smooth-looking, hair.

"Easy!" He laughed to himself, whilst lifting his whiskey into the air, and winking at me. "Alcohol kills the nerves!" he then explained, as he enjoyed a sip of his drink.

"And kills the brain!" I told him as I rolled my eyes and shook my head.

I perched myself on the edge of a very long, but extremely comfortable sofa. I started to admire the exquisite room I was in, as I tried to settle down. A roaring fireplace filled the room with warmth. Large, arched windows that were lined up along the exterior wall, allowed light to flood in, and provided a stunning view of the late Lord Edward Hamston's estate. Old bookshelves covered a large section of the wall at the opposite end of the room, which towered over the giant alcohol cabinet with a couple of emerald green armchairs placed at an angle in front of it.

The warmth of the fire began to make me unwind a little, but then my wary eyes caught site of a portrait, and I stiffened up again. A large portrait that was hung high, of the late Lord Edward Hamston, was glaring down onto the room. His face looked aged, and weary. His stern expression however, showed off his authority, power and provided a very clear message that he was not a forgiving man, nor a man to get on the wrong side of. His grey hair sat waved above his wrinkled forehead and his white bushy eye brows, yet it was his eyes that caught my attention the most. The cold, mean stare made me think about his life story. The struggles and successes he had. The nightmares, and dreams he thought long and hard about. I couldn't help but think of the madness that possessed him, simply because of his hatred for people.

In fact Lord Hamston was the reason to why I was here, meeting four other very well known assassins. Despite the fact that Lord Edward Hamston was a gentleman, and was well respected among people and his community many years ago, he had a dark, deep secret that in the end ate him alive and drove him insane. The torture he put himself through was incredible, but the story itself is one of sorrow and heartache.

Lord Edward Hamston's story begun when he was a young man, aged 23. He lived with his family in this manor. His life was perfect, in fact it was more than perfect! He had everything a young, lively, upbeat man could have wanted. A good, caring family who would do anything for him. A beautiful, adoring, girlfriend called Lilly, who he cherished so much with all his heart. Loyal and honest friends who knew how to have a good time. He had everything going for him in life.

Also Edward, at this time in his life, was learning more about the estate that he would inherit someday, and he showed great potential and capability that he wouldn't allow the manor to fall in disrepair, or into debt. He was described as a very bright gentleman, with a business head that sat firmly upon his shoulders. He never seemed to run away from responsibilities, and was able to keep all aspects of his life well balanced. People greatly admired Edward. He thought nothing could go wrong in life, but unfortunately his good fortune wouldn't last forever.

One late evening during autumn, Edward and Lilly were returning to the manor from France, where they had a romantic, long weekend break that was unforgettable. Whilst the two blissful lovers were in France, Edward had proposed and asked for Lilly's hand in marriage, and of course she accepted with delight. They were both on cloud nine, and were full of new hopes and aspirations for their future together. It was all they talked about on the journey home, and both of them had never felt happier.

Edward, when he was alive, had told me that he couldn't wait to get back home, because he had an extra surprise for his perfect, delicate

Lilly. Before he left for France, he had asked his friends and family to throw a surprise engagement party for the love of his life, and to celebrate the wonderful news. He knew she was the one for him, and was sure Lilly would agree to marry him. When they drove up the gravelled drive way, towards the main entrance of the manor, he gazed over to Lilly and told her there was another surprise waiting for her. Her face lit up like a candle in the dark.

As soon as they pulled up outside the manor their smiles were abruptly removed from their faces. There were horrifying, blood-curdling screams and desperate shouts and pleas for help coming from inside the manor. It sounded like the depths of hell just beyond the other side of the front door. It was as if people were being tortured, suffering, put through incredible amounts of pain. Edward knew his friends, and family members were inside. His heart raced, as he had no idea what to expect, or what was happening to them all, but he knew he had to investigate and help those who were in the house. He wasn't prepared to run away, or leave those he cared for.

Lord Hamston ordered Lilly to stay put, and not to move a muscle, as he wanted her to keep out of harms way, but it wasn't like she could move anyway. She had just frozen stiff with fear. Her face was pale, and she looked frightened and confused. She didn't know why there where so many voices bellowing out from behind the doors in such a nightmarish way. Edward's adrenaline pulsed through his body and took control of him. His heart violently pumped away to the point were it felt like it could have shattered his rib cage, and torn through his chest.

Without thinking, Edward aggressively barged through the front doors with all his strength, whilst panic was playing havoc with his emotions. Nothing could have prepared him for the sight he had to endure next. Blood. So much blood. Blood drenched and covered the floor like lakes and rivers. Bodies upon bodies littered the entrance hall, like autumn leaves on the ground. Blood splattered marks redecorated the walls, and limbs were scattered about as if they were nothing. The stench of sweat, fear, and death filled Edward's nostrils. A smell that he never forgot for the rest of his life.

Men in black suits who looked like they were attending a funeral were dotted about the place. In their possession they had smoking guns that had blasted people apart. Some of the men carried machetes with sharp, long blades that sliced everyone into pieces like a butcher chopping up meat. Some men even had heavy, thick metal chains to choke and batter Edward's loved ones to death. The sight was more than overwhelming for poor Edward to take in, and he just stood still in horror not knowing what to do, or what was going on.

Then a man dressed in a white suit caught Edward's eye. He stood a few steps up on the stair case, in a splatter free zone watching all the chaos unfold. He stuck out like a sore thumb. It was almost as if he thought he was god. This man had a straight face, and didn't show a flicker of any reaction, remorse, regret nor sentiment. Evil.

As if Edward wasn't scared enough, he was cruelly faced with his mother, Lady Amelia, being forcefully held up by her hair. A man in a black suit had a clump of her mousy, greying hair in a big knot in his hand. He brought her to her knees, whilst raising her up from the floor by her hair. Lady Amelia looked like she was dead already, as she was so shell-shocked in her surroundings, and witnessing the death of so many people she knew, she couldn't do or say anything. She didn't even flinch with pain as she was dragged to her knees. She was whiter than linen, and limper than a dead plant. It was almost like she was ready to die, and had given up trying to survive; maybe she didn't want to survive after the terrifying ordeal.

Before Lord Hamston had a chance to do anything, a long, blood-soaked machete was raised into the air. Edward could just about make out the expression on his mother's face. Amelia used her last bit of energy to screw up her eyes as tight as she could, and let out one last spine-shattering scream which echoed in a haunting way. One quick swipe of the blade and the scream stopped. Edward could hear the echo of his mother's scream, and listened to it until the echo finally died. The man was still holding his mother's head mid-air. The loud thud of her body hitting the blood-spewed floor filled his mind with rage, hatred, and pure distress. Then the black-suited man carelessly dropped his mother's head onto the floor, as if it was rubbish, and Edward roared as loud as he could.

All went quiet. Nothing happened. Edward wanted to faint and collapse, but his adrenaline was too much for him to handle, it was the only thing that was keeping him up right. The 20 or so men, dressed in black suits looked at him along with the white-suited man. Before he knew it Lilly had heard the heart-wrenching shout from Lord Hamston and ran to his side. She then let out a whimpering sound and within seconds tears streamed down her face like waterfalls. The white-suited man gave a simple nod of his head, and with that, all the black-suited men charged towards them both.

Edward roughly grabbed Lilly's hand and dragged her along whilst he ran for safety, but they were out-chased and outnumbered. Edward suddenly felt a sharp, stinging sensation that flooded his aching body. A wet feeling was trickling down the front, and back of him, he wanted to fall down, but was unable to. He peered down and to his horror he was faced with a machete blade impaled through the middle of his torso. Lilly yelled, as the blade was harshly yanked out of his bleeding body causing Edward to fall to his knees and then sway side to side. He felt his life leak out of him.

Lilly rapidly crouched down in front of him, and grabbed Edward's arms in an attempt to move him. She desperately tried to pick him up, and get him pack on his feet. It was no good. She was too small and weak to even move him an inch. Edwards's dull, dying eyes lazily stared into hers. Lilly's eyes looked like they were drowning in tears of sadness. Edward could feel his world spin violently, and fall apart. He didn't want to lose sight of his love, and certainly didn't want anything awful happen to her.

Out of the blue two men grasped hold of Lilly's thin arms, and lifted her away. They shouted abuse in her face, and insensitively laughed loudly. She frantically kicked her legs into the air, screamed and screeched, and bit and wriggled as much and as hectically as she could, to try and break free. She couldn't get away from the men's impossibly tight grip. Against her will she was heartlessly thrown into the car that they, Lilly and Edward, had happily arrived in.

Edward wanted to shout after her but his mouth was drier than the desert. Every word he tried to say was choking him. He watched his graceful, pretty Lilly vanish into the distance and out of view. No more long flowing light blonde hair. No more soft, pink lips. No more lightly shaded blue eyes. No more gentle touches with her smooth milky skin. She was never seen again after that night. Edward collapsed on the steps leading to the main entrance and everything had turned dark as he lay still helpless and dying.

Against all odds, Edward survived the entire hideous ordeal thanks to a brave, loyal servant called Billy. Billy had got out of the manor, and was waiting for the evil gang to leave so he could go back in and help anyone who had survived. He also had the sense to stealthily, yet efficiently fetch and call for help. Edward was the only one he could help, as the others had all been murdered in such a ghastly manner. The demonic gang did a good job of making sure no one could live another day to tell the tale.

The police started a serious investigation into what had happened. Officers had told Lord Edward Hamston that the person who was responsible for this despicable, cold- hearted slaughtering was a big underworld crime lord known as The Angel, which explained the white suit. It was almost like a sick joke. They explained that the reason to why this had happened was because the Hamston family funds were running low, and they were close losing the estate. This news shocked Edward, as he was learning about the various forms and ways of making money, and was assured by his own father and the financial advisor who was a close friend of the family, that the estate was in good hands and was thriving. He had always assumed that there was plenty of money, and his parents certainly seemed to be well settled and not stressed about any financial difficulties. What good actors they were! Edward felt inexplicably betrayed by his parents, and those who knew of this secret.

It turned out that Edwards's parents got so desperate for money they sank to the lowest of lows in high society. They borrowed money from a crime lord. Edward wished so hard that he could rewind time, and make them avoid making a deal with The Angel. His heart sank to the pits of his empty soul. If only they had told the truth, or even spoken to their own son who had so many intelligent ideas, so many lives may have not come to such a gruesome end. Edward did feel a sense of anger, yet pity towards his parents, because instead of opening up, they put their reputation, status, and authority above all else. If it wasn't for them, Edward would still be holding Lilly.

Time passed and Edward's mother and father couldn't repay The Angel, so everyone had to pay with their lives instead. The Angel was unforgiving and not a patient man. He didn't like being made to look like a fool, or weak. One thing was for sure: it wasn't just the killing of Edward's family that happened that night, it was also a big brutal boost to his limitless reputation, almost a publicity stunt to show other people how powerful and cruel he was.

To make matters worse the police couldn't do anything, or should I say wouldn't. Lord Hamston told me when he was telling me his horrific story, that The Angel had men on the inside of the police force and many an officer had been killed, tortured, and made to suffer for trying to arrest him. It was not just the officers that paid the price for meddling in The Angel's affairs. The officers' families were made to watch the officer die brutally, and then the family would be butchered shortly afterwards one by one. All police officers stayed away from any cases that had The Angel's fingerprints littered all over the scene of a crime. The Angel was untouchable.

However, Edward was not going to let The Angel get away lightly with his unspeakable actions. If the police were not going to do anything, then he certainly was. Untouchable made it sound like a challenge to Edward, and after all he had nothing else to lose. Everything he loved and held close to his heart, had been snatched away, nearly including his own life. Also the thought that Lilly might still be alive drove him to push harder, even though the chances were very slim.

So for months he plotted, and planned his revenge. Edward would dream up evil ways to punish this man for killing his friends, family, and even some of his staff, and of course ripping Lilly away from his life. His loyal servant, Billy, became more concerned each day as Lord Hamston seemed to be going slowly mad. He lost the ability to communicate properly with people, his social life disappeared, and he became a recluse. The hatred just rattled around in his angry mind every second of every painstakingly draining day. How much he wanted to kill these men was unbelievable. It was the fuel that kept him going, and in a way kept him alive. Some nights he wouldn't get a wink of sleep;

some days he wouldn't touch a piece of food. He became obsessed with The Angel.

Eventually, Lord Edward Hamston, managed to put his plan into action, and he did get his own back. One bitter-cold winters night, every one of The Angle's men paid the price for what they had done. Each man dressed up in a black suit seemed so familiar to Edward. They had been living in his mind for months on end. As he bumped each one of them off, and watched them die in pain, as their rotting souls were sent to hell, he gained a sense of enormous pleasure that overwhelmed him. Being covered and splashed in these men's blood seemed to enlighten his moody, mental mind. Each soul he took away from the coffin of these twisted, bloodless bodies, was another soul of Edward's friends and family put to rest.

When it came to The Angel, he wanted him to suffer the most. He knocked The Angel out with one heavy blow to the side of his head. Edward felt a slight crunch of the skull as he knocked him unconscious. Edward tied him to a chair in a dark room, leaving just one dim light on. The light shone down on The Angel. Edward found it amusing and rather ironic. It was almost like looking at a biblical picture, in his crazed mind. The types of picture where angels are always shown in the bright light of God. He knew he would never get to see God, only the deepest depths of hell were he belonged.

It was now time for Edward to play god, just like The Angel had done before hand. The chair to which The Angel was tied underneath the dim shining light, wasn't a normal wooden chair. Edward had found an ancient, wooden chair that looked like it had been through the wars. Shards of prickly wood, which would splinter you just by looking at it, were sticking up from the top of the rough seat, and round the edges. It would feel like sitting on a load of thorns. If the crime lord struggled too much there would be more wood in him than bone. Lord Hamston was going to make him pay, by torturing The Angel as slowly as possible whilst inflicting as much pain as he possibly could.

Edward flicked out a pocket knife, and admired the blade on it. The light kept bouncing off the edge of the blade, as he imagined how good it was going to feel sticking it in. He thought about digging the tip of the knife into The Angel's skin, and then moving the knife deeper and beneath The Angel's nerves and flesh and then giving a sudden slicing motion, and pulling the blade out. Edward stared mercilessly at his victim who was sitting on the wooden, spiked chair still unconscious. Not an ounce of compassion, or doubt went through Edward's mind, only sinful revenge.

Randomly, within the next split second, Edward plunged the knife into The Angel's body, and started to tear him apart. It was as if something had possessed him. Each jab pierced The Angel's skin, split his muscles, and cut his veins and nerves. Each stabbing motion was like anger therapy for Edward. He carried on till The Angel's body was covered in bloody, deep cuts. Edward watched intensely as The Angel's annoying white tattered suit began to turn red as his blood oozed out of him. Then Edward wanted The Angel to feel the throb of agony, and feel startled and staggered, so he woke The Angel up by slapping him brutally over and over again, whilst standing behind him.

The Angel came to his senses, and started to yelp and cry in difficulty when he realised what had happened to his body. It only made Lord Hamston laugh incredibly hard. Edward removed himself from the light and stood in the darkness so The Angel couldn't see him. He silently walked around the circle of light till he reached the front of The Angel. It was almost like playing mind tricks on him. Edward was enjoying playing around with his prey. He was full of joy and happiness watching this criminal struggle for his survival. Nothing could have been better, especially as Edward knew he was going to die, and he would be present to see it happen.

The Angel's eyes darted about in pure panic, as he couldn't stop groaning in pain. His breaths became sharp, shallow and shaky. After a little while of Edward torturing him, and playing tricks, and making him suffer, his tormentor stepped into the light. The Angel knew exactly who Edward was, which only made him freak out even more. Edward grasped The Angel's jaw bone so tightly he could have crushed it with his bare, strong hands. He yanked back The Angel's head so fast, and roughly, he could have given him whip lash, or even have broken his neck. Edward then tied The Angel's head to the back of the chair so his head could not move anywhere, and his eyes were staring up at the light. It was a little tricky to do, as The Angel struggled and tried to prevent Edward achieving what he wanted to do, but it became easier, as The Angel grew weaker from lack of blood.

An old, rustic but tough bit of rope was placed across The Angel's sweaty forehead, and tied neatly to the back of the chair. He tried to resist against the rope and set his head free, but it was physically impossible as he began to feel tired. Before he knew it, Edward gently pulled out a small vial, and began to tease The Angel's, by gently shaking it from side to side in front of his face. The Angel once again, tried to break free by wiggling around, but only caused himself more pain, as shards of wood snapped off the chair, and lay, impaled deeply in his skin.

Inside the vial contained a strong, vile, potent acid, and Edward was going to make the most of it. Calmly, Edward started to let a few drops of acid drip into The Angel's mouth. The Angel attempted to scream, but the more he did the wider his mouth became, which made Edward's job a lot easier and more exhilarating. He admired The Angel's tongue as it burnt, and sizzled away disgustingly. Holes also began to form and grow in his teeth. Every inch of pain Edward could bring to this man, was a moment to hold onto.

The Angel thought he would try and be clever, in his frantic panic and fright. He attempted to clamp his mouth tightly shut, so no more burning acid could get inside him. This did not bother Edward in the slightest, after all, he had acid! Edward carried on pouring the acid onto The Angel's closed lips, and watch his mouth erode away. With a sadistic smile on his face, he knew that this crime lord was not going to get the better of him. The Angel's lips now no longer existed, and the acid erased the whole of his mouth and skin, leaving nothing but bare bone behind.

The mixture of cooking, rotting flesh, mixed with lethal chemicals excited Edward. He carried on tipping the little bottle and listening to the sound of the acid eating away at The Angel's face and the inside of his mouth. There was not a more satisfying noise. The acid started to burn his teeth away, and before he knew it, Edward tipped the rest of the acid down his enemy's throat. The Angel couldn't help but swallow. Edward stepped back and watched the gruesome performance.

Blood carried on spewing out of the deep cuts, and the acid was destroying his insides, like putting ice on a hot frying-pan. The screams of agonising pain stopped, as his voice box had been destroyed. Edward could hear him trying to gasp for air, but it was impossible for him to breathe. A minute later the struggling stopped. His eyes were still wide open though. Edward carried out one last action to this man. He heartlessly smashed the glass vial across his eyes and the bridge of his nose, and peacefully strolled away, as the last tiny bits of acids corroded his eyes and nose away. What a mess!

Shortly after that wonderful event, Edward was faced with another situation. He didn't know what to do with his estate, and the money issues. He knew now, there was no money to be repaid, and he wasn't prepared to surrender the manor either. He felt it was something he must fight for, and keep hold of. He had now inherited the debt that his parents had left him, and even he couldn't think of a way out of it. It did become a major worry, which he grew extremely irate about, as he couldn't enjoy and bask in his sweet victory against The Angel.

One day when Edward started to get desperate for ideas and money, he was approached by a stranger in the little, nearby local village he lived. The stranger gave him an opportunity to make some money. Whoever this man was, seemed to know that Edward was responsible for killing of The Angel. Edward didn't like the fact he knew, as he had no idea how he found out. Maybe people heard about the death of The Angel, and automatically linked it back to him. It made him wonder if the police would investigate, and interview him too, although when he thought harder about it, the police owed him one, as they could get on with their jobs and live peacefully, and more effectively too.

This man made a deal with Lord Hamston. He offered a fairly large sum of money to kill a certain man who was well known around the village, but he wasn't known for any good reasons. He was a nightmare, and a pain in the arse to everyone. His name was Brut. Brut was a drunk! He slept with men's wives, even worse he despicably raped, and took advantage of other women. He was a bully. He used his weight and threatening looks to get his own way and intimidate others. No one wanted to stand up to him because he was an ugly, scary, thug.

Edward accepted the offer, but told the stranger, under strick instruction, not to breathe a word to another living soul, or he would come after him. Edward completed the job, and was paid handsomely. Through one brutal killing, he made others very happy. He enjoyed killing the bad people to make others more relaxed, and at peace. It made him feel oddly wholesome, and gave him another purpose in life. He gained so much work, he was raking in the money. He started to travel further and further afield, killing people on request, in exchange for money. He then grew to call himself an assassin. It was odd to think that Edward had The Angel to thank for his new profession, and lease of life.

Ever since Edward drew his first drop of blood, he had urges to kill. He was like a wolf, once he got the taste of blood he just wanted more of it. So he was happy, glad and relieved it became a career for him, whilst achieving some good. He trained himself for years, perfecting everything there was to know about being an assassin. He never failed a mission, and was soon becoming renowned around the world among other assassins. Some assassins admired him for his dedication, determination, and daring ways, but other assassins were displeased with him. They saw him as a rogue, a danger, a want-to-be-assassin. So much so, that some people had tried and attempted to murder Edward just to get him out the way, but none succeeded, proving his power, and that he was worthwhile to call himself an assassin, and eventually he was left alone.

One night Edward's servant, Billy, bitterly fell out with Lord Hamston, and was making a right ruckus. Billy didn't agree with Edward's murderous actions, and believed that killing was not right, morally wrong, and that Edward showed characteristics of a mad person so he threatened to tell the police. Those were soon to be Billy's final words. Edward acted calmly, and pretended that he didn't care, and asked Billy to leave the drawing room, and to stop acting like a soppy child.

As Billy stomped away from Edward feeling furious, Edward bolted towards him. Quickly, Billy spun his heels, and was faced with his Lord's face in his. Before, he could react, and take in what was happening he could feel himself moving backwards. Edward had a tight hold on his puny arms. Warm heat pressed up against Billy's back. It suddenly hit Billy that Edward was pushing him towards the lit fire. Fiercely, Billy lashed out in fear for his life, harshly resisting Edward's pushing, but Edward had just flipped and lost control of himself. The strength of his body was much greater than Billy's narrow framed body. Billy hollered out cries for help, which were ear piercingly loud. No matter how hard Billy tried to get away, and push himself away from the dancing flames, it was no use.

Poor, young Billy even resorted to begging for his life, but it was as if Edward didn't know him. It was almost like he had forgotten that he was about to kill the man who had saved him, from the clutches of death. Edward had changed into a different person. The power, reputation, and madness had finally broken him. Lord Hamston's expression on his face made him look psychotic, and his eyes were empty as if he had no soul.

Billy was literally leaning into Edwards's body as the heat of the fire made him feel sick. Edward paused, and examined Billy for a brief moment and let him hang there in his arms. Billy's eyes meet his, and before he knew it there was one final hard shove and Billy flew backwards. The fire ate his scrawny, exhausted body, like he didn't even exist. The hot flames twirled and twisted around him. It almost looked like the flames were wrapping him up in a tight cocoon. In seconds the smell of burnt human flesh gathered in the room.

After watching Billy cruelly burn to death, it was then that he had realised that Billy was right. He stood back in astonishment, still inhaling the dirty air. Edward admitted to himself he had turned mad, and that it was as if his feelings had disappeared; as if they had died the night that he should have died. He stood frozen not knowing what to do. He then, to his surprise, realised that there were no feelings of remorse, or sorrow for what he had done. It was as if death and killing had become a hobby, just a simple part of life.

Ever since the late Lord Edward Hamston had told me this story it made me realise that this man was someone that you couldn't fully trust, but a couple of years after the death of Billy, he decided that he wanted other people to do his dirty work for him. The police had become suspicious of Lord Edward Hamston. So he sort of 'adopted' me and four other young people, not all at the same time. He trained us up into people who would do him proud. We almost became his own children, but like I said this is not a man you could fully trust. I had been in his care since the age of 12 years. Thanks to him I felt like I too had a purpose in life. I am now an accomplished assassin.

I don't consider myself to be mad, and I know for a fact that I am still very well connected to my emotions. I just bury them deep down inside me most of the time and try to ignore them. Feelings and a conscience is not good in my line of work. It makes everything a lot harder than it needs to be. You have to have a clear, sharp thinking mind to be someone like me. A killer.

CHAPTER 2

THE DEAL

"I T'S A SHAME WHAT happened to Edward, isn't Grace? Couldn't believe it when I heard the news that Edward had recently died. Bit of a bummer really!" Ricky pronounced, whilst pottering towards my direction, and studying his surroundings carefully. His eyes too, became fixated on the giant painting of Edward, which loomed over us both. "Here," he huffed pushing a crystal cut, whiskey glass underneath my nose. "You look like you need one." I peered up at Ricky with a stern facial expression that clearly showed the lack of trust I had in him. He slightly backed off, whilst releasing the glass into my hand, trying to act like he wasn't a threat towards me. "Don't worry, I haven't poisoned it or anything. I'm not the one you have to watch out for!" I couldn't help but let out a slight anxious giggle, whilst silently agreeing, as I knew too well he was probably speaking the truth.

Five minutes had passed very slowly and tensely. I spoke very little within that small amount of time, but if I was being honest, Ricky was doing most of the talking. I knew Ricky could be a chatter-box at the best of times, but something gave me the impression that he was simply chatting endlessly, because secretly he was worried as well. Assassins are not people to trust, and we like to keep our weary distance from one another, but as Lord Edward Hamston had recently passed away we were all called together for a meeting. I could only presume this meeting was a reading of a will, or something along those lines. Certainly wasn't going to be a joyful occasion!

I started to think whether I'd miss Edward or not. After all, we were all like his own children in an odd way. It was hard to say if his parting was going to be tough on any of us. Only time would tell, and reveal all. My mind then began to wander off in a trail of thoughts. Ricky's voice eventually was blocked from my ears as he carried on talking. My mind was now firmly set on thinking about the other three assassins, who were soon to join mine and Ricky's company, very soon.

One of the assassins who would be joining us was a woman called Hazel Clarence, more commonly known as Lady Luck. She wasn't the most talented assassin among the group. In fact, it seemed like she had survived just on luck itself, hence her nickname. How she managed to get away with some of her killings was a miracle. She'd complete her missions by the skin of her teeth. I found it rather annoying that she never seemed to put much effort, or skill into her line of work; not like the rest of us. She did have one 'talent' that she enjoyed using quite often to lure her prey into a false sense of security. *Seduction*! A woman like her, with her stunning curves, big bosom, swaggering hips, and a soft, innocent toned voice, could pull any man with one killer wink of an eye.

Then there was Karl Fletch, but everyone called him Gizmo. His extra name does indicate what he specialises in. Gizmo had amazing knowledge of the ins and outs of anything mechanical! He also loved his technology, therefore he was always experimenting and fiddling about with anything electrical. Gizmo was insanely intelligent too; I would even describe him as a genesis. The way his mind worked was chaotic but beautiful. Because of these aspects that he had high attributes in, he was a lethal assassin. Yes, physically he couldn't win a gun, knife, or fist fight, or anything like that, but he didn't need to be able to. Gizmo could kill people without being anywhere near them. I would say Gizmo was definitely the one I was most afraid of. He has been known to set up some pretty nifty traps, and torture techniques as well.

For example, Gizmo was once given the task of eliminating a man called Joseph Lingway. Joe came from a long line of criminals and over the years became incredibly powerful, and near enough untouchable. That was no problem for Gizmo as his brilliant mind came up with a fearfully cunning plan. He had recently been filling his bulging mind with the exploration of infrasound, which was the study of low frequency sounds, and the effects the vibrations could have, particularly on a human body.

Gizmo noted that the low frequency sounds would cause certain vibrations that would have an effect on the human body, but not on the ears, therefore not being able to detect the sound, as long as the sound levels were bellow 20Hz, 20 Hertz. This would cause people to suffer symptoms of Vibroacoustic Syndrome. The effects of the infrasonic outputs would mainly affect the fluid parts of the body at first, and would cause humans to be able to feel invisible beating waves hitting their body, and inflicting pain. It even had the potential of damaging internal organs, making them feel like jelly, but depending on the volume, make-up, and the power of the infrasound, it proved it could affect any part of the body.

Gizmo learnt that at a 130 dB, 130 decibels, it would cause direct pressure to the inner ear, making people's hearing become distorted, which affected people's ability to understand speech. At 150 dB, subjects began to feel nauseated, and the body would also begin to vibrate. The main area that was most subject to the vibration was the chest and the abdomen. 166 dB, breathing problems occurred. The low pulses affect the lungs. Finally, at 177 dB the infrasound would induce artificial respiration at an abnormal rhythm, causing other health problems.

On top of all this gruesome, but useful information Gizmo had obtained, he became aware that if the vibration was to pass through a substrate, such as the ground, the vibrations would pass through the body via the skeleton, causing major damage to bones and joints. With all this fresh new information to hand, he wanted to try it out and this target, Joe Lingway, was perfect to try it out on.

Gizmo had meticulously and perfectly made and planted a device, which would play the infrasound, underneath the floor boards to a small, enclosed pool shed at a hotel that Joe was staying at in Rio.

Gizmo had also managed to invent a minuscule device that would lock the door behind Joe, after he had enter the shed, by motion detectors. Gizmo knew no member of staff would go inside the pool shed at this time of night, because there was no need for them to do so. He managed to lead Joe into the pool shed at 11:45 pm, by leaving a trail of recordings to catch his attention and lead him inside the shed.

Meanwhile, Gizmo was sitting up in his hotel room, cleverly out of sight, and out of the way, and was watching Joe walk towards his death. As soon as the door was locked behind Joe, all Gizmo had to do was push a button which triggered the sound to play.

Gizmo had a rotating knob on his little control pad, so he could increase the power and impact of the vibrations. I could only imagine what was going through Gizmo's mind as he casually looked on from afar, as his master plan was working like a dream. Gizmo eventually turned the device to its maxim, making sure no one else was around or close by who might have been able to feel the effects of the vibrations, and after a little while he turned the device off. He knew for a fact that Joe had died. No one could have survived that. He did wait to see if there were any signs of movement, but there were none. Joe's bones, joints, and organs had been destroyed. The mission was a success, and the assassination baffled police. The device itself was simply turned off and left under the floorboards and was never detected.

"So this is where the party's at!" A loud, thick, booming voice bellowed through my mind, snapping me back to the present day. Ricky was the first to greet Tank. His humongous, bulging, muscular body made Quick Shot look so pathetic and weak. Tank always wore a tight tank top, and baggy jeans, so people could get the full display of his muscles, which he was ever so proud of and never modest about. Tank was ridiculously strong. He was so strong in fact, he could probably blow a puff of air, and knock our heads off! He had thudding veins that popped out of his arms and the sides of his head, and had shaved tribal patterns amongst his short hair, as a haircut.

Despite his size and thuggish looks, I got along well with Tank. His real name was Aiden Dill. The only reason why I got along with Tank was because he was the only other assassin that I had spent time with. Not by choice however. I had been under the care of Lord Hamston for about five years, and then he came across Tank. I was then given the task to look after Tank and help him with his training, as Tank was not a fast learner, and Edward grew impatient with Tank's ways.

So after my own long, hard, back-breaking training sensation with Edward, I would take time out and bring Tank up to speed and help him improve. I never knew how Lord Hamston felt about me training Tank, I didn't dare ask either. I could never tell if he disproved of it, or whether he was glad that someone could get through to Tank. Tank had always been one sandwich short of a picnic.

I gradually stood up, and when I was fully straightened Tank's heavy looking eyes looked at me. His face lit up with glee,

"Ace!" he cried out to me, and rushed over as fast as his tree trunk legs would carry him.

"Hello... TANK!" I winced as he scooped me up into his big arms, and swung me into the air, whilst giving me a loving hug. My feet were dangling off the floor, and I felt as if I was being crushed by a boa constrictor. Tank had a bad habit of forgetting his own strength, but a feeling of euphoria washed over me as I was glad to have Tank by my side. It had been many years since I last received one of his bear hugs.

I could hear Quick Shot chuckling away to himself in the background. He was still standing by the doorway. I glared evilly at him, over Tank's massive shoulder, to warn him to be quiet. He immediately stopped laughing, but I could tell he was biting his lip, as his eyes focused on the floor.

"I'm so happy to see you," said Tank as hr clumsily put me down.

"So am I." I smiled up at him. For the first time today I felt a little bit more relaxed and at ease. Having Tank by my side was like having a faithful companion, almost like a pet dog!

"You too actually know each other well then?" Quick Shot raised an eye brow whilst taking a couple of paces forward,

"Yeah, she's my friend!" Tank replied in a slightly goofy voice. "She helped me with my training years ago." He chucked his hefty arm around my shoulders nearly knocking me forward. "People got annoyed with me, because they said I was slower than a snail travelling backwards, but Ace helped me!"

Quick Shot had a surprised expression on his face whilst muttering, "So you do have a heart, Grace!"

"Shut your face Ricky, it's not the time nor place to drag up the past," I barked back angrily.

You see, myself and Ricky have a little bit of history together. We had been seeing one another for only a couple of months, but Ricky allowed his heart to slowly get involved, and it was more than I could handle. I had never been in a position like that before, and I didn't like it. The feeling of falling for someone made me sick, and to settle down was something I never wanted to do at that point in my life. I still didn't want any serious commitment, or relationships of any sort. I was at the top of my profession, and nothing was going to stop me enjoying it. I then ended it and wanted nothing more to do with him.

I tried to explain that having emotional attachments would throw me of my game, and I couldn't allow myself to get like that, plus he should know better as well. Ricky took it as meaning that I was using him for sex, which wasn't the case. It was so important for me to keep my distance from my own feelings. It was how I managed to concentrate, and that was why I'm at the top of my profession today. Again it left another bitter after-taste for Ricky, as he thought I loved my line of work more than him, which in retrospect, I did.

Quick Shot rolled his eyes, took a massive gulp of his whiskey.

"Oh lookie!" he shouted sarcastically, "I think that there… what you're feeling right now is, annoyance, or possibly anger?"

"Fuck sake!" I blurted out, "don't you ever let anything drop! We were over years ago, and it was only a couple of months of sex!"

"See you were using me!"

"NO I BLOODY WASN'T, YOU WILL NEVER UNDERSTAND!" I screamed, and to my horror I realised that I had truly lost my temper. "You always know the best way to bring the worst out in people." I could feel Tank trying to pat me on the back to calm me down. I politely smiled and whispered to him, "I'm okay, it's just some children never grow up." Before any more drama could kick off Lady Luck showed up.

Her entrance was so glamorous and glorious like always. She gracefully swept in, whilst her brunette, slightly curled hair, lightly bounced and brushed against her slim shoulders. She wore a red dress that tightly hugged and squeezed every curve and line of her body. Her bosom was proudly protruding out, and her long legs were on show for everyone to see.

"Good day Gentlemen. Hello my darling Ace." She softly spoke, almost sounding like the famous Marilyn Monroe. "Boy, the atmosphere is tense in here. Did I hear a little shouting match going on my darlings? I don't want the drama to start without me." I didn't say a word, no one did. Lady Luck peered over at me, and then at Ricky, slowly looking him up and down whilst pouting her thick red lips. She must have over heard the shouting in the corridor as she approached the room. She casually strolled over towards Tank and I, and as she did, I watched Ricky almost blush, and he ogled her behind. *Pathetic!* Hazel settled herself down beside me as I sat.

"You certainly have got a glow about you darling," she said, whilst admiringly,

"Thank you."

"Maybe its previous lovers that brings it out in you." She chuckled to herself. I just simply looked away and stared at the floor dully, and biting my tongue viciously. "Oooo, drinkies, I wouldn't mind having one."

She suddenly looked over at Ricky, dropping a hint that he should be a gentleman, and get her one, but all Quick Shot did was shrug, "Drinks are in the alcohol cabinet, it's over there love!" Quick Shot told her bluntly as he tilted his head.

Hazel let out a loud sigh, and rudely told him, "One day you will understand women." She sexily started to strut over to the drinks, and as soon as she was out of ear shot, I tugged at Tank's jeans pocket. He looked down at me, puzzled.

I whispered in a bitchy tone, "I don't know who she thinks she is, bloody prima donna. If anyone's an expert on past lovers, it's her; she's had plenty of them!" I threw myself back in the sofa, wishing I could get out of here and soon! I have an Ex in the room, and now a soppy tart who is a sorry excuse for a woman. Tank sat down alongside me, and said the last comment I wanted to hear, especially coming from him.

"She's very pretty!" I watched Tank watching her. Lady Luck was bent over the alcohol cabinet, swaying her bottom about.

I sighed tiredly, and told Tank, "I promise you, she maybe pretty on the outside, but her insides are full of daggers waiting to stab someone in the back."

"Really!?!?!" Tank sounded flabbergasted. It was as if Tank thought I was being literal. His voice sounded like a child finding out that Santa Claws didn't exist. Mind you Tank really wasn't the sharpest tool in the box. It wouldn't surprise me if he still believed in Santa!

"NO." I placed my hand on my forehead, and tried to think of a way to warn Tank away from that slag. I did care about Tank. I felt like he was a younger brother, which made me feel like it was my duty to scare him off of people like that. "Let's put it this way." I leaned into Tank, and spoke a little slower. "You wouldn't want her for a steady diet, you'll get hurt." Tank pulled away from me, and sat still for a moment.

"What like heartburn, or a stomach ache?" I took a steady breath in whilst dropping my head, and I decided it would be easier to agree with him.

"Yes." I huffed. There was a brief moment of silence, until Tank pointed something out to me.

"I think Quick Shot is going to get a stomach ache."

"What?" I frowned looking at Ricky. Ricky's mouth had dropped wide open. He looked as if he was catching flies. His eyes were stuck on Hazel, like glue sticking paper together. "He's got more sense than that surely." Tank just shrugged as a silent reply. "Come to think of it, this is Ricky, and he'd shag a crack in a china plate if he got the chance to...men!" I felt like pulling my face off at this point. I didn't know how much longer I was going to be able to keep myself under control. The stress levels in me were rising.

Hazel then danced her way over to me again. I took another deep, calming breathe in an attempt to keep myself nice and calm before she threw another mindless comment into the open air. It was amazing how normally I am level-headed, cool, and collected, but today, this situation and these people were just making me go bonkers.

"Darling." There it was again the annoying '*darling*'. She obviously doesn't have a good vocabulary! "You know, you look like you have put more weight on. Why is that?" I looked at her in complete astonishment. I didn't know how to react. Did Hazel know she was being rude and insulting? It was like she was completely oblivious to what she was saying to people. Hazel was just opening her big mouth, and bumping her gums because her brain wasn't engaged.

"She is not big, I am." Tank stood up, and started to show off his muscles. Flexing and bending his arms and pecks, doing his usual show off routine.

"Darling sit down, no one cares." Lady Luck spat, turning her head away looking disinterested, whilst flicking her hand sharply up into the air, showing the palm of her hand to Tank's face, as a sign for him to go away. My blood begun to boil. I saw Ricky walking over, to get closer to us, so he could listen in on the ear bashing that Tank and I were receiving. Tank looked disheartened, and placed himself on the very end of the sofa in an attempt to keep his distance. It was like he had been playing with fire and burnt himself. I couldn't help but feel sorry for him, but I hoped he had lost interested in that snobby tart, and would stay away from her, yet I felt I had to say something to Lady Luck, because I wasn't going to put up with her behaviour for much longer.

"Hazel, don't be so harsh to Tank," I gently told her, trying to pretend that her past comments hadn't riled me. Lady Luck let out a slight amused laugh.

"Oh, he's not hurt, he's just a big bruiser. I'd be amazed if he has feelings darling."

That was it! I felt sorry enough for Tank as it was, but now, she had leapt off the line! Tank would never stand up and shout at a woman like Lady Luck. Not because he was a friendly giant, but because he was not witty enough to deal with her words firing out at him, like bullets being fired out of a machine gun. No matter how hard I tried I couldn't bite my tongue any more or I'd bite it off.

"Look, listen here."

"AHHH, Gizmo there you are!" Ricky rushed over to him interrupting me.

A small, skinny, creepy looking man walked in. His hair was jet black, with a lot of jell in it. In fact he had enough jell to style all of our hair cuts. He was wearing a scruffy T-shirt, and plain black trousers. He wore thick black framed glasses and had stubble growth across his chin.

"Hi there everyone." He snorted. His short legs carried his tiny body over to a coffee table as he abruptly announced, "Everyone please gather around. I was given this disc at the air port by a member of staff there, they didn't know who left it for me." We all looked bewildered, and confused, but Gizmo carried on talking. "However there was a letter attached to the disc." He pulled it out of his pocket, and with his small hands opened it, then laid it out on the table for all of us to see.

I examined the writing quickly, and it didn't take me long to figure out whose writing it was. The curls and flicks of the pen-written letters gave it all away for me.

"It's Edwards's hand writing, I know it well," I announced.

"Indeed it is." Gizmo replied. The curiosity grew in me, and started to take over. Ricky's voice then filled the air as he took charge, and started to read the letter out. It was very brief.

"The disc that I have left you will provide you answers, and a speech from me, as I want to say my final goodbyes to every one of you." Ricky paused for a moment, as we all assumed it was very strange for Edward to want to do something like this, and then carried on. "P.S. I would like you to open my favourite bottle of port, and drink a fond farewell to me, it's the least I ask of you."

Ricky placed the letter back down on the table. No one spoke for a little while. In my mind the note seemed to kind and pleasant to sound like Edward, although, there again, if he knew he was dying he may have wanted to leave us with something sweet. Ricky spoke once again, his voice had a sorrow sound to it.

"I'll go and get the bottle."

Sharply, Gizmo asked, "How do you know what his favourite bottle of port was?"

"I used to drink with Edward late in the evenings. We passed many nights swigging back drinks, and we used to drink plenty of the port that Edward is talking about in the note." I studied Ricky's body language, and I noticed that so far he had been putting on a brave face. He looked like he was reminiscing about their times together. Quick Shot was obviously fond of Edward; more than any of us.

"I'll prepare the disc for all of us to watch," Gizmo said, quickly pulling all sorts of bit and bobs out of a boring looking, black backpack.

"Darlings?" The annoying pitched voice echoed through the room.

"What?" Ricky replied whilst slowly walking towards us with glasses and an old bottle of port. The label was in tatters and peeling off the side of the bottle. There was an air of concern in Hazel's voice.

"What actually happened to Edward?" She took a dramatic sharp breathe in, "I was never told." Tank tried to explain what he thought might have happened.

"I think he killed himself."

"Why would he do that!?!" She sounded horrified. "Look at this place, why would anyone kill themselves when they live in a place like this? Granted it needs updating but still!" I looked at Hazel, and wanted to slap her! The levels of disrespect she was showing was unreal.

"You really need to think more about what you're saying," I told Hazel sternly.

She didn't really show any reaction, and ignored me, which only fired me up even more. It was as if she was asking for a fight, and I'd have no problem tearing her pretty little face to pieces. She certainly would not have a smug smile, nor any beauty after I'd finished with her! Finally though, Hazel did shut up after about five minutes of ranting, and her telling us why Edward shouldn't have killed himself, but to be honest none of us fully knew what happened to Lord Hamston. The silence was lived short when Lady Luck opened her large mouth again. She poked me in my side with her long nail, which made me shiver.

With a confused look on her face she asked me, "I have always been meaning to ask you something, why do people call you Ace?" At this point in time I was about to spit venom, and I could see at the corner of my eye everyone's eyes watching me tensely.

I then answered the question, snappily, "Because I'm the best at what I do."

"I don't see how darling, it's a rather brash statement." She looked at me with a face that I wanted to rip off. The others picked up on the fact that any second I was going to flip and scream the place down. I began to feel venomous anger within me.

Luckily Gizmo piped up, "Everyone, the disc is ready to play."

An image of Lord Edward Hamston was projected onto a space on the wood panelled wall.

"Hello to you all." The posh well spoken-man greeted us. "I know this is probably an inconvenience to all of you, and I am sorry about that." I found it chilling to find Lord Hamston talking to us now even though he had passed away. "I will assume that you are wondering what has happened to me." Lord Hamston peered away from the camera for a brief moment and stared straight back into the camera lenses. It was almost like he was trying to compose himself, and remain confident and cheery. "I have fallen ill with cancer." My heart stopped. I was so shocked. As far as I was concerned, Edward was well in himself and was as fit as a fiddle. He never let on this fact to any of us, that he had such a crippling illness.

He carried on talking. "The cancer has developed too much for doctors to stop it, there's nothing they can do about it. I didn't want to tell any of you about this. As you know I have always been full of secrets, and fairly enclosed about my personal dealings." My eyes quickly darted around the table. Everyone looked just as surprised as the next person. "But this is my way to tell you all what happened to me, and to say my final goodbyes."

Hazel started to whimper and shudder next to me. "All raise your glasses please." Everyone grabbed hold of a glass, and raised it up into the air. Edward had a glass as well, and made a toast. "To my hard work and your success." Then he tentatively took a sip. Everyone else copied Edwards's words and actions, and we all drank the port. The strong taste burst in my mouth, as I could feel the warmth of the alcohol trickle down inside me.

"Now, down to business." Edward abruptly spoke aloud. His voice changed drastically, and straight away I sensed something was wrong. This uneasy feeling was driving me crazy, but Edward sounded like he had a plan up his sleeve. I was all too familiar with his mannerisms, and so was everyone else. "I assume you also think that you will be getting money, or a part of the estate as you are like my family." He started to smile. The crooked smile suddenly struck fear into my heart, as a massive amount of doubt suddenly blasted across my mind. "I shall tell you what I will leave you." A sadistic look covered his eyes. I began to feel sick with panic. Something wasn't right and I just knew that I wasn't going to like what I was about to hear next. "Your lives," Edward announced.

"What?" Tank grunted in confusion.

"I have poisoned the bottle of port which you have just drunk from." My fears were confirmed. A terrible feeling ran through my body.

"YOU BASTARD! YOU FUCKING BASTARD!" Ricky bellowed out, slamming the glass harshly down onto the table, whilst the others turned white.

"The poison will have already started to work, but don't threat! There is a way to save yourselves." My fists were clenched up so tightly, my knuckle had turned white. "I have some unfinished business that needs taking care of. There are a number of people that I never got the chance to eliminate, so now I am passing the tasks down to all of you." Edward slouched back into his arm chair, and banged his feet up onto a table. It was almost as if he was making pleasant conversation with a friend, instead of threatening us with our lives. He seemed so relaxed, and at peace with himself. "Now, if you all complete the list of people that I want you to kill, you will be given a bottle each with a cure for the poison." He clamped his old wrinkly hands together, and placed them close to his face. "The poison is a slow working poison, and it will take 3 months to kill you. I, of course, invented the poison, so don't try and act like smart arses by attempting to find a cure."

I felt like I was in the worst nightmare anyone could dream about. I already felt like I was in the depths of hell.

"Obviously these killings will not be easy, hence the incentive for working for your lives." Edward peered up, and said in a slight sarcastic voice, "In fact these missions that I am sending you on are practically suicide missions." He let out an evil chuckle and joked, "But I guess it doesn't matter if they are, you'll die either way if you don't achieve what I want." A hard solid lump formed in my throat, which made me want to vomit my guts up. I couldn't even begin to tell you how much rage was pulsing through my veins. The betrayal was horrendous. I felt like Edward had stabbed the knife into my back, and given it a good twist on the way out. "Oh yes." Edward began talking again. Each word he spoke, I ended up hating him even more. "I'm just about to piss you all off even more."

"Fuck sake!" Ricky blurted out, it was almost like he had Tourette's, but I didn't blame him for his reactions.

"You will all have to work together as a team to be able to complete these tasks that I have left for you. It will be a hundred percent impossible for you to do it all by your lonesome." That was it. I couldn't work with these people, I certainly didn't want to. This was my idea of a punishment, for all the bad things I had done in my life. *I fly solo*. I don't have any lackeys! That would probably get me killed. I was livid with the situation that I had been stuck in. "For the information and names of the people that I want you to go after, head to my work office in the east wing where you will find everything you need." Gizmo let out a massive sigh, as Tank look like he was going to explode into thousands pieces. "There is a little bonus for you all though." Everyone's ears picked up, praying for any type of good news. "You will all be sleeping and living in my beautiful manor while you are working together. You'll need to as you'll be working together, all hours of the day and night."

Those were not the words I wanted to hear. His way with words was cruel and bitter. It was like his tongue was a dagger, stabbing each and every one of us. "See you guys in hell." He let out a villainous laugh, then Edward vanished from the wall, and that was that.

BANG! Everyone jumped out of their skins as Tank's fist smashed in the wall with fury where Edwards face had been. His iron like fist went through the wall with ease. Everyone froze. No one breathed, moved, or spoke. There were loud snapping noises of wood breaking off the wall as Tank yanked his fist out. He had left a massive gaping hole behind.

"I'm glad that wasn't my face!" Ricky joked trying to lighten the mood a little, but no one wanted to hear jokes.

Gizmo snapped, "This isn't the time for jokes!" No one spoke again, for a little while. The silence was deafening, and then Gizmo flew off the handle, jumping and flaying his arms around. "You poisoned us didn't you?" He violently pointed and shook his stubby finger in Ricky's face.

"Wait, what.... are you accusing me of poisoning everyone, and then myself?"

"No I'm accusing you of poisoning us, and not yourself, you're the one that got the bloody drinks!"

Everyone coldly stared at Ricky as he then shouted, "How fucking dare you accuse me of doing that, and anyway it could be you that set this up!"

"Oh yeah, how?" Gizmo started to square up to Ricky. Ricky deliberately stood so close to Gizmo it dwarfed him.

"You were the one that was mysteriously given this note and disc by some stranger."

Then a loud thud happened next to me. I felt the floor bounce slightly. I quickly looked and saw Hazel had collapsed. "Oh fucking great, she's so bloody dramatic," Ricky spat out in the heat of the moment. I crouched down next to her and examined her. "Why are you even bothering with her Grace?"

"Because Ricky I want to make sure it's not the poison that has done this to her."

"Of course it isn't!" His voice began to get slightly higher pitched with frustration. "You heard what that old bastard said to us, three months, and then we die." I stood up with a sense of purpose as something flash through my mind.

"Oh god, what a clever man." Gizmo then followed my statement up with a question.

"What's so clever?"

"Don't you see what Edward has done as an extra challenge?" Tank, Gizmo, and Ricky looked at one another, exchanging looks. "He's chosen people he wants dead, and he knows we have to work as a team, and look at us now, already we are bickering and fighting like children." They all looked at me in horror. "We have to work together so I suggest no more bloody fighting. If we want to save our lives we are going to have to save one another's lives too."

"Crafty git," Ricky muttered under his breath as he walked round the table, and started to pace back and forth. "I still can't believe that we are in this situation. Assassins don't work together."

"I know, it's almost like he is testing us." I thought hard for a second or two and finished off my sentence by saying, "It's almost as if he didn't want his training and hard work and effort to be wasted." Tank grunted,

"Wow!" He walked over to me and cutely told me, "I don't mind working with you Grace, I like you."

I simply replied with a forceful smile. "Tank can you pick up madam here, and we will all make our way to Edward's office, and check out these files."

"Yes, yes, yes." he enthusiastically agreed, as he bent down. His arms acted like a digger. He scrapped up Hazel effortlessly, and followed us out of the room. Not a lot was said on the way to the office. I think everyone was deep in thought, shock and worried sick.

As we all reached the office, and entered the room I took a deep breath. I was full of dread. I was not looking forward to finding out whose lives will be short-lived. On a large oval table there were four folders clearly laid out on display.

"This must be it." I rushed over to it with the others close behind. Tank dropped Lady Luck in a cushioned chair, and quickly joined us. As my eyes darted across names I just felt like killing myself. By the sounds of it so did Gizmo,

"We are in so much trouble," he stated, "These guys are untouchable and a death trap."

"Hey!" Ricky shouted out, "we can do this." Everyone looked at him in disbelief. We were all so faint-hearted about everything. "Remember the story that Edward told each and every one of us, about him killing The Angel. He described him as untouchable and he managed to kill him by himself." I felt admiration towards Ricky at this point.

"Look, Ricky I appreciate you trying to pick all of our moods up, but let's face it we are officially screwed!" I placed my hands on the edge of the table, and gripped it tightly. "Edward was probably the best assassin that ever walked on this planet. I mean he fooled us for goodness sake."

I just physically, mentally and emotionally couldn't think positively at a time like this. I felt like my anxiety was crushing my insides.

"Yeah, but you're forgetting something." He grinned. I started to think that maybe Ricky was going a little mad from the stress. "There are five of us!" At this point I couldn't be bothered to reply I just wanted to curl up into a ball, and sit, and hide in the corner, and get my mind together.

"Come on Grace, or should I say Ace." He stretched out his arm slightly across the table to grab my attention. "Look, I'm about to pay everyone a compliment, and these don't come often, so listen." He stopped talking for a moment and gathered his thoughts in his mind. It was almost like he found it painful to give someone a compliment. "We are all pretty damn good at what we do, I mean all our reputations precede us." Gizmo had a smile slowly forming and tugging at the corner of his mouth. "We are all amazing in our own special areas. If we combine them together we would be fairly unstoppable and even better than Edward himself." Tank agreed, and his mood suddenly improved. They began to feel more encouraged and motivated. "And I'd love to show up that old git now more than ever, and we need everyone to be motivated and willing to try their hardest." I laughed at the remark towards Edward, and gave a little nod towards Ricky.

He was right. There was no point of hiding, and trying to shelter ourselves from the reality of the situation. Ricky's eyes brightened up, and made him look a lot chirpier than normal. It was strange how Edwards's death, and the shock-horror of being forced into this predicament, had taken my mind off of the types of characters around me. I was pleasantly surprised by Ricky's little motivational speech. Maybe he wasn't a total arse after all.

A weak slightly shaky voice then called out from the corner of the room, "Darling that was a great speech." Hazel picked herself up off the chair, and carefully made her way over. She was stumbling slightly. She stood next to Ricky and admired the files on the table. "So where do we start?"

"Here." I stuck out my hand, and pulled the closest file towards me and spun it round so I could read the name. "Gabriel Luke Hencher."

"This is going to be a toughie," Gizmo commented turning his nose up at it slightly.

"Well, he's the first one to go," Ricky replied. "Right let the war begin."

CHAPTER 3

GABRIEL LUKE HENCHER

W E HAD ALL HEARD of the name, Gabriel Luke Hencher, and there was one very good reason for this. He was a renowned business man. Successful, wealthy, bold, yet he had always been involved with some very dodgy characters. He was a multi-millionaire, and could afford the best of the best. Unfortunately for us, that meant he could afford the best security for himself, and also for his assets and properties. Most people were under the illusion that Gabriel was a legit business man, and worked hard to get where he was. We knew otherwise.

Gabriel was a proud owner of a number of popular casinos, clubs, and bars, all of which were classed as hot spots, or 'the place to be'. His venues drew in hundreds of people every night, even the odd celebrity. We read up on Gabriel's file that Edward had left us. It listed his properties, business, details about his life, but we were not left the reason as to why this man had to die. I grew even more suspicious, as killing a man in cold blood was bad enough, but not knowing why exactly worsened my mood, especially as my own life was now massively at risk.

What I knew, and my 'team' knew, would be enough to want this man dead though. Gabriel was involved in a very successful bank robbery many years ago. He had stolen hundreds and thousands of dollars from an American bank, when he lived in America. The newspapers from the time of the robbery, reported that the police caught the criminals who committed the crime, but myself and the others knew the truth. Gabriel was a sly bastard! He got away with the robbery, hence why he had so much money to be able to start up his own ventures, and he used his mates in the process to be able to obtain this money from the robbery. This man was not to be trusted, and money was his number one pleasure in life. He didn't care who he had to stitch up, or double cross to get it either.

It turned out that Gabriel had a plan, behind the of the bank robbery. He didn't care if his mates, who were working beside him, were dropped into boiling water. In the plan for the robbery, Gabriel was the getaway driver. When his partners in crime amazingly managed to rob the bank, they came charging out of the building and chucked the bags of cash into the back of the car. Gabriel simply sped off, and left his friends behind in the main road. His friends assumed that something had gone wrong, and that there was a reason as to why Gabriel had driven off so frantically, leaving them venerable and in the open. It turned out that Gabriel's secret plan had kicked into action.

All Gabriel had to do was speedily drive round the block and hide the car which concealed the money in a small, quiet alley way, so it was out of sight. It was clear Gabriel was no fool, as he had done his research, therefore he knew that there were no CTV cameras around that specific area. He then clambered into a different car, which he had parked beforehand, on the road by the street curb, and drove back to the bank. Police sirens were ringing in everyone's ears, and began to fill the air. As police approached the scene of the crime, Gabriel spotted his 'friends', and then carelessly ran them down with his car.

The police naturally rushed over to Gabriel's side, and enquired what was going on. Gabriel lied to them and claimed he saw the bank robbers leave the bank, so he stopped them by hitting them with his car.

He also acted up to the police, telling them that he had seen a driver, driving off with all the money, but couldn't give a good description of the car itself. Gabriel got away scot free and was even rewarded for his brave actions. The police couldn't find the money, and after years of trying to retrieve it they had to stop looking. Gabriel then moved to the UK, and started a new life. He built his casinos and clubs from the money that he had stolen, then started making his fortune overnight.

In my opinion this man deserved to go down. It was good to know that our first target we were now pursuing was an evil, sly, conniving man with no morals. It was like having fuel for the fire, yet still why would Edward randomly choose this man for us to kill?

"This man is an absolute…"

"Yes we know," I abruptly interrupted Ricky's sentence before he could offend mine, or someone else's ears, but he stubbornly continued to speak.

"All I was saying is, this man shouldn't be alive anyway. Its amazing how no one has tried to kill him already."

"That's probably because most people have the impression that he's legit," I answered back.

"I can find out his plans, and where he will be tomorrow night if you want, and get blue prints for the building he will be in," Gizmo offered sounding excited and raring to go.

"Great stuff." Ricky jumped up with joy, "Oh, I don't know about you guys, but I feel pumped!"

"Yeah," Tank boomed. Gizmo dashed off out the room, and started to get straight to work. Everything was happening so fast, sometimes my mind struggled to keep up with what was happening. On the other hand, the sooner and faster everything was completed the better.

Later that night after eating our meals Ricky pondered, "Has anyone seen Gizmo?"

I replied, "He has been working solid. I asked Tank to take Gizmo's food to his room." As I sunk into a chair, trying to unwind from the hellish day, I couldn't help but still feel shell shocked from the brutal events that had happened.

Then to make me feel even more foul-tempted a squeaky, stupid, slow voice spoke.

"Darlings, he must have a break soon, it won't do him much good working like that." Hazel wandered into the room, pulling out a little golden pocket mirror, which was the shape of a heart. She admired herself endlessly in it. I crossed my arms tightly across my body and glared at the ditsy woman. Suddenly to our surprise we heard a voice cry out.

"I GOT IT, I HAVE THEM!" Excitedly Gizmo came dashing towards us, leaping about with piles of papers. "Look!" He threw the papers across a table, as we all looked at him with befuddled expressions on our faces. "I managed to hack into his email accounts, and I found where he will be tomorrow night at ten," he blurted out. "He is going to be at one of his casinos. The Golden Bar."

"I know that place, it's wonderful!" Hazel perked up. "I have been there many times. Once, I went there with this very…"

"Not the time Lady Luck!" Gizmo butted in. Hazel rolled her eyes and remained quiet, whilst throwing herself back into a chair, looking like a stroppy teenager because she didn't get to finish her story. Pathetic!

"I have the blue prints of the building." Gizmo rolled out a large piece of paper with a detailed outline of the building and the rooms.

Something then hit me.

"Have you realised something? This building has no window." Ricky, Hazel, and Tank leaned in and examined it closer. You see, for an assassin windows are brilliant! You can shoot through them whilst being well hidden; they make easy access points to certain rooms without being detected, and they come in handy to exit through, or to escape after a killing. No windows to a building always made me feel rather uptight.

"I don't like this place already, it would be like walking into a box with no easy way in or out," Ricky announced. Clearly he was feeling the same way as I was.

Gizmo then told us, "Look, we have to get him, and we can do this. I'd rather do it sooner than later. You don't know how this poison may affect us, or when it might start to do so."

"How do we get in?" Tank asked whilst scratching his head, looking rather dim.

"There will be bouncers at the front door." Gizmo grinned strangely, as if he was looking forward to tackling this challenge, whilst pushing his glasses up his small, pointy nose. "All together there are twelve bouncers, which will more than likely double up as body guards for Gabriel." Gizmo then pointed out their positions, where they would be standing, and areas the guards would roughly be watching. "The first floor is where Gabriel's office is." He showed us the stairs that led to that particular floor. After the stairs there was a rather long lengthy corridor. The corridor makes a sudden left turn, which would led us to Gabriel's office. His office was above the casino floor, and looked down upon it. I suppose that way Gabriel could see who was leaving, and entering his casino, and double checking that people were spending their money.

I patted Gizmo on the back, and gladly told him, "Well done, you've done a fantastic job."

"It's what I do best!"

"You didn't answer my question," Tank huffed. "How do we get in?"

Hazel gently slouched deeper into her chair and suggested, "How about using good, old disguises?" She clamped shut her shiny mirror and popped it away in her cleavage. Everyone peered round the table as Ricky spoke, "Not a bad idea, there will be a lot of people about, and I'd rather keep my identity a secret. So hiding my face isn't such a bad idea."

I then sarcastically spat, "Hiding your face would be a brilliant idea!" Small chuckles circled around the room, as Ricky pulled a silly face my direction, showing he didn't care much for my bitter comment. I carried on talking, whilst ignoring his childish reaction. "Don't forget Gabriel might have heard about Edward passing away, so he is either going to be very relaxed, or very concerned. I'm worried. Why do we have to kill these people, and why does Edward want them dead?" Ricky watched and listened closely, I could feel his eyes staring at me. "Have you got a question Ricky?"

He then suddenly straightened himself up, and quickly replied, "Oh, no-no, I was thinking very hard that was all." He then extended his sentence and looked over to Hazel, "You said you had been to this casino before."

"Indeed I have."

"Then you will have to completely change your appearance." She simply nodded and smiled in a dopy way.

We then began to plan in detail the best way to approach Gabriel. Also what to do when we had him in our grasp. Also we had to make sure that the bouncers not aware of what was unravelling in front of their eyes, and to make sure we got in and out safely. On top of that we had to be undetectable.

"Yes, we have it, we have got the plan of action!" I sighed in relief. It was perfect, I felt so confident with what we had all conjured up.

Gizmo smiled.

"Great stuff."

"I think everyone should go to sleep now," yawned Tank. He looked like he could have fallen asleep right there and then.

"Not a bad idea," Ricky agreed whilst half letting out a yawn. "We will need our rest." Everyone agreed and headed to their rooms.

I started to reminisce whilst I walked down a stretch of corridor, within the manor, remembering what it was like growing up here. I remembered sneaking out of my room late at night when Edward was fast asleep, and just walking around innocently and pointlessly. Sometimes for the sake of it I use to try and slide down the corridors in my socks, to see how far I could travel. Nothing had changed a bit to this old manor. I turned round the corner about to enter my old bedroom and found Ricky standing in my way. I jumped unexpectedly.

"What are you doing here?" Ricky looked down at the floor, and let out a little sigh. He then began to talk very quietly.

"I just wanted to apologise about earlier, making those sarky comments." He lifted his head slowly and carried on apologising. "I guess today has just been such an emotional day, and those remarks I couldn't help but make, and I'm sorry." I simply kept a straight face and slightly nodded, not making any eye contact with him. "Also I just wanted to say I'm glad you're on this team; it won't be easy between us, but I realised that you are a crucial part of this team, and I couldn't wish for anyone else to work with." A little smile tugged at the corner of my mouth. I didn't want to smile, or forgive him, if anything I wished he'd just leave me alone.

I felt a little awkward standing so close to Ricky. It had been such a long time since I had been this close to him. He looked exactly the same from years ago. His lips still looked soft and tempting. His hair was still smooth, slick and silky, not a grey hair in sight. No wrinkles or crows feet had appeared on his slightly tanned skin. His skin still looked immaculate, and his eyes were still stunning. He had beautifully shaped dark brown eyes which I found so charming and mysterious. My nostrils were then filled with his sweet masculine scent. I hadn't realised that for a moment we had just been standing there looking into one another's eyes. Nothing was said between us, and the tension grew more and more. It was almost like I was in a daze, transported back in time, when he and I were so close.

I wasn't a hundred percent sure, but I was fairly certain that within a split second Ricky was going to lean in to kiss me. I rapidly broke the eye-locked gaze, and stepped back. It was getting too much for me to handle. I abruptly said to Ricky,

"Good night," and scooted past him, feeling more awkward than I felt originally. I could then feel my checks beginning to fire up and blush. I assumed that was caused by embarrassment. I pushed open my bedroom door, and was about to shut it immediately behind me, but his voice called out for me quietly,

"Grace." I hectically poked my head out of the little gap that I left myself between the door and the door frame.

"What?"

Ricky had a cheeky, and heart filled grin on his face, and said something to me that made me shudder, and sent tingles up my spine.

"I meant it when I said I am happy that you are working with me." The stare started to grow back again, like an annoying weed that won't die. I couldn't help it. I just couldn't control myself as, I found myself just hopelessly gazing into his eyes once again. "Good night Grace."

"Night." I replied and slammed the door shut behind me. "What, is going on!?!" I whispered to myself. I cupped my slim hands over my tired face, and slipped down the door until I was curled up on the floor. I had my knee pressed up against my chest, my elbows resting on my knees, and my head slumped in my hands. I let out a long big sigh in an attempt to clear my head, but it didn't work. I now had Ricky on my mind, which was the last thing I needed. "I can't let him play with my mind like that, it's silly," I ordered myself. "There was nothing there the first time round, and there will not be a second time, and I'll make sure of it." I began to try and make sense of it all, "It must be the mixture of stress, and old faces, and this place, and everything that's happening at the moment that is making me act oddly." I paused for a split second, "No, I'm not acting oddly, he is. I don't know what he is playing at, well his hopes will be short lived."

I finally managed to pick my aching head up out of my hands, and I was taken aback. I was faced with my lovely old bedroom. I forcefully pushed myself up then started to look about me. A small smile from the mixture of pleasure and delight appeared onto my stressed, flushed face. I took a couple of paces forward and told myself, "This is where it all started." The many nights that I spent here when I was a younger. Nothing had been changed or touched since I grew up, and left this place and travelled the world. This room felt like home to me.

This one area was the longest place I had ever lived in. It beats any hotel room that I placed myself in. I gazed about and saw my four poster bed that was very grand, with dark blue drapes down the sides. I loved that bed when I was young, I felt like a little princess in a castle. I had never seen a bed like it before back then, and I remembered the burst of excitement when I learnt that this massive room was all mine. Alongside the bed were two normal classic-looking bed side tables, and opposite the bed was a massive wardrobe. The front of the wardrobe was covered in mirrors. I thought back to the time when I used to dance and prance in front of it as a child, and growing up I even sat in front of it talking to myself, to motivate and psych myself up for the day ahead.

Again, in this room like many others there was a huge window that took up one side of the wall. A bench with royal blue cushions stretched from one side of the window to the other. The night sky was always breathtaking to admire out of this window, as the silver moonlight lit up the grounds to the manor. Long, heavy curtains were placed on each side of the window, which made the room darker than the shade of black when they were shut, but despite their heavy nature, they were so smooth and velvety. There was also my own private bathroom suite through a little door.

For the first time today, I felt truly happy and relaxed and at one with myself. The confusion and stress of the day was left far behind when I started to focus and rebuild my strength. I was falling in love with my room all over again. It gave me the feeling of innocence and peace.

After washing, and changing into my night clothing I got into my bed. I lay still on my back as I could feel my head slowly sink into the soft, fluffy pillows, and the duvet snuggled me in making me feel warm and welcomed. I let out another long sigh that filled my soul with hope. It started to feel like everything would be okay. I then started to entertain the thought of how comforting old memories were. The feeling of positivity came back to me, and I really did feel like myself again. Whatever happened the next day I was prepared for it, after all the shock of everything had began to melt away.

The next morning I awoke feeling refreshed. As I was getting cleaned, and changed I was preparing myself for the day ahead. I decided not to think too much about the people that I would be working alongside with. The thought of me working with the other assassins made me feel agitated, and gave me a dreadful headache. *Just take them as they come'* I thought to myself. It was the best way of dealing with them at the time.

I wandered out of my room and began to head to the kitchen to find something to eat for breakfast. I was walking down the corridor minding my own business when Gizmo wearily crawled out of his room, appearing in a dull, dark green top, and loose fitting jeans.

"Morning," I pleasantly said.

Gizmo starred at me oddly, and replied, "You have changed your tune since yesterday."

"Morning to you too Grace!" I joked mimicking his squeaky, geeky voice, as I peered down at him. We began to walk side by side. "Sleep well?" I asked, but Gizmo was still looking at me with a strange look upon his face, as if I was on drugs or something.

"Yeah." He grunted. I learnt there and then that Gizmo wasn't a morning person. There was a moment of silence as he was trying to keep up with my walking pace. "I don't want to sound rude…"

"But you're going to be, aren't you?" I giggled to myself. I never understood why people said the phrase. It is like people use it to cover up an insult. Gizmo carried on talking.

"Yesterday you were on edge… not yourself, and well, you had a face like a slapped arse! But today you are all peachy and happy. Why?" I took a moment to think about it and came to an assumption.

"If I'm being honest, I was in a vulgar mood yesterday, but only because I wasn't sure what was going to happen, was forced into a room with you lot, no offence, and I knew I had to face my 'ex'. On top of that people like Hazel drive me insane. I can't stand air-heads, and we were betrayed and poisoned. So, do forgive me for not being full of airs and graces yesterday!" I explained bluntly. "Last night though, brought back some great memories. Just staying in my old room brought everything flooding back to me, and I guess in an odd way it lifted my spirits."

"I thought you thought, that things were going to be good after Ricky made his little speech yesterday."

I tilted my head and thought a little more whilst giving Gizmo an answer, "I guess it did do me a some good to know that people are willing. I wouldn't say it was Ricky's doing though, but deep down I didn't feel great." He had an expression on his face that showed he'd understood what I meant. After all we were assassins.

Finally we reached the kitchen. It was the least favourite room of mine within the grounds. It was very old fashioned, almost Victorian styled. It was dark, dingy and very bland. The brick walls were exposed. There were no attempts to brighten or cover them up. There was a little white door that led out into a small courtyard which the servants used to spend time in years and years ago. The door rattled loudly and also whistled too as a draught made its way in.

Tank had already beaten everyone to the kitchen. When he saw Gizmo and I enter the room Tank splattered, "Morning Grace, Morning Gizmo." He had a mouthful of food, and as he spoke chunks of it were sprayed out. I'm sure Tank didn't even notice, he just roughly whipped his chops, and carried on shovelling his food down.

"How are you today Tank?" I asked as I started to forage for some food.

"Yeah great." He smiled, "I feel really good, really, really, really good." I looked at Tank. Every time I did he always reminded me of a slow minded child. The day that I look at him, and I see a fully grown man, would be the day I'd probably have a heart attack! Never the less, it was also a relief to hear that the majority of us felt good. It showed that the poison hadn't taken effect yet.

"Always good to hear."

"I can tell you are better," he told me, whilst digging his spoon deep into what looked like a hot bowl of gloop. I could only guess that he was eating porridge.

"I sure am," I answered whilst screwing up my face as Tank ate another massive mouthful of grey gloop. It looked so thick that you could have used it for wallpaper paste!

"Good because I don't like it when you are sad," he said meaning it as a sweet good-hearted comment. He cared about me a lot, and had always looked up to me. Some time had passed as I was tucking into my coffee and biscuits. Watching Tank gulp down that food put me off eating. Then I could hear Hazel's irritating laugh.

"Guess who's joining us now!" Gizmo grunted under his breath. I happily laughed to myself, and felt a little bit relieved. I was glad I wasn't the only one that didn't particularly like her. The door was pushed open in a dramatic fashion to deliberately catch all of our attention, but I carried on looking away and sipping at my warming coffee.

"Morning my little darlings." I cringed, and pulled an unpleasant face as she tried to make a patronising comment to us, but at the corner of my eye I could see that something wasn't right. I could tell that Gizmo and Tank were just sitting very still, and very quiet. I couldn't help but glance over my shoulder, and then I understood why the room suddenly became very silent and awkward.

My mouth dropped. There was Hazel leaning and draping herself across Ricky like a sash. Ricky just looked at us all without saying a word. Hazel then danced her way over.

"Well you ducklings aren't very chirpy this morning." Again no one gave her a response. She leaped up on a chair with a big soppy smile on her face. I just looked at her in disbelief and then at Ricky. "Come on big boy, I bet you could bring some life to these people." The words kept flying out of her mouth as she was completely unaware of what shock she had caused the group. Everyone knew exactly what had happened. It didn't take a rocket scientist to work out that they had slept together last night. I physically could not speak or move. Hazel pulled up a chair alongside herself, and told Ricky to sit next to her. I watched Ricky intensely as he slowly made his way over to her, and did what she told him to do.

He hung his head down and didn't look at anyone. Not even me. I hoped and wished he felt deeply ashamed and humiliated. She then threw her dainty delicate arms around him and ordered,

"Tank get me a cup of tea." Tank didn't say anything. He gingerly stood up, and started to make some tea.

"No," I muttered to myself. "Oh no you don't." I slammed down my cup in anger. Some of my coffee violently splashed out of the mug. "Tank don't make anything for her, she has got legs and hands." Tank stood there wide eyed.

"Darling what is wrong?" She started to bat her silly long eyelashes. I suddenly got the urge to rip her eyelashes off and bash her dolly like face against the wooden work top.

"I'm saying go and make your own tea, there's nothing wrong with you."

"Darling, I'm just so tired."

"Well guess what," I growled venomously. I could feel my heart rate increase, and myself feel hot and bothered. "Tough tits!" The rage started to fill my body up. "Maybe you should have spent last night lying on your back for the right reason." Tank gasped in horror at the fact that I had the nerve to talk to Hazel in such a rude way. I just felt so betrayed and upset. Gizmo peered on as he slowly shuffled backwards out of the firing line.

Hazel at first did nothing. She just sat there with a blank look on her face, and then to my annoyance she started to smile, and chuckle to herself like the immature school girl she really was. Ricky remained quiet, and still wasn't looking at anyone. I could feel my hands becoming sweaty and clenching up.

"Why are you getting angry about this Grace?" Hazel then tilted her head and rested it on Ricky's shoulder. He quickly looked up at me. His eyes were filled with worry and panic with a hint of an apologetic attitude. I was about to explode, but found myself lost for words. All I could say was, "You're nothing Hazel, and Ricky. You're both nothing." I evilly glared at him with pulsing anger, "You should fucking know better. You're both pathetic." I threw my chair back, and stormed out of the room. I felt like I was leaving a trail of fire behind me at the speed I left.

I slammed the kitchen door shut behind me, and found my legs beginning to move faster. Before I knew it I was running away from them all. Weaving through corridors, up sets of stairs, avoiding standing decorative objects. My adrenaline had taken over and I needed to get rid of it. Tears began to flood down my face as I finally reached my room. I banged the door shut, threw myself onto my bed, and buried my face amongst the duvet. Then to my horror what had happened had finally sunk into my mind. I had just made a big scene out of something I shouldn't have, but it was too late for regrets now. It then hit me that I must have had feelings for Ricky. Why would I react in such a jealous angry rage?

"Typical," I whimpered to myself. "When I think I have pulled myself together, this happens." I bashed my head against my springy mattress repeatedly at such a force it could have given me whip lash! I was just so full of heart ache. I couldn't understand it. It must have been from last night's encounter with Ricky. It must have brought back old memories and feelings.

I then began to think things over. "Bastard!" I screeched out as I shot upright. "Bloody bastard." I realised, and I was fairly sure he was only after one thing last night. Sex! Why else would he come to my room and use his charming allure? Instead he went to the slut's room where of course he was going to get a shag because she can't keep her legs shut. Disgusting, disgraceful bitch. She has lack of morals and is so selfish.

So not only was Ricky after sex, like most men are, but he has caused me to make a massive embarrassing scene, and on top of that Ricky, and the others, are now going to learn that I have feelings that I didn't realise I had for him, which might wreck my reputation. This was my worst nightmare coming true. Nothing else could make me feel so small and stupid. The thought that I was going to have to show my face at some point filled me with dread. I would rather rip my face off, and just call myself Miss Anonymous! Also I had a job to do with them tonight. I couldn't bear the pressure pushing down on me once again, crushing every bone in my body.

Knock, knock, knock. A gentle tapping sound came from my door. I didn't reply as I wanted to be left alone. I found myself choking up, not being able to speak, as my throat had grown tense. I knew if I spoke my voice would sound shaky and distressed. I was in such a desperate need to be by myself, that when the knocking on my door continued, I broke down and cried. Hot tears ran down my flustered face. Then the door opened and someone entered the room.

"Grace?" a low voice softly murmured. Again I showed no response, and shortly after, I felt a large hand rest upon my quivering shoulder. "Are you okay?" I knew it was Tank attempting to comfort me. I nodded whilst pushing away my tears. The bed suddenly slumped as Tank sat his huge framed body down on the bed. Neither of us said anything to one another for a little while, but then he wrapped his arms around me gently and pulled me close to his chest. The hug he was giving me was lovely. I thought the last thing I would have wanted was human contact, but it was just what I needed. His warmth spread through my mind and soul. "Please don't cry," he whispered as he then began to stroke my hair. I found it soothing.

I plucked up the courage and started to speak, and I asked in confusion,

"Why did I do that Tank? What was I thinking? What's happening to me?" I was so desperate for answers to my questions that I forgot Tank wasn't that smart, and wouldn't be able to answer them in a million years. I was surprised to hear what he said next.

"You will find your answers with time, you'll always get the answers you need in the end." Strangely enough I found that comforting too. I looked up at him and whimpered, "Thank you."

Tank just smiled and nothing more was said.

A few hours had passed, and once again I managed to pick myself up off the floor. *'It's now or never'* I told myself in my mind. At some point I would have to face the others, and just hold my head up high. I was going to make sure that they didn't get the better of me this time round. Nothing was going to stop me. I had been pushed over and trodden on enough. It was time that I took charge and lived up to my assassin's name, Ace. I took a deep calming breath, adjusted myself and left the security and safety of my own room.

I stormed, and marched about looking for the others. I walked with a strong purpose, and determination. I finally heard their mixture of voices coming from the study. I dashed over to the doors, and before any doubts had a chance to protrude into my mind, I launched myself through the doors. By the way everyone reacted they were not expecting to see me any time soon.

"Right, let's get ourselves organised." Everyone stood still, as if time had frozen. I grabbed the plans that Gizmo had drawn up, and rolled them out across the table. "Gather round, I want to go through this one more time to make sure everyone knows what they are doing," I barked. Still no one moved. I then shouted angrily, "Am I talking to myself, or have you all gone deaf? Get your arses round this table this instance." Everyone rapidly jumped, and rushed over quicker than you could blink. I felt as if I was dealing with badly behaved infants.

As we all started to go through the plans, and getting the weapons and disguises prepared, I had noticed that Ricky's eyes wouldn't stop following me around the room. I did find it agitating, but I suppressed and swallowed my emotions and soldiered on. I really was determined not to let him get the better of me, but wondered whether suppressing my emotions would trigger an emotional outburst later. Needlessly to say I, carelessly shoved my doubts to the back of my mind, and soon forgot about it all, as I became increasingly engrossed in the action plan and preparations.

I felt good taking charge. Better than good even, and no one was going to stop me. The plan was brilliant, the weapons I chose for myself I was more than confident with, and the disguises I was very pleased with too. I was convinced we wouldn't be recognised with them on inside the casino. I didn't recognise myself at first when I took a quick glimpse in the mirror. I found that I was slightly taken aback, and startled. I even made myself jump backwards with shock, but that was perfect! It was the effect I was hoping for. If I didn't recognise myself, who else would?

I wore a red haired wig, which was styled to look like it was clipped up, with a couple of curly straggles gliding down the sides of my face. Obviously I wore make up, but the type of makeup that would suit a red-haired person, so very earthy colours were applied to my face. I even put light foundation on my face, and arms to lighten my skin tone, and wore light, thin tights to create the same effect. I wore a slim, dark emerald green dress which was low cut at the front showing ample bosom. I also wore contact lenses, to turn my eyes from blue to a beautiful, striking light green. Tonight, I was going to be a deadly, foxy, red head!

My first weapon of choice was a mousegun. It was very small, so I safely concealed it within my bosom, so it wouldn't be detected. It was my back up weapon. If I found myself being caught or trapped, or possibly have my weapons taken off me, or even if I ran out of ammunition for my other weapons, I knew I had a reliable back up gun. I always thought it to better to be safe than sorry. The mousegun was mainly designed to be used for self-defence. It's not very practical for long distance shooting or actually assassinating anyone.

To accompany the mousegun, I had a couple of Glock G23 pistols. They to me, were a well-balanced gun, and good to use in most situations. You couldn't go wrong with them. Very low recoil, good accuracy, had a fast fire rate, 15 round clip, and had a scope too. It was easily portable, and so they were strapped to my upper thigh with a holster, with my dress covering them. Easy access for me if I needed them, yet again hidden away from prying eyes.

I also had a couple of neat, yet handy gadgets. Inside the heel of my black velvet shoes were compartments that had extra ammunition, just in case I ran low, even though I was hoping that tonight wasn't going to be a blood bath. Also I was wearing what seemed to be a couple of innocent, pretty bracelets, but they had a secret button. As soon as the button was pushed on the bracelet, three small blades would suddenly appear, allowing me to stab and slice people if need be. I felt more than safe with what I was equipped with, and these weapons seemed to suit the plan and the job at hand. The only thing that unnerved me and made me feel unsettled, was the fact I had to work with the other incapable buffoons.

A couple of hours later, when everyone was ready, we eventually gathered in the entrance hall and we were all stunned and pleasantly surprised how well our disguises looked. Tank and Quick-Shot were all dressed up in suits. Even Tank had a wig on to cover up his shaved patterned head. His wig was mousy colour, and was slightly spiked. Hazel on the other hand, well she still look like a tart, but changed the colour of her hair, and did the same as me, changed her skin tone, whilst slimming down her lips and went for minimalistic make up, but wore large jet black sun glasses, which had little jewels on the corner of them. Gizmo remained in his normal nerdy clothing as he would remain in the car, and feed us information through ear pieces.

"We all look brilliant," I piped up. "So are we all ready to complete our first mission?" Butterflies started to develop in my stomach as I spoke those words. The realisation started to kick in that this was the big moment. We were about to start our first mission and there was no going back.

"Yes," Tank replied, whilst patting me on my back. The others agreed and we started to make our way out of the entrance. Before we got into our vehicle, which was a black BMW, Tank bent over, and cheerfully whispered in my ear, "Well done." I knew what he meant by that. He was proud of the way I was handling the situation, between Ricky and I, and getting on with everything, and making the most of the situation, like I told myself to do. I was feeling oddly smug for myself with being able to do so as well.

Before I knew it we were outside the casino, Golden Bar. Crowds of people were flocking in, all laughing, and chatting away with excitement. The name of the Casino was written and lit up inside a bar of gold. There was something about this casino that looked very Las Vegas styled! Giant palm trees lined up alongside a red carpet that led you into the building, as the building was flashing with bright colourful lights. It was very dramatic. It struck me as a bit over the top and almost tacky.

There was a buzz in the air. Ricky and I were the first people to leave the vehicle, and enter the Casino. Each step I took towards the building, I started to feel ill with anxiety, but I couldn't expose it. I knew I had to remain in character, and stay as calm as possible to avoid attracting attention to ourselves. I slapped on a false smile, and swaggered into the casino. It was unusual for me to feel so emotional, and such a wreck whilst being on a mission. Most of the time I would feel the adrenaline pulsing through me, making me excited, and I'd normally be enjoying myself.

Then Ricky linked our arms together whilst we drew closer to the entrance. I shuddered with displeasure. I could feel his eyes burning the side of my head as he continuously stared. I knew he wanted me to look at him, but I refused to do so. As far as I was concerned he was dead to me, but whilst on a mission, unfortunately, he couldn't be. As we approached the bouncers I avoided eye contact with them, but kept smiling like an idiot possessed. We managed to get past them with ease, and no hassle which I was so relieved about.

I then began to think that the security to this casino wasn't as great as Gizmo led us to believe. I couldn't see that many bouncers about, and barely any CCTV cameras around as well. In fact, I felt a little bit disappointed. It was as if we were expecting security to be as tight as fort Knox, but I couldn't allow myself to get into the frame of mind, that this was going to be a walk in the park. The worst thing to do on a job was get too confident and cocky. It leaves you open and venerable, and the chances of making silly mistakes heightens.

Myself and Ricky headed to the bar and took our places. We both slyly, yet casually, watched our surroundings, whilst trying to look comfortable together, which was very hard to act out. Tensions were made worse when Ricky finally decided to speak to me.

"I am really sorry." I thought he was about to say my name out a loud which would have made me into a nervous wreck.

"Don't start now." I spat, whilst gritting my teeth together, creating the illusion that I was still smiling.

"You don't understand."

"And I don't want to." For a split second I gave him a stern look. "If you keep on about this I will kill you." I laughed afterwards as I saw a barman heading towards us. I was trying to keep up the act that Ricky and I were happy, and full of joy in one another's company, although at this point I think I would have rather of thrown myself off a cliff, into an ocean of cactus plants! I tried to make the threat look like a joke, as I became aware that the barman may have overheard what I had said. Ricky just sat there and did nothing. He looked like a piece of rotten fruit; weak, slumped, miserable, and pathetic. I just thought to myself *'if he keeps this attitude up, we are going to look strange, and if we survive, I'm going to kick his arse afterwards!'*

"Can I get you both anything?" the bar man asked us politely, with a charming smile upon his young face.

"Yes please Darling, a white wine for me Darling." I sarcastically said, deliberately trying to annoy and provoke a reaction from Ricky, by talking and copying Hazel's actions and voice. Ricky wasn't playing along with it though, or taking this mission seriously, so I gave up with him. "What do you want Darling?" I said whilst half placing my hand on his lap, slowly rubbing and caressing his upper thigh, and leaning into him, just to get his blood boiling. There was a double meaning behind what I said to him, and he knew it.

"Whiskey." Ricky then grumpily grunted, and then glared at me coldly. The bar man spun round, and was fixing up our orders; god knows what he thought of us two. I could imagine him gossiping to his work colleagues about us, which would attract unwanted attention to us. "That's immature, and insensitive," he muttered under his breath, with a whining tone.

I then leant in even closer, and whispered in his ear, "If you're not going to act like a couple, or very good friends at least, then I thought I would act like someone you clearly like, and have taken a sudden fancy to… oh like… hmmmm… that bloody, stupid, tarty, air-head of a bitch. Hazel."

The bar man returned back, and slid us our drinks across the bar. Ricky was staring at me intensely. I just wanted to chuckle to myself, knowing I was upsetting him. Irresponsible on a mission, but I really couldn't have cared less at that point in time.

"That will be six pounds twenty please." The bar man put out his hand, waiting for the payment. I then peered over at Ricky whilst he looked like he was grinding his teeth to crumbs.

"Be a Darling, and get the first round. Thanks big boy." I then grasped the glass of wine, spun round on my chair, and was watching everyone getting on with their lives.

A voice suddenly filled my left ear, from my secret, near enough invisible earpiece.

"Okay, Lady Luck is about to enter the building, and start playing her part now. Over." My eyes watched prudently, as Lady Luck then arose from the active crowd of people. She easily mixed in with the other people, but I couldn't help but find it easy to pick her out, as my hatred for her acted like a radar. After a little while, myself and Ricky started to manage to pretend to enjoy ourselves. Clearly seeing Hazel must have stirred something in him, as he finally got his act together. It was a challenge for the both of us, to act like chums. I also think he got his arse into gear, because he couldn't stand me mimicking Hazel. It must have been horrible for him to endure, whilst I found it delightfully amusing.

Gizmo's voice once again spoke to us. "Lady Luck, have you found the head guard yet? Over." We watched her as she placed her necklace close to her mouth. Hazel and I had secret microphones hidden in our necklaces, which would work if we pressed a tiny little button on it. It looked like we were playing with our necklaces, if we were to communicate through them. For Ricky and Tank, their microphones were hidden inside their shirt collars.

"Yes, I have spotted him." Her soft voice spoke. It made me cringe hearing her voice so clearly in my ear, even though she was a fair distance away. For me that would be the best torture techniques for anyone to use on me, apart from Ricky. "I'm about to make my move on him," She announced. We watched thoroughly as she erotically started to stroll towards the main guard. He was standing by the stairs that myself and Ricky needed to get up, to be able to get to Gabriel Luke Hencher's office. The guard was very well built. He looked dangerous, and very strong, and no doubt about it, armed. Hazel started to flirt, and seduce the guard, as she did everything in her power to lure him away.

"This must be fun for you to watch," I heartlessly joked at Ricky's expense. He then grabbed my hand tightly, and forced me towards him and bitterly muttered, "I don't have feelings for her." There was a moment where he just held me close to his warm, tense body. I whipped his hands off mine, then turned my back on him slightly. I didn't want him touching me in such a manner. I then focused on Lady Luck. Her efforts and skills were rewarded, as she tempted the guard away from his post. The stairs were completely free for Ricky and me.

"Lady Luck has done it, send Tank in." I communicated wearily to Gizmo. I now started to feel more and more positive about this mission, so far everything was going according to plan. It was running like clockwork. Ricky and I just had to wait for Tank to complete his part of the plan for us to be able to get on with ours.

Tank loomed in sight, and heavily yet confidently wandered into the casino, making his way over to a roulette table. We watched in great anticipation. Five minutes had passed, and the room was chock-a-block with people laughing, chatting, shouting and screeching with excitement and adrenaline. The odd person moped and sulked in lonely corners of the bar, after losing large fortunes. Gambling is a fool's game!

"THIS GAME IS FIXED!" Suddenly an angry voice cut through the happy, buzzing atmosphere. Mine and Ricky's head were fixed on the situation that Tank had managed to create. "You are cheating. This casino sucks!" Tank cried out at the top of his voice. Other people started to peer round and examine the situation. As Tank started to become louder, and drew more attention to himself other people started to gasp in horror believing that Tank was hard done by. He looked rather humorous playing this role of a frustrated gambler. He was stomping his feet harshly, flaying his arms around in the air ridiculously. Even his face began to turn slightly red from the amount of shouting he was doing.

Bouncers were then flagged down to escort Tank off the premises, but Ricky and I knew at the back of our minds that Tank wasn't going to go quietly and quickly. He would try and drag out this situation as long as he could, to distract as much security as possible.

"Come on." Ricky nudged me. We both stood up, and tried to shuffle our way through the crowds without looking suspicious. I was looking around, and admiring people's games, as if I was looking for a free table to play on. We finally snuck through the crowds, and got to the place where the main bouncer was standing. I dashed forward and up the stairs, as Ricky took a rapid look around to double check no one had latched onto us. My heart was pounding and the adrenaline flooded my mind like water filling a glass. I felt pumped.

As we stealthily ran down the long corridor I whispered into my miniature microphone, "We are in the corridor making our way to Gabriel."

"Roger that," Gizmo replied sounding slightly relieved.

The corridor was very bland and boring. Nothing here to thrill anyone. The only decoration that was about was the odd plant pot with shrubs growing out of it. At least the plants gave a little life to the area. We finally got to Gabriel's office door, but to my horror there was a number pad on the wall. We had no code. No code, meant no entry. How could Gizmo over look this?

"Gizmo you idiot," Ricky huffed. "There is a security lock on this door and we need to punch in a code to gain access. Please tell me you have a code for it." There was nothing but silence. "Gizmo, hello?" I looked up at Ricky as, our eyes met one another's with panic. We both had the same sickening worried expression on our faces. "Gizmo?" He had gone silent which struck fear into my heart. Had someone found him? Has someone found out about all of us? Was our cover about to be blown? As if, like magic, Gizmo's squeaky voice spoke to us. I let out a long relaxing sigh.

"Don't worry, I'll figure something out." Ricky replied abruptly.

"Good but don't be too long. I don't want to be hanging around here any longer than need be."

My heart sunk suddenly. I could hear something. Something I really was hoping not to hear. Footsteps! Footsteps were slowly making their way over to us. Ricky and I both ducked, and shuffled against the wall. We crouched next to one another besides a plant pot. The pot was large, thankfully, but wouldn't be able to give us safe cover for long. I placed my hands on my guns, and was ready to draw them out at any moment.

"Hurry, someone's coming." I quietly spoke to Gizmo urging him to help us quickly. My breathing became slightly erratic, yet I tried to control my nerves. I took a brief moment for myself, and shut my eyes. One long, deep lung full of air inflated my lungs, and threw my breathing into its normal pace again. *I mustn't allow myself to lose control*; then it hit me.

"Gizmo," I burst out quietly. Ricky watched on in desperation. We were like trapped rats. "Did I see an air vent along the corridor somewhere?" Ricky then looked at me, then looked like he was praying to himself in his mind.

"Correct. There is one, but you will have to go back on yourself." The footsteps continually carried on coming towards us.

"We can't do that it's too risky. If we fire our guns once, Gabriel is going to do a runner."

"Trust me, just follow my lead."

My eyes started to dart about. As I looked down over my right shoulder, I noticed small round pebbles in the plant pot. I grabbed a hand full, and clutched them tightly. I then started to slide myself along the wall and began to head back on myself. Ricky followed closely, like a shadow. It felt mad going towards someone that could easily appear round the corner at any second. We didn't have a lot of room to move about either, and there was no way to sneak past the bouncer who was walking towards us, so distraction was the first thing that came into my mind.

I got to the corner of the wall. The air vent was just across from us but we couldn't make a mad dash to it otherwise we would be exposed. I quickly made a simple flick of my wrist, and threw a stone down the corridor that bounced off the wall, and made a small banging noise. The footsteps stopped dead in their tracks. I held my breath, desperately hoping that he didn't see me throw the stone. I could hear no movement so I quickly peeked my head round the corner. The bouncer dressed in a navy blue suit, with an ear piece had his back towards us.

I took a couple of steps out into the open, away from the wall, and lobbed another stone as far as I could. Praying that he wasn't going to notice these tiny stones flying past him, but it seemed to work. There was a slight thudding noise as the stone hit the carpet in the distance. The bouncer once again stood very still for a brief moment, and as soon as he heard another noise he began to walk away from us, to investigate the noise.

I legged it to another plant pot which was conveniently placed underneath the air vent in the ceiling. I balanced carefully on top of the pot, and reached upwards. I stretched as far as I could, and I began to move the air vents grill that was blocking my entry. As soon as I pushed it to one side I pulled myself up with difficulty. Then the footsteps began to come back to life again. They got louder, as I started to help Ricky up into the air vent.

"God sake, come on Ricky!" As I pulled him up, and finally got Ricky safely into the air vent, he quickly placed the grill over the hole behind him. We watched nervously as the bouncer walked underneath us scratching his head in confusion. He too was making his way to Gabriel's office. My heart rate started to calm down as I knew we were out of sight, and well hidden.

The air vent was extremely narrow and cold. We had to be very wary of not making any noise as we crawled towards the office. Very fast I muttered,

"We are in the air vent."

"Well done," Gizmo replied, sounding slightly down hearted that he hadn't come up with an idea fast enough. I knew I wanted to have words with Gizmo after this assassination. His neck was on the line with me. I couldn't believe Gizmo over looked the fact that the door to the office was secured by a code. I thanked my lucky stars that we got out of that tricky situation without anything going disastrously wrong. I assumed that Gizmo didn't pick up on the pad, simply because he rushed everything. I then began to think to myself *'maybe that's why Edward gave us three months worth of life, because these jobs will take time to plan.'* We avoided a disaster by the skin of our teeth. Ricky then opened his big mouth.

"It's been such a long time since we have been left alone together like this."

"What in an air vent?" I snarled sarcastically. "And for what it's worth, it's probably a good thing that we haven't been left together in such a tight spaces."

"Why's that?"

"I might just kill you, and boy I certainly feel like doing that now if you don't stop making stupid comments, and start focusing on the job at hand!" Ricky remained silent after that, and I was overly grateful for it.

The most crucial part of the mission was about to happen. The killing of Gabriel. I was looking forward to it in a weird way. It would mean one less scum bag to deal with. I then could hear muffled voices talking. I knew we were very close to the office. I saw beams of light penetrating through the darkness ahead of me. It was the light coming from the office below, I was sure of it. I rapidly crawled my way over to another air vent grill and gazed down.

I could see a desk with paper work piled up on it. A black phone, flat screen computer monitor, a large leather chair that sat comfortably behind the desk, and wads of money lying about the place carelessly. Also there were some T.V screens at one side of the room where CCTV cameras were filming people gambolling, drinking, and making Gabriel richer. I had a sense of pride that we had got past the cameras without being noticed, or spotted as looking odd or suspicious.

"I'm glad you managed to sort out that fool," a voice which sounded rich and deep said. It was Gabriel. The target was right underneath me. In moments to come he won't be warm and vertical! Ricky and I waited patiently as the bouncer and Gabriel started to talk to one another. It was a nightmare. I just wanted to put a bullet through this guy's head, and make a run for it. I was growing more impatient by the second.

"I do not know where Dave has got to either sir," the guard told Gabriel. Gabriel tilted his head to one side and pinned his index fingers together whilst resting them on his chin. "He has been gone for about twenty, twenty five minutes."

"Have him killed when you find him," Gabriel ordered. "I can't have my main guard be half arsed about his job," he explained, sounding disappointed. I cruelly smiled to myself thinking that he is probably already dead, if Lady Luck has successfully bumped him off.

"Yes sir."

I began to think that the staff probably couldn't trust one another. Watching this bouncer take the order of killing the main bouncer must not have been the first time this has happened. Gabriel seemed to be someone who wanted the best of the best. So in that case, he would want the best protection. I took a closer look at Gabriel, as I tried to see what he looked like in person. We had seen a picture of him from his file, but with the bundles of money that he has, he must be wearing some amazing quality stuff, which I will be shortly about to ruin.

He had jet black hair, with a little moustache, that was joined with a thin beard that outlining his broad square jaw line. He was covered from head to toe in tacky, distasteful jewellery. He had a heavy chuck of gold hanging round his neck and his knuckles were covered in thick golden rings. I was amazed he could raise his arms because of the amount of jewellery. He struck me as a typical man that had it all and wanted to show it off at once. Expensive jewellery, a very well made navy blue suit that had a pastel pink silk shirt underneath it. I felt like I was about to shoot at hundreds of thousands of pounds worth of person tonight. It was a great feeling, and was only willing me on even more. There was not a chance I was going to miss this geezer!

The bouncer then spun round swiftly, and was about to exit the room, but at the last moment Gabriel randomly said,

"Oh, congratulations." The bouncer then looked round at Gabriel looking puzzled. "You have been promoted to my new head guard." A crooked smile appeared on the Guards face, but he didn't look over all pleased with the news. Who could blame him? Then Gabriel sadistically grunted, "Don't let me down, because you know what will happen."

"Yes sir, thank you sir," he replied, and then shut the door behind him. Ricky and I waited for a few moments to make sure that Gabriel's new head guard was out of earshot. We didn't want anyone to hear the gun fire, even though the gun has a silencer on it. We also realised that Gabriel was a very efficient man. Not only did he have bouncers to look after the casino, but he managed to double them up to be his guards. Clever man!

The time felt right to complete the last part of this operation. I gave Gabriel one final last look, and couldn't help but count each final breath he was taking in his last moments of life. I gazed over at Ricky, and gave him a slight nod. He then passed me a thin piece of paper with steady hands.

On the piece of paper there was a message written. It was placed in Gabriel's case file when we started to study and look into Gabriel's background. Edward had left us all under strict orders to deliver this coded message to each person we killed without fail. We had no idea why, or what the message meant. It was a load of random scribbles. It made no sense what so ever. We couldn't make a logical link between Gabriel and Edward, so I was under the impression that myself, and the rest of us were now working under contract from someone else. Maybe Edward made a deal with someone before he died, a last minute business deal, but even then that didn't make sense. Why would anyone take on last minute work, when you know you were going to die very soon, and why threaten his best assassins with their lives?

I wasn't going to argue with reality though. This had to be done, or I was done. I took one brief final look at the note, and then slipped it through the gaps in the air vent. As I let the piece of paper slip from my fingers, I helplessly watched. It floated down like a feather and immediately caught Gabriel's attention.

"What the…" He frowned, as he too watched the note glide down, and gently land on the floor. I now held my gun close and began to aim. Ricky too was doing the same. If I missed the shot, he would hit him. Gabriel walked towards the note, like a lamb to the slaughter. He cautiously bend down and picked up the piece of paper, and looked around him anxiously as he stood up again. He then peered down and began to read the note. Any time soon, I was going to pull the trigger, and rip a bullet through his head. I was ready.

A few seconds later Gabriel started to scream. It was horrifying. I wasn't expecting that reaction. He began to shake uncontrollably and furiously, and in the process he dropped the coded message. He then began to shout out, "NOOO! Oh god no, please no." It was as if he was begging. It then became very apparent to me that he knew he was about to die. I looked through my scope and focused, trying to drown out the frantic panic that Gabriel was filling the air with. I knew it was only a matter of time before one of his guards over heard the commotion, so time was running out. I could feel the added pressure build within me.

I had the perfect head shot and was about to pull the trigger. In the next second or two, I was going to see his brains splattered all over the place. Instead, he suddenly ran towards the door. I had never seen a man bolt so fast. He escaped my line of sight within seconds. It was like watching a wildebeest flee from a starving lion. I couldn't fire in time, and tried to follow him through my scope, but couldn't. *'Shit!'*

I then heard a silent shot and the next thing I saw was Gabriel suddenly stopping. I was confused for a brief second, and watched as he slowly yet clumsily, turned around. I saw blood. Blood was draining from his chest. He then fell against the door, and slid down it, leaving a line of blood smudged on the door. He then looked upwards, looking like a ghost, and stared at the air vent. He was starring right at us. His eyes and face were a haunting sight. Something you'd see in a nightmare. I felt my eyes were locked with a dying man's eyes. I wanted to look away but I couldn't. There was something in his look that sent shivers down my spine. I was used to seeing dead people and people dying, but there was something in his look that upset me and made me feel sick. It was as if his eyes were trying to tell us something.

All of a sudden, the stare was broken as his head dropped, hanging motionless. I still couldn't help but stare. My eyes were transfixed on his bloody body. What was going on with me, why was I feeling like this? Was it some very bizarre effect from the poison? Before I could bog myself down in any more thoughts Ricky proudly whispered, "One for me." His smugness pissed me off, and I just look at him with an unamused expression on my face, and barked, "Move!"

We quickly crawled back along the air vent, and made sure the coast was clear, before dropping out of it into the corridor. When we dropped down into the corridor I spoke to Gizmo,

"Mission completed." Then asked, "Are Tank and Lady Luck out of the building?"

"Yes." I could hear that Gizmo had a smile on his face, and to be honest, I felt like smiling too. Ricky and I made our way down the stairs, and were just about to walk onto the overcrowded casino floor, I almost leapt with joy knowing that we were almost finished. Then an aggressive voice boomed from behind us.

"Where have you been, this is a restricted area?"

My mind went blank as I felt so confident that we could just walk out of here. Ricky then butted in very quickly.

"We were looking for the toilets." The bouncer just stood there, very still, not saying a word. I just felt like running out of this place, but there again it would be best to try and remain looking normal. "We bumped into another bouncer in the corridor, and he said that the toilets are just over there." Ricky then pointed towards where the lavatories were. I stared at the guard intensely hoping he was going to buy our lies. "We have had a lot to drink, this casino is great!" He tried to butter the guard up, seeming so innocent.

"Come with me," the bouncer ordered, with an expression that showed that he didn't believe us. My mind was now set on the dead bodies in the building. If they were found before we could get out, it was all over for us.

The butch bouncer marched us both towards the bar area. I felt a surge of panic grow within me, as I didn't know what to expect. It was starting to become impossible to control my nerves any longer. The bouncer who looked like a gorilla, then pulled the bar man who served us early, over to one side.

"Have these guys been drinking here?" The bouncer was checking out our excuse. He was double checking that we were not lying to him. Luckily this was the bar man that had served us earlier; otherwise the situation would definitely not be looking good. The bar man smiled at us both.

"Yeah." The bar man gave me the impression that he was fed up. It led me to believe that this wasn't the first time the bouncers had approached the bar staff for an alibi. The bouncer then coldly looked at us both and walked away with nothing else to say. I could tell it pained him to leave us alone, but more than ever we really had to be making our get away, but we were free! Within that moment, Ricky and I spun round and made a dash towards the exit. I was not willing to spend a second longer in this place.

Ricky and I then made our way out of the casino, and boy oh boy, was I glad to see the back of it. We both made our way back to the BMW, and clambered into the back of it. Gizmo was sitting in the front of the car, and he shuffled round to face, Ricky, Hazel and me.

"What took you so long to get out?" Gizmo grunted abruptly. "We began to worry that you had been caught." Tank started the car, then drove away from the scene of the crime. I just glared at Gizmo.

"Don't tell us we took our time!" I didn't like his attitude. Ricky then piped up, and defended me, "You mucked up, and put our lives in danger."

"Your lives are already in danger."

"Yeah but it didn't have to be put into more danger, did it?"

"Look," Gizmo hung his head slightly, clearly feeling disappointed in himself, even slightly humiliated. "I didn't know about the security door. I must have over looked it."

"It's not good enough."

"Look, you guys looked over the plans, it's not just my fault."

"But you were the one that was so willing to do the research, and the planning. It's what 'you do best'!"

"But you,"

"Will you both shut up!" I snapped, wanting to bang their heads together. Fighting like this wouldn't solve anything. "We just need to take more time on the planning process."

"But," Ricky again spoke,

"No!" I looked at him harshly, "Don't argue with me!" I felt like a teacher telling off a naughty school boy. "I know what you're going to say."

"Which is?"

"I don't want to spend more time on the planning, because it eats up time, and the more time we take up the more we are closer to death." There was a very sombre atmosphere in the car. "The fact of the matter is, we need to. We have been given three months to actually do this properly. If we don't do the planning properly we will keep running into situations like tonight, and we might not be as lucky next time round." No one spoke after me, and as far as I was concerned it was the end of the subject. I was sure that it was all a reality check, and time for us was like gold dust, so we might as well invest it wisely.

"Oh, and for the record Ricky, thanks for your help out back there." I didn't want to give him any praise, and it hurt me to say that one line, but I felt obligated to do so. After all he had fired the shot that killed Gabriel, and it was a perfect shot too.

"What are you talking about?" he snapped, but not in an angry manner. My eyes widened, as I felt confused. He then told me, "You did the hard work, all I basically did was lie to a guard, and put a bullet in someone!" He grinned

"Exactly, you were the one that killed Gabriel, you've got the glory."

"Grace, shut up." He rolled his eyes tiresomely, "If it wasn't for you getting us out of the corridor by the air duct, then I wouldn't have been able to make the kill" I looked at him with a small, but unaware smile on my face. "I guess that's why they call you Ace." I gave him a little nod to show my appreciation and then looked away.

"Well at least my little darling is safe." Hazel dramatically expressed whilst flinging herself round him again. I swear she was deliberately trying to get under my skin, or was jealous of the fact that for once, Ricky had paid me a decent compliment.

Then to my surprise Ricky sharply barked at her, "Get off me." Ricky then proceeded to shove her off him, and followed it up with an annoyed glare. Hazel just stared, shocked, at Ricky, and reluctantly removed herself from him. He then hung his head and looked at the floor, avoiding eye contact with anyone else. I saw an evil glare that Hazel passed on to me, but I shrugged it off and peered out of the window of the moving vehicle. I felt a little smug though. Maybe Little Miss Perfect felt like she had just got a slap round the face, and maybe Ricky is coming to his senses again, and realising what a cow that woman is.

I then started to think about what would be facing us next. I didn't want any more close calls like we had today, and I hoped that we could all work along with one another, and pray that the rest of the missions would be straight forward. I doubt they would be. At least there is one less mission to worry about. One down, three more to go!

CHAPTER 4

REALITY CHECK

As I lay in bed that night I couldn't help but smile. A lot of things started to fall into place, or at least it felt like it was. It made it easier for me to accept the situation that I had been hopelessly placed in, although I was still not happy with it of course. It's a heavy burden for anyone's shoulders. At least the first target had been eliminated, and yes it wasn't straight forward, but at least it was done. It gave me some belief that we could complete all the assassinations and save ourselves.

Also I couldn't help but think about Ricky's actions in the car earlier that night. Maybe he does have a conscience! God only knows what was going through his mind earlier, and I loved Hazel's reaction. Boy, I felt so good and highly amused; it was almost entertaining, but do I still have feelings for him? I have no idea. My dramatic explosion in the kitchen suggests I do, but I didn't want anything to do with getting emotionally attached to him. After all I still don't know whether he was after sex, or just trying to express himself. All I knew for certain was men are a lot of hassle, probably more hassle than they are worth! They drive you coo-coo for no apparent reason.

The next morning I had woken up before everyone else, so I spent breakfast alone. In a way I was slightly pleased that I could stomach food without watching Tank chuck his food down his throat like a pig. I then decided to go to the study and examine the other cases. I was sure the others wouldn't mind, and I figured if we chose the easiest mission, and leave the hardest till last, it would allow us to have more time and practice as working as a team. Like I had said yesterday planning is key, and we were foolish thinking we could rush through the plan and handle things head on. A good plan equals fewer risks.

I entered the silent study, and made my way over to a side table were the files where in a pile. I grabbed them, placed them in front of me and started to work. Flicking through the case files was interesting. I found it somewhat odd that a person's life could fill just a few simple sheets of paper. It made me think that we are all insignificant in some ways, and I wondered what my few pages would look like, if I had one of these case files on me. More than likely nothing, or very little, as I am practically invisible, and I make it my business to keep my life to myself.

I came across Mr Gabriel Luke Hencher's file. As I stared at the picture of his greedy, fake face, my mind automatically flashed back exactly to the moment where the bullet split his skin tearing through his chest. His eyes. The eyes still haunted me. It was like a rabbit caught in a set of headlights. It made me shudder. No matter who we are, or how powerful, or rich we may be, we all fear death, even myself. In a way death is the essence of life, it unites everyone. I just pushed Mr Hencher's file to one side. Out of sight out of mind.

I then chose our next victim. Mr Oscar Brown. He seemed to be the most straight forward to kill. We were even provided with a home address. BINGO! He seemed like a normal man, in fact there seemed to be no reason to kill him at all. He was a legit business man, earned just over an average wage working as a salesman. Had a family of three. A wife who worked in a bakery, and two children aged 5 and 8 years old.

No criminal record, no bad stories about him; he was squeaky clean. If anything this guy seemed like your everyday man. Unfortunately a jobs a job. What has to be done has to be done. He must have done something to piss someone off though, and not in a minor way either. I hoped it wasn't a mistake that Oscar made years ago, and we were the bad aftertaste from it.

"Yo-yo-yo!" I heard Ricky's perky voice call out from behind me. I glanced over my shoulder casually. He looked bright, breezy and ready for the day ahead. He happily made his way over to me, then sat alongside me with a cup of strong tea.

"When did you decide to turn gangster," I joked as I shook my head. I peered back down at the paper work.

"What do you mean, I have always been gangster homey," he sarcastically replied trying to sound like a rough, tough man. I rolled my eyes up at him, and to my embarrassment he even tried to do silly hand actions to match up to his 'gangster personality'. It looked awful. He had his arms crossed like a knot, and random fingers pointing out at all directions. It was like his hands had gone into a spasm. Then to take the joke too the next level he started to rap! "Yo, my names Quick-Shot, but you can call me Ricky, my gun is so hot, and my..."

"Just shut up please," I cut in whilst half grinning at his expense. He let out a little laugh to himself, then I started to try and focus once again on the paper work.

Ricky peered over and asked curiously, "So is this going to be our next guy?"

"Indeed he is, but I have no idea why anyone wants this guy dead." Ricky gave me a complex look.

"How do you mean?"

"Well, this guy is just your average Joe, look." I carelessly shoved the paper work in front of him, and talked him through it all. He was just as baffled as I was, but then conclusively he summed everything up by saying, "Unfortunately this guy has got to die, otherwise we do, plus this is the nature of our profession. When have you ever started caring about the people we murder?"

"I don't know, just something doesn't... feel... right." Half way through the sentence something caught the corner of my eye, and distracted me whilst talking.

"What's up now?" Ricky asked concerned. I didn't like what I saw. In fact it started to make me shiver with panic, and confirmed some of my fears that were floating around the back of my head. I stretched out my arm and squashed a piece of paper between the table and my fingertips, and pulled it closer to me slowly. In my mind I was hoping desperately that this piece of paper wasn't what I thought it was, but deep down I was sure I knew exactly what it was. As soon as I dragged it directly underneath my nose, I took a sharp breath in.

"It's one of those coded messages again." I didn't breathe for a moment, but Ricky carried on chatting.

"Why are these coded messages such a big deal?" I watched as his mind started to ponder and work.

"I don't know, but there is definitely something bad going on here, I just have that feeling."

"Don't be so dramatic!"

"Do you remember the face that Gabriel made, when he saw that coded message? He looked like he had seen a ghost," I snapped aggressively. I wanted him to take me seriously, and understand my doubts. "I have seen petrified expression before when killing people, but none quite as bad as that," I explained in a calmer tone of voice. Gabriel's face started to vigorously burn an imprint on my mind once again. It felt as if this was going to become a regular, unwanted vision. "Plus whoever invented this code made it especially hard to crack. It even stumped Gizmo. You don't do something like that over anything small. I've never seen anything like this."

There was a brief moment of silence until Ricky started to rapidly dig through the other folders. It was as if something I had said, had sunk into his mind, triggered a thought, and caused him to suddenly go on a frantic rummage through the pieces of paper, like a mad man.

"What are you doing?" I asked, watching him suddenly go mad. He answered, "I'm just checking if these coded messages are in all the files." As his hands rummaged through the paper work he said, "There's one here." A few seconds later he repeated himself again, but in a much more subdued way. "There one in here too." I sat back in a chair, and started to think out allowed uncontrollably.

"There is something much more serious going on. Edward didn't tell us the full story and it's too bloody late to ask him what this is all about."

"Shit!" Ricky threw himself back into his chair, then cupped his hands over his face in disbelief. "I think you're right." He grumbled, sounding as if he wanted to wake up from this nightmare. I then felt like my mind was working overtime, trying to figure out what was going on. It was as if we were all in the thick of something, but what was that something? I gently, and thoughtfully, picked up the photo of Oscar Brown, and started to speak to the photo, as if I thought he was going to reply, or give me some form of answer or direction.

"What have you done to get yourself tied up into this mess? Why would you know Edward? Why would he want you dead?" Madness was setting in.

"WAIT!" Ricky blurted out, startling me. "Why do you think Edward wants these people dead?"

I frowned at him, and simply told him, "Because of the coded messages, I bet you that Edward knew what these meant, and I can guarantee that he's behind all this."

"But you can't say that."

"And why not Ricky?" I could hear the anger and frustration in my voice build, but my mind was too tired to feel the emotion.

"Because someone may have used Edward to get these jobs done. Someone may have provided these messages, and case files etc." I just sighed and shrugged my shoulder heavily.   "So you're saying someone forced Edward to record that video message, then took the time to make these case files, with the coded messages, to get us to do someone else's dirty work? It's a bit farfetched by any means."

"Not unheard of though, and it's possible."

"I still think that this is all down to Edward. You know what the man was like." I placed the photo of the bland, boring looking man onto the table, rested my head on my hand, and looked at Ricky. He stared straight back at me, with a clueless expression on his face.

With that, the study door opened but neither of us bothered to look round to see who had entered the room. Our minds were drowning in thoughts and guesses.

"Thought I would find you guys here." I looked over and Tank became very still. The small cheeky smile that once balanced on his bulky face slowly fell off as he worriedly commented, "Oh no, what's wrong?" exactly at the point Gizmo shuffled past Tank to get into the room.

"What?" Gizmo snorted rudely, "What's happened now? Oh god, please tell me there is nothing wrong." He rushed over, and slammed his hands on the table. "What's happened?" It was like he was on the brink of having a nervous breakdown! He was so demanding and bad tempered in his approached. I just thought to myself *'short man, short temper'*

Ricky and I just looked at Gizmo with a vague looks. Nothing was said, but I just placed the coded note under Gizmo's pointy nose. He glared downwards, and then at me. His eyes kept darting between, me, Ricky, and the note.

"These notes are in all the files, and I believe we are involved in something that is much bigger than just simply killing a few people off." Gizmo didn't say a word, he just froze as his eyes focused, and squinted onto the coded message.

"You mean this situation has got worse?" Tank gingerly asked as he walked over to us all to look at the note, and our faces.

"There's a good possibility."

After we all discussed what was going on, and studied Oscar Brown, we were no closer to finding out what was really going on.

"Whatever is truly happening it's obviously bad, not only did Edward poison us to make us complete these missions, but he may have done it because if we found out what was really happening we may have tried to pull out." Gizmo concluded. He spoke in a sad voice, and I could see the sorrow and pain on his face. In everyone's faces. All of our heads were thumping away. I felt like a sledge hammer was smashing my brain apart.

"Hang on," Tank muttered quietly whilst his eyes then started to move around the table, and the room. All our eyes met his intensely.

"Where is Hazel? Has anyone seen her?" We all shook our heads, not really caring where she had got to. Although I was surprised, and slightly amazed that I didn't realise she wasn't here. The room was much quieter without her!

Ricky then kindly offered, "I'll go to her room and see if I can find her." We just nodded in agreement, as none of us were that keen on finding her.

A couple of minutes later there were loud voices screeching down the corridor, and filling up the room with horror and anger. I could hear voices full of rage. I jumped to my feet and sneakily ran up to the study's door. About a couple of metres away Hazel and Ricky were standing at logger heads. I ran over and yelled, "WHAT IS GOING ON HERE?" My voice cut through the bitter shouting and everything fell silent. You could hear a pin drop.

"It doesn't fucking matter," Hazel bellowed whilst dramatically flaying her arms in the air, and she began to storm off. Ricky just looked at me with a befuddled expression and half shrugged in confusion. I couldn't tell whether Ricky was acting, or was genuinely just as horrified as I was. Ricky then made the fatal error of making a mean remark.

"That bitch is crazy."

"THAT BITCH, YOU CALLING ME A BITCH!" Hazel had overheard Ricky's snide name calling. She threw herself round, almost contorting her body, then marched straight back over. "How dare you!" Hazel was red in the face with fury. I took a pace back, and gave her a moment. Her eyes were full of hatred and spite. She started to violently point her finger in Ricky's face as she attempted to scream the manor down. At this point I could feel Tank and Gizmo behind me looking on, and watching this situation unfold in front of us.

"How could you say that to me?" She screeched, piercing everyone's ear drums. No one had any idea what she was yelling and throwing a tantrum about. I only assumed that Ricky would know as he had obviously said something that had seriously wound her up.

"Hazel?" I softly spoke as I reach a hand out towards her in an attempt to sooth and gently calm her down. She then slapped my hand away viciously, faster than a snake spitting venom. I was taken aback.

I didn't know what to think or do. "Hazel, please calm down and just talk, shouting is not going to help matters."

"Oh yeah! Yeah sure! Miss bloody perfect." My mouth dropped wide open in astonishment, as she hurled spiteful cold abuse at me. I didn't want to hear what I was hearing. What had I done that been causing so much friction between us?

"Listen Hazel, I have no idea what your problem is but you need to ease up."

"No, no, no, no!" She stubbornly refused just as a child would. "You would love me to bow down in front of you, and kiss your fucking arse but I won't." I screwed my face up, and tilted my head slightly as I had now completely lost the plot to what this was actually about. It now seemed she had a problem with me, and I had no idea what I had done to upset up so much. She had suddenly gone on a war path.

Hazel just stood tentatively still, the only movement from her were the tears that were forming in her blood shot eyes.

"Hazel, you're going to have to fill in the empty gaps here, because I have no idea what you are talking about."

"YOU'RE SO MUCH BETTER THAN ME!" She wept out aloud. Everyone exchanged expression around one another as Hazel's head dropped effortlessly.

"What are you talking about?" I felt like I was stuck in some bizarre world.

"Grace is the Ace." She sniffled whilst evilly glaring at me sideways on. I felt on edge, and that anything could happen at any point. I was on high alert as she had an insane look in her eyes. Was it the poison that had made her snap and lose her sanity?

"That's because of my profession. I worked bloody hard to get where I am, but I had to sacrifice a lot in life to get where I am."

She then slowly shook her head angrily blurted out, "Bollocks!" Now my eyes matched my mouth, both wide open in disbelief. I knew Hazel could be unpleasant, but this was a completely new level of it. I didn't know Hazel had it in her to be so aggressive and by the amazed stunned looks on everyone else's faces they were thinking the same. Hazel started to remind me of a drunk that has had too much to drink, and has got vile and angry over nothing.

"Don't give me that sob story you want to talk about hard times?" she screeched in a high pitched voice. "Then I will give you a heart breaking story."

"Look, Hazel I don't know what's going on with you."

"Fuck off."

"Please stop using bad language." Tank tried to calm her down but not surprisingly she then attacked him. She pushed myself and Ricky aside and tried to square up to him. I saw Gizmo starting to cower away. Hazel looked like a pathetic tiny ant compared to Tank, but it didn't stop her having a go at him.

"You're nothing." She started to leap up and down in frustration. "You are just a big dummy!" She then randomly started to laugh cruelly and sadistically, "No wonder you ended up in an orphanage, no one wanted you, no one would take you, and no one could ever love you. Your parents probably stuck you in there because you are so thick and ugly and they were ashamed."

I watched as each word was like a stab to Tank's big heart. I could see the pain scream out through his face. His eyes sank as his bottom lip lowered. He stepped back, staring at the floor, not able to make any eye contact with anyone or anything, as if he was too embarrassed or hurt to do so. That was it. The final straw. She was not going to say another word to Tank like that. How dare she hurt him like that! In one quick movement I grasped her shoulder and dug my fingernail into her skin, then roughly forced her backwards. I could feel my rage build and my blood boil. The force with which I pushed her back almost caused her to fall onto the floor.

"Hazel, snap out of it." I yelled. I knew yelling wasn't going to help matters so I lowered my voice at the last second. "You have great skills that you use well in this line of work." It pained me to say it as I thought she was always useless, and I loathed the fact I had to compliment her, and give her attention to get the peace and quiet back again. "What you do, we can't do, but there is no reason to act like this. None." Hazel then forced herself into my face, my hand was still tightly attached to her shoulder.

"You have everything." She started getting even closer. I could feel her hot breath on my face, and it repulsed me. "You are the best at what you do. You even have friends in this business, you even have someone who is like family, and you even have someone that loves you."

At this point her forehead was against mine. I could clearly see the depression and the sorrow in her eyes, but then I could hear the grinding of her teeth. Suddenly with no warning I felt a sudden blast of pain on my left cheek. I slightly stumbled back in shock, trying to figure out what happened, whilst loosening my grip on Hazel. I then realised she had slapped me. With that I threw her onto the floor, whipped out my gun, and pressed it against her head. It was a natural reaction for someone like me, but I also got a sick sense of pleasure from it too. Feeling like I was in control, and having the gun pressed up to her soft skin, made me feel a whole lot better yet my anger didn't lessen.

"I am not a woman to mess around with." I threatened her. Hazel just laid there unphased.

"You know what annoys me the most about you? You have all of that stuff, and you don't even realise it. You're so disconnected from reality." I let out a growl of frustration and forcefully shoved the gun harder against her head. "Go on shot me." She whispered, tempting me, "See how far you get without me." I then froze. I wanted to pull that trigger, and remove Hazel from my life. She was like a tumour, causing me pain, worries, and heartache! I realised she had me wrapped round her little finger, and she knew that as well. Without Hazel, half of the assassinations wouldn't be completed, but I found it so hard to yank the gun away from her head. I felt irritated, so much so I just wanted to shoot her there and then, but I couldn't. A large hand was placed on my shoulder as I heard,

"Let her go," Tank said carefully. I knew he was talking sense. Maybe he was the only one who was able to think straight. I listened to Tank and trusted him. I put my gun away, and stood upright. I frowned at Hazel as she lay on the floor helpless and alone. No one was going to help her up off the floor. Tank wrapped an arm around me to let me know that everything would be okay. I always felt secure with him.

"You're right Hazel, we will probably need you in some of the missions." I analysed the fact that I had taken everything on board. "But we don't need you on this one; your skills are not needed." I felt like I had bruised her ego just by saying that simple sentence. I felt as if

I was dismissing her from her duties, which once again gave me a sense of control and power. I watched carefully as she picked herself up off the floor. The elegance and beauty had vanished, and for the first time ever I saw a normal human standing in front of me with real emotions. "You need to leave and calm down." Nothing more was said. Hazel did what she was told and walked off peacefully although I was sure she was secretly crying, as her back was facing us.

"Are you okay Grace?"

"I am now, thanks. What about you? Those comments were cruel."

Tank simply shrugged and smiled, "Maybe my parents did dump me for that reason, but who knows. I'd like to think they did it for a good reason though, but I will never know. After all they are still my parents, and maybe one day I will get the chance to meet them, and have a true family. It's what keeps me fighting to survive." I just looked at Tank, as I could see the same expression of pain return to his face. It obviously saddened him, and felt raw, but it was good he had a dream, and some hope and something to spur him on, especially in a time like this. I was moved by it all, but managed to keep myself sensibly composed. Tank patted me on my back, then led me back into the planning room.

As I was about to enter the room I allowed Tank, and Gizmo, to enter the room before me. Before Ricky could re-join the group, I pulled him to one side, and asked him sternly.

"What did you say that kicked that off?" I gave him a look that showed that I meant business.

"She started to throw herself all over me again. I just told her to get off me, but she wouldn't. I then came clean, and tried to explain to her that it was a mistake, and a moment of weakness on my behalf, and that all of this had to stop."

I didn't know what to say in reply. A part of me wanted to tell him off, and say that a moment of weakness is still not an acceptable excuse for sleeping with someone, and then giving them the cold shoulder. There again a selfish part of me felt relieved that it was over between Ricky and Hazel, and I didn't have to put up with her stupid flirting any more. I finished off by questioning, "So that was it then? Emotions ran high."

"Well hers did."

"Fine, just keep your distance from her," I warned him. "We don't need any more fuck ups." Ricky agreed, then we tried to put it all behind us and attempted to move on.

Sitting back at the table with one man down felt odd, but I knew it was for the best. Leaving Hazel to stew, and think about what she had done might do her some good. She might come to the realisation that she was upsetting us all and causing unnecessary problems.

"I know!" Gizmo suggested excitedly, "I could try, and crack these codes and see if I can find out what is actually going on."

"Fine," Ricky grunted whilst sounding fed up. "But don't forget we have missions to plan."

"Yeah a lot of planning needed," Tank piped up pushing that point forward even more.

"Yes, yes, I understand." Gizmo held his hands up in the air as if he was surrendering. "But these codes could be important, and I for one want to know what I am involved in."

"Yeah, even if they are important, we would still have to do whatever is required of us, whether those codes are more bad news or simply nothing," Ricky lectured.

"Okay, any spare time I have, I'll have a go at cracking the codes, okay?" Gizmo huffed, sitting with his arms tightly crossed. Even though he had said that, I could see Gizmo's genius mind at work whilst studying the coded message.

"You know what guys, I think we should start planning this mission tomorrow," I announced anxiously. I wasn't sure how the idea would go down with the others. "We will need a fresh mind to properly plan, and not leave any mistakes to chance." Everyone seemed more focused on the coded notes then the missions themselves, especially Gizmo. Everyone did agree though, which I was relieved about. I assume that everyone's heads felt just as bogged down and messed up as mine. I needed some time alone, in fact I was desperate for it. I casually left the room and walked away. I needed some fresh air to sort myself out, and to try and clear my mind from the chaos that was erupting in it. I wanted to solve and sort things out and then just sweep it all to one side of my mind. I knew exactly where I wanted to go as well. My all-time favourite spot in this manor. As I wandered outside I already started to feel happier.

I soon found myself by a large pond outside in the grounds of the estate. The massive excessive pond was linked to a little lake which travelled through the village close by. The water was fairly clean and sparkled. I sat underneath a huge drooping willow tree, feeling enclosed and concealed. The sound of the water and the song of the birds were so relaxing. The whole surrounding area had a blissful sense of tranquillity. The gentle sunlight beamed onto my face, and the crisp, brisk, cooling breeze caressed my exposed skin. I felt at one with nature as I watched fish swimming around minding their own business and birds butterflies fly around and around enjoying their freedom. I did nothing for ages apart from sit and admire the beauty and the wonders of this stunning pond life.

I then heard snapping of twigs and feet scuffling around behind me. Remaining sitting cross-legged on the cold, slightly damp grassy ground, I twisted round sharply. Ricky's face suddenly emerged from the other side of the willow branches.

"Hello there, you little adventurer!" he shouted out, disturbing the quiet. I just turned round and carried on admiring the wild life. "I thought I might find you here." He stood next to me as he gazed around himself. I didn't say anything back to him. He then placed himself next to me on the ground. "I remember you saying that this was your favourite place to be when you wanted to escape, and feel calm again." I felt pleasantly surprised as I finally gave into the fact that I would have to talk to Ricky at some point, or he would just be talking to himself all this time.

"You actually remember me telling you that?" He charmingly smiled towards me.

"Yeah of course I do. I always listened to everything you told me." I politely grinned back at him, and found my cheeks warming up a little. *'Am I slightly blushing?'* I wondered as I swiftly swept my hand across one cheek, hoping that Ricky wouldn't notice. Luckily I don't think he did, but I felt touched that he would remember such an insignificant fact.

There was a moment of silence. Normally being stuck with Ricky alone, he would talk constantly. He would win for Britain if there was a nibbling your ear off contest!

"Are you okay?" I asked him. He turned his head and looked slightly confused that I asked him that simple question.

"Yeah, fine," he answered seriously, and then followed up jokingly. "Apart from being poisoned, and having a crazy lady on my case, because I had a moment of weakness, etc, but yeah I'm terrific."

"Moment of weakness?" I questioned raising my eye brows. It was something I felt compelled to bring up with him.

"Meh!" he grunted, "It doesn't matter, but I thought I'd come down here, and try and calm down myself." He took a breath in, "This whole mess we are in is hard. It's challenging and I don't want to crack, Grace. It could be the worst thing to do." It was then that I realised that I wasn't the only one that was suffering. Of course everyone else would be feeling exactly the same as I was. I was alienating myself. I knew if Ricky was feeling the burn of this situation then so was everyone else.

"Hazel was right," I admitted with a defeatist attitude. "I am totally blind about reality." Ricky didn't reply he just carried on staring at me. "She was right about friends, I mean look, we are sitting and talking and the same for Gizmo, he is a little odd but I don't dislike him, and Tank is like family. He's almost like a brother to me, but someone being in love with me?"

"Oh, she blowing things out of proportion." Ricky quickly jumped into the conversation again. I couldn't help but pleasantly smile at him. "I mean, you know what she is like, she knows our past, and she's trying to drag it back into the present day."

"Right."

"And I know you don't get back with your ex's, because there's always a reason why you break up with them in the first place."

"Yeah."

"And she's crazy. I think she is trying to make everyone feel more stressed and uncomfortable so we match her levels of insecurity."

"Okay Ricky, I know already." I couldn't help but silently laugh to myself. It became clear to me, like glass, that Ricky was still in love with me. He was just trying to list a bunch of excuses so he didn't make me feel uncomfortable. It felt like a young school girl and school boy trying to tell each other they like one another for the very first time. It felt awkward, but oddly I felt a buzz. It was as if I was excited, and I could feel an odd bond between us two, without any more being said. The innocence of love was starting to boil out of me, but I didn't feel bad about it this time. This time I was almost tempted to accept the fact that Ricky makes me truly happy within, and that secretly he always had done. I have just been so heavy-handed with my emotions and feelings that I never listened to them properly, but everything was coming to life now.

Ricky saw the fact that I couldn't stop smiling. I was like a grinning idiot.

"Why are you so happy?"

"No reason." I wasn't going to tell him how I felt. I thought it was best to get the missions completed, and then maybe I might see what happened after everything was completed.

"Erm.... anyway, I'm going to head back, do you want to walk back with me?"

"No I am fine, I will be back a little later."

"Alright." He then placed his hand on my shoulder, and used me to help himself get up, but then playfully pushed me over. In retaliation I threw a stick at him and missed.

"You haven't got aim as good as mine," he laughed and winked cheekily. With that he started to make his way back to the manor. I suddenly felt slightly lonely without him by my side, but at last I was now able to admit to myself that I truly and honestly have strong feelings for him. Maybe the reality check that Hazel has given me has opened my eyes, and mind, to new and exciting things. I think most of all what I have learnt is it is okay to live your life.

As I looked back at the glittering pond, an ugly but graceful herring swooped down majestically, and harshly snatched a fish away from its home. It was fascinating to watch and witness, yet I had no idea that one natural action would trigger off a massive chain of thoughts. Doubts, and deep thoughts filled my mind.

What I just saw started to make me reflect on my own past as I knew how how that felt to be cruelly taken away from your family, and home and be left with nothing. Also what I was doing for a living? Is it right to kill people whether they are bad or good? Maybe it is my purpose as I was given a second chance at life thanks to Lord Edward Hamston. What would be the chances of meeting someone like Edward and then be trained to be a mean, lean, killing machine? I couldn't help but think in depths about the pain we were about to inflict on Mr Brown's family and himself. I started to doubt what I was doing for a living, and what I had done with my own life. Ha I wasted my life? I had become somebody in this world, but it felt like I had become someone for the wrong reasons. It's not much of a life that I had. A small part of me wanted to give this life up, and move on and do something much better and bigger with myself, instead of sticking a bullet through someone and receiving cash for it. For the time being though I would have to make do, as I was having to do this against my own will.

CHAPTER 5

MR OSCAR BROWN

I WAS AWOKEN THE NEXT morning by the heavy hammering of rain, but no matter. Yesterday, after finally embracing my emotions instead of fighting them, I felt more human, more at one with myself, more alive. It made it easier for me to accept the reality of the situation I had been hopelessly placed in, which allowed me to think more clearly. I have to admit I did feel disheartened that I chose now to do this. It was a shame that being poisoned made me realise how much of my life I had actually missed as I only thought, and consumed myself with, my career. It was a crime!

Needless to say I was revving and ready to get going today. I felt like I was off to a flying start, even if it did mean cunningly planning and plotting to murder an innocent, hardworking family-man. Deep down I knew I had to, and so did everyone else. It would mean one step closer to saving mine, and the rest of the groups lives.

A little later on that morning I was surrounded by my fellow assassins, apart from one. Hazel. We gathered, and assumed that she was in her room, sulking. No one had seen, nor heard from her, since her '*little*' episode from yesterday. I don't know whether that's because she was too proud, and full of her own self-importance, or possibly she was dying of embarrassment, and felt like a humiliated clown, or for once she may have listened to someone else for a change and did what I had told her to do, which was to stay well away from us for the time being. No one cared though, as she was not needed for this mission. Her seductive skills, and the ability of having the gift of the gab was no use to us, and everyone knew it. I wanted to make sure that this man's death was done respectfully with no problems.

Planning and discussing was much easier without Hazel about the place too. There were no silly, '*Oh darlings*' latched onto every pointless, worthless sentence she spoke. There were no aimless stories that were invalid, which would side track us and cause us to lose focus. Plus we could all get a word in edge ways, and speak our minds before we forgot valuable points of concern that needed to be aired. Maybe that was another reason why the planning on the first mission wasn't much of a success. Mind you after yesterday, I think everyone was glad that we were not on the receiving end of an ear bashing, and tongue lashing from Hazel, especially at the start of the day when we needed to think straight with clear minds.

As time rolled on, we had all made steady but promising progress with the planning. I noticed that Tank didn't look like he was feeling like himself. Something was troubling him. It was obviously something he didn't want to voice at the table in front of the other guys. His body language was very sheltered. His arms were tightly crossed as his bulky shoulders seemed to be hunched up. He had a moody dark look upon his face too. It worried me when he had that expression on his face. Even though I knew he wouldn't harm a fly in this room, let alone a person, but he did have a mad streak in his eyes. My sweet, jolly Tank had covered himself up under a blanket of anger it seemed. What was the cause of his anger? Nothing immediately sprang into mind.

"What's wrong Tank?" I enquired caringly after Gizmo and Ricky had left the study to fetched coffees and teas. His big, brown, cow like eyes looked into mine as he started to enlighten me.

"I'm worried about Hazel." I almost shot back in my chair in shock and awe.

"Really?"

"Yeah." He huffed as he suddenly looked very subdued.

"Why is that?" I screwed up my face. Then a thought came crashing into my mind like a tank blasting through a fortress wall. "Please don't tell me you have feelings for her." I almost started to feel like praying in hope that he hadn't gotten attached to her. "Do you remember what I said to you when you were eyeballing her up when we first got here?" I sounded and felt like a nagging mother. I was trying incredibly hard to push my point forward, and deeper into his mind that she was nothing but trouble. "And you remember the problems she caused between Ricky and me?"

"Yes, yes, I know," he grunted stressfully. I picked up the fact that he was seriously uneasy about something to do with Hazel. It was starting to bug me, but nothing could prepare me for what Tank said next.

"I feel... sorry for her," he reluctantly told me, whilst giving me a look knowing that I was going to feel disapproved.

"Why?" I could tell by Tank's reaction he wasn't too pleased with me. So I tried to back up my reaction by expressing myself to him. "I mean, Tank, you of all people must understand why I am a little shocked to hear you say that." Tank just sat still, he didn't say a word, or move an inch. He became very moody. I felt like I had to carry on explaining myself. "What she said to me was bad enough. Her heartless actions had caused a lot of awkwardness and friction within this working team. Also some of the comments she made, made me cringe, and that's hard to do!"

Tank looked away, and seemed to be pretending to look out of the study window, even though I could tell his little mind was working away, and thinking about what I had just said. I cupped both of my hands against one of his mighty hands. He looked at me and then grinned slightly.

"I know you are thinking about everyone in this group." He paused for a brief moment. It was as if he was trying to pick his next words very carefully, which was a quality not often displayed by Tank. "It feels like no one has given her a chance." I tried to figure out what he meant by that comment. "She may be reacting like this because of a certain or a bigger reason." Suddenly he grasped both of my hands comfortingly as he spoke wisely, "If you want this team to work, well, then try and patch things up with her." I admired Tank for his gutsiness and kind heart. An uncontrollable smile stretched across my face and I beamed with pride. Those smart words and advice came from Tank's mouth! The young man who was like a boy. Finally as I stared at him. I saw him for the true man he was for once, and the small idiotic boy that I thought I knew had vanished.

"Just go and talk to her for me," he bargained. I hesitated for a few seconds, but finally gave in. For Tank, I would mostly do anything.

"Fine, but only when we finish this mission." I couldn't refuse Tank's request after being so impressed by his maturity that had suddenly bloomed and came to light, right before my very eyes. He then leaned in towards me and solemnly spoke.

"Promise me."

"I promise. You have my word."

"Thank you."

Almost a week had past. It had gone by so quickly I had lost track of times and dates. Vigorous planning had taken place every day for hours on end, making sure that nothing could go wrong, and tonight was the night that the dirty deed had to be done. I was filled with a sense of displeasure and guilt. Killing an innocent man was going to prove much harder than I had originally thought. The only comfort I could yank out of the darkness was it should be a quick and clean death for Oscar.

The plan was simple but deadly. Ricky, Tank and myself were to pick the lock at the front door, and gain entry into the house. Tank would make sure that the two children would remain in their bedrooms, which were right next door to one another. I had to drug the mother, only to knock her out so she didn't wake up, whilst Ricky would shoot Oscar in the head. We hoped that we could do it without Oscar waking up, so he wouldn't even realise that he was dead. Then we could leave and never think about it again.

All of us, minus Hazel, reluctantly climbed into the car and Gizmo started to drive out of the long drive way. The sound of the tiny little stones crunching underneath the tyres only made me feel sick. *'Here we go'* I just thought to myself.

"Are you alright Grace?" Ricky nudged me. I didn't want anyone to touch me or talk to me, so I gave a simple nod and remained silent in the car. I was trying desperately hard to get into my killer mode. It was more difficult than normal. I remember not that long ago that sticking a bullet through someone never phased me. It was almost like shooting fish in a barrel, but now being more alert and aware of my emotional surroundings it was killing me inside that I had to do this.

Eventually we arrived at our destination. We had placed the car in front of a large, lush, green bush, opposite the target's house, hoping that if anyone heard or saw us enter the house they wouldn't notice the car so much. Across the small, quaint lane was a very old but adorable little cottage. A perfectly square cut lawn lay flat alongside a garden path, with shrubbery lined up on either side of it.

"Has everyone got everything?" Gizmo enquired.

"Yeah," Tank answered abruptly. He seemed eager to get this done, and over with just like I was.

Ricky then reminded Gizmo in a clear voice, "Now remember Gizmo, keep an eye out for any suspicious neighbours, or anything, let us know immediately."

"I know, and I will."

As we stealthily got out the car, and crossed the road quieter than a mouse, I wanted to vomit. The journey up here had only unravelled my nerves even more. I couldn't let the others see, or know about it, after all I still had a reputation to uphold, and I was sure that if they knew how vile I felt it would have discouraged them to go through with this, and make it harder on themselves. *'Pull yourself together you stupid cow'* I kept telling myself repetitively. *'You're not a coward, you never have been and you never will be.'* I yelled this in my mind in an attempt to psych myself up for this.

We had reached the front door. There seemed to be no movement inside the cottage which was a good sign. It meant that they were all in bed fast asleep. The front door was thick, very old, and wooden. It also seemed very heavy looking, and I became wary that an old door like that would make a lot of noise when opening it.

"Be careful when you open the door," I finally managed to say. Where I had been so quiet my mouth felt dry, and my throat felt tight and tense. Ricky nodded and understood what I meant. He crouched down in the darkness, and started to gingerly unpick the lock. Worryingly Ricky then anxiously muttered, "Something's wrong."

"What do you mean? Why is something wrong?" Tank snapped. He sounded aggressive. I looked at him trying determine what mood he was in, but I couldn't see his facial expressions. It was too dark.

"For whatever reason, the lock pick won't unlock this door." I didn't know why we couldn't pick the lock either. Maybe the lock was far too old for it to be picked open with a modern device. Then an idea flashed across my mind.

"The back door," I quickly spoke. "There should be a back door that leads into the kitchen that might be easier to get into." I remembered the blue prints that Gizmo had presented to us of Oscar's house during the planning stage, and I could remember the layout of the house clearly in my mind.

"Fuck this!" Tank blurted. I was taken aback. What the hell had gotten into Tank? "Let's just smash down the door."

"NO!" Ricky and I jumped. I could see Tanks silhouette of his fists clenching up. I started to feel extremely uneasy as I hated the fact that we were lingering around the front door for too long.

"We can't make any noises that would wake anyone up." I tried to reason with him, and then Gizmo spoke to us through our wireless headsets.

"What's going on? Why are you guys not inside yet?" His voice was full of concern. I felt like running away, and leaving this far behind. The build-up of emotions made my brain feel like it was going to explode, and I wasn't sure how long I could keep this brave exterior up for.

"We have a problem," I replied trying to sound calm, but I could hear my own voice shake with stress. I saw Ricky peer up to me, as he heard the shakiness of my voice clearly. He stood up slowly, as I cleared my throat and tried to speak confidently. "We can't seem to pick the lock. We don't know why."

"I don't know why there is a problem." Gizmo's puzzled voice echoed in my ears.

"This is stupid." Tank started to speak loudly as I started to stare at the floor, not able to look at anyone any more. *I'd rather be in hell then here'* I thought to myself as I felt like crumbling and falling to the floor.

Gizmo then suddenly ordered, "Speak quieter Tank, and calm down."

"No," he shouted. "We spent forever planning this, and we can't even complete the first bloody part of it."

"Please be quiet Tank." Ricky spoke softly; I was unable to say anything. I could sense that Ricky was still watching me closely. "Ace came up with a plan B Gizmo. We will just go through the backdoor that leads us into the kitchen." But with that, Tank suddenly took three very large paces away from the door, and then to my horror, charged full steam ahead into it.

My heart was suddenly in my mouth as the door flung open making a loud crashing sound that seemed louder than a bomb going off.

"Shit!" Ricky panicked in astonishment. I felt like I could have fainted there and then, but then a burst of adrenaline brought me back to life, as I saw Tank bolt up the stairs. Ricky and I had no choice but to chase after him. The plan had gone horribly wrong. I was terrified how this would end. I knew in my heart and mind it wasn't going to be pretty thanks to Tank's abrupt, thoughtless actions.

"What the hell is going on?" Gizmo yelled frantically in fright into our ears.

"Tank's gone mad. He barged down the front door and ran off up the stairs." As we had got half way up the stairs, there was a loud bang. A gun had been fired! Shortly following a haunting scream filled the house which made my hair stand on end. Then another shot was fired, and the screaming had stopped dead. As we got to the landing Tank walked out of a bedroom with blood covering him. The blood had splattered over his face and clothing as we saw his gun smoking. We stood still in terror.

"What the fuck Tank!?!" Ricky bellowed out. It was like witnessing something out of a horror film. I couldn't believe what had happened. My brain couldn't process what was occurring around me. "How could you do that? We were going to do it with dignity, like that poor man deserved. Instead you blow their bloody brains out like they were common criminals you.... you..."

A door then opened a long side me and Ricky as a small voice cried out weakly, "Mummy."

A little boy stood there. My heart skipped a beat, as I tried to usher the boy back into his room, but he wouldn't move. He was just as shocked as we were. The small, innocent child looked at me and Ricky, but the sight of Tank covered and dripping with blood sent the child into a deep state of shock. At first the little, blond haired, big blue eyed boy looked as if he was going to faint, but then screamed, and floods of tears rolled down his face, catching us all off guards.

I suddenly ran over to the other door, and stood firmly against it, in a desperate attempt to keep the other child from leaving her bedroom. I didn't want any harmful or disturbing images to pollute the other child's mind. I only wish I had thought faster to protect the other child. Ricky saw me try and protect the other child, but then we were both distracted by Tank once more. I found myself being afraid of him. He shoved Ricky to one side, then proceeded to stormed into the child's room without a thought, or a care in the world.

"NOOOO!" Ricky shouted as he viciously jumped onto Tank's back, and tried his hardest to yank, and drag him out of there.

BANG! My heart sank deep, and shattered into a thousand pieces. Hot tears pricked my eyes and began to stream down my face. My eyes started to feel like they were burning, my inside ached, and I couldn't move. To make things worse I could hear movement in the room behind me. I slouched down the door and sat in front of it like a big rock. I felt a depth of despair and sorrow pulse through my veins. There was a banging sound from behind me as the small, young child tried to get out.

"Mummy! Daddy!" A little girl's voice wept out. Even the young minded, inexperienced child knew something was wrong. Her little angel like voice made me cry and sob even harder. I couldn't control myself. She never asked for any of this to happen to her or to her family, and I couldn't help but think what the rest of her life would now be like, and how much damage and destruction we had caused her. We were like an ugly, deep scar; we would have a permanent effect on her life forever. She was now left alone, with no one to care for her. I knew too well how that felt from my past and the damage it had inflicted onto me. If she ever grew up and wanted revenge, I would let her take my life. I hated myself more than words could have expressed.

"You bastard! You cold hearted, son-of-a-bitch, bastard!" Ricky voice boomed. "How could you? How?"

"What's going on? Guys, what's happening? There are lights turning on in every house. You have seemed to have awoken the whole street!" I couldn't speak. I felt like I had no right to communicate with any human ever again after the nightmare that had unfolded in front of me. Ricky rushed out the room, and looked down at me. His constant watching over me was a way of him trying to protect me. I was still a blubbering wreck on the floor.

"Come on Grace we have to go, before we are spotted or arrested by the police." I just ignored him. I couldn't move a muscle. I felt as if I was rooted to the floor. Plus I didn't want to get up and run off, just in case the little girl ran out and saw the bloodshed that had taken place.

"Hang on." Ricky then got hold of a large trunk and forcefully shoved it in my direction. "If you stand up, we can put this in place of you." Ricky understood me and my thoughts. I picked myself up, wiped away the tears, and put the heavy lump of a trunk in front of the little girl's door. "We have to go!"

I saw a little photograph of the girl who was trapped behind the door. It had fallen over as Ricky was pushing the rectangular trunk. I picked it up, and took a quick look at it. She too had golden blonde hair, with beautiful blue eyes, and pale linen-like skin. She sounded like an angel and she looked like one too. I placed the photo into my pocket and started to force myself away from the door. It was near enough impossible to do so.

Then Tank walked out in front of me. I stopped and stared at him. I had no words to say to him, in fact I didn't want to be anywhere near him. I couldn't stand the sight of Tank. He didn't say anything either, he just looked at the floor, and walked down the stairs as if nothing had happened. This wasn't the Tank that I knew and loved. This was a stranger who has lost his mind. Ricky then grabbed my hand and tried to make me move faster down the stairs, I snatched my hand back. I didn't want any human contact. I didn't run down the stairs either. I walked coyly down them. Each step I took towards the knocked down, broken front door the more guilt flooded my mind. I felt like I could have drowned in guilt.

As I walked out of the house, I could hear the screeching and crying from the girl. It was like she was begging for her parents to come and rescue her and attend to her needs. The tears started to pour from my sore eyes again. I then saw Gizmo and Ricky at the car windows. They were trying to hurry me into the car so they could speed off into the distance. I could see their mouths moving. Their lips were aimlessly moving up and down and up and down, but I couldn't hear their voices. That little girl's scream was already haunting my mind; it was all I could hear.

As I got into the car, Ricky tried to talk to me, but I couldn't talk back. I stayed silent, and wanted to remain silent. Nothing was said between anyone after they had all seen the state I was in. Ricky was pulsing with rage and frustration. Gizmo was on edge and looked like he was going to have a nervous breakdown. Tank seemed to have no expression at all. Not an ounce. He didn't look pleased, or proud, he didn't look shocked or sad. He was like a dead man. I couldn't stand being sat in the same car as him, and couldn't wait to get back to the manor. I just wanted to hide away and cry like those poor children did tonight.

CHAPTER 6

DRUNKEN TRUTHS

A S SOON AS WE arrived at the manor we were immediately greeted by Hazel. She was standing dead in the centre of the entrance underneath the giant chandelier. She looked nervous. I assumed she was eager to hear if the assassination had been completed. We all walked closer towards.

"So, is it done?" Everyone just looked at one another with sorry expressions drawn across our faces. Hazel's eyes suddenly welled up in fear, as I could tell that she thought Oscar Brown was still alive.

"Yeah, it's done." Ricky spoke gently. The awkwardness and the sorrow filled every ounce of my body as I just wanted to vanish out of sight. I no longer wanted to be there amongst company. Then Hazel couldn't help herself and enquired about the assassination.

"Did something go wrong darlings? You all like you have seen a ghost."

"It wasn't done the way we wanted it to go."

"What do you mean?" I couldn't help but suddenly lose control of my emotions once again.

"It was all thanks to the hands and the well-equipped Tank," I growled spitefully.

I gave a sharp stare towards Tank, who just stood still. He still had no expression on his face. It was as if he was completely clueless as to what he had done, or had forgotten. I began to walk away when Tanks voice rang in my ears as he told me naively, "Well at least it's done."

I bite my bottom lip hard, so hard I could have easily drawn blood. I span round, and looked at him in astonishment. Ricky and Gizmo just stood to one side, looking tense and concerned as to what my reaction was going to be like. Hazel was placed on my other side as her eyes darted around; looking stunned at the fact that I was now filled with hatred towards Tank.

"Yes, yes. The killing of the one man we were told to kill is done." I spoke calmly trying to keep myself in order, but then the sound of the little girl's and boy's voices shot through my mind, and the mother's high pitched, petrifying scream cut through the war in my head like bullets. I couldn't help but lose my temper. I spat out heatedly, "But the killing of three extra people was not necessary." Tank then quarrelled with me, bitterly.

"For all you know it may have done some good. I could have done them a favour."

"OH bloody yeah!" I gasped in disgust. "What would that be then? What good, or delight did you bring to that family?"

"That boy would have woken up with no father, that woman would have woken next to a dead husband, I stopped them waking up to it." As Tank howled at me, I died a little inside. It felt like a part of me had been ripped out and trodden on, and it hurt, a lot.

"Tank what's happened to you?" I eyeballed him as he just gawped back. The veins in his head where sticking out, and pulsing. I could see he felt just as exasperated, and angry as I was. "Don't you see, the killing of the one man was enough, and yes that poor family would have woken up to a nightmare, but they still would have had their lives." I could hear Hazel slightly sob in disbelief, as Gizmo and Ricky hung their heads in disgrace, as if they had failed. "That little boy could have been something amazing, and yes there would have been no father, but he still would have had a mother to love and care for him." I felt like crying again, but my eyes were so dry and sore it was impossible. Every time I blinked it was as if my eyelids were lined with sand paper.

I dug deep into my pocket, then pulled out the photo of the little girl. I hastily inspected it, but as soon as I saw her little, lit-up face I felt violently sick.

"Now there is this little girl, all alone, and no one to love her, and it's all your doing." I chucked the photo on the floor. The photo glided along the marbled flooring, and landed at the top of Tank's shoes. "Take a good look at her Tank! Why did she deserve that?" A hard, sickening lump formed in the middle of my throat that made me feel like I had to stop talking, but then I could feel something else in my pocket. I managed to yank it out. I looked to see what it was. It was the coded message that we were supposed to leave behind at the house. I haphazardly threw it on the floor as well, and with that I left them all looking towards the floor at the little girl's picture, and the note. I walked away, and left them all behind feeling dishonoured and dirty.

I soon found myself sitting alone with a bottle of wine attempting to drown my sorrows. I just wanted to numb reality for a bit. I wanted to escape the hustle and bustle of this chaos. The room I was sat in was like being in a rustic pub. There was a bar chuck full of booze, a pool table, card table, and even a darts board. The lighting was dim, and the smell of alcohol, and stale cigarette smoke filled the air. About an hour had passed, then Hazel found me. She coolly sat next to me not saying a word. She admired the bottle of red wine of which I was drinking from, and then seized a wine glass and helped herself.

"I'm sorry about what happened darling."

"It's not your fault," I answered without looking at her. My eyes were firmly fixed on my wine glass as I took a massive gulp from it. The silence grew once again and I began to feel awkward, but I didn't care. I didn't know if that was because of the alcohol, or because I was just too worn-out.

Another five minutes had passed of just pure alcohol consumption and stillness until I plucked up the courage to address Hazel. I was still feeling rather hostile towards her, but I remembered that Tank wanted me to talk to her. I couldn't believe that I was about to do something Tank requested me to do after his cruel, blood-thirsty, slaughtering, but I felt like it had to be done.

"I'm sorry for being such a wreck the past few weeks." I huffed rubbing the side of my face. "Just being here, it's..."

"Weird?" Hazel spoke, finishing my sentence. "I understand that darling." She finished, whilst swirling her wine around and around in her glass. "We all feel as if we are not ourselves." She then took a big breath in, then said something that cheered me up slightly. "I am so sorry for everything I have done to you, and all the pain and problems I have caused you. I know you think I'm a bitch. I see it in your eyes, but you're right to think that, I am, but I don't mean to be." I pleasantly smiled at her, as I dived down deep and tried to find something friendly to say back to her.

"You were right the other day though." Hazel frowned at me looking baffled. "I had so much already in my life, but I never realised it, and because of you I have been tempted to stop being an assassin," I explained, but Hazel didn't see this as a compliment, if anything she looked like she was fired up again. "I don't think I explained myself well, it's probably because of the drink." I then started to sum myself up. "You made me start embracing my emotions, stop trying to push them away. It is as if you have given me my life back, and because of this I want to live my life to the fullest, instead of living in the shadows." Hazel leant backwards and nodded slowly as she took everything in.

"But... you're Ace, you don't, or should I say can't feel emotions in this line of work. It is bad enough for any assassin to listen to their emotions."

"I know that, just as much as you do, and I know I have a reputation to uphold, but I am so sick of it now." I exhaled loudly. "I don't want to be Ace anymore; I just want to be plan, simple Grace Summers." Hazel smirked at me, as her eyes lit up with joy. She almost looked as if she was about to burst with excitement.

"I'm so glad you have admitted to the fact you don't want to be in this game anymore!" She took a ladylike sip of her wine with her pursed lips, and carried on talking. "I have been thinking about leaving this all behind as well."

"What you? Why?"

"Look at me." She laughed as she chucked her arms up, and down her body, and then roughly pointed at her face. "I'm aging!"

"But that's no reason to quit," I told her firmly. "You still have plenty of years left in you." She then rapidly swung the last of her wine down her throat and stood up.

"You are sweet darling," she said whilst softly patting me on my knee, almost being slightly patronising. "But you know, just as well as the others do, that I have got so far in this line of business because of my looks." I didn't know what to say to follow that comment up. There wasn't really anything good to say that came into my mind. I knew that she had no real talents, and yes, she did get by on her looks, but I was anxious about saying anything, just in case it caused another scene between us. "No one is going to find me attractive, or alluring when I'm old. Have you ever heard of a sex-goddess granny?" She joked, and I couldn't help but find myself laughing with her too. "No, I need to do something with my life as well, my looks will go sooner or later, and then I really would be screwed in this line of work."

With that the door to the room opened. It was Ricky.

"I'll come back in a bit if you want," he quickly shouted out.

"No darling. Its fine, come in, I'm off anyway." Hazel turned back around and looked at me. She looked at me with kindness in her eyes as she then whispered, "You've got a good heart, use it well." She gave me a wink and a cute little grin, and then walked off swinging her hips from side to side. Once again I noticed that Ricky's eyes didn't know where to look as Hazel approached him. I just laughed to myself. I now felt like I was beginning to understand Hazel, and why she was such a mess. I felt sorry for her as well. It was clear now that underneath all that confidence and make-up was a timid, worried, insecure woman. I was surprised at the fact that she was in no denial that she had no skills to be an assassin as well.

Then it hit me that Tank was right. It probably did do us some good to have a brief chat with one another, and to get to know and understand each other a bit better. I felt like I should say something to Tank but even now, whilst slowly numbing myself with alcohol I couldn't face him. Even thinking about him was causing me too much pain.

"What was that about?" Ricky asked looking surprised to see us two talking.

"Just had a little chat, and now we understand one another better than before," I replied as Ricky perched himself next to me on what was Hazel's seat. I didn't want to completely reveal what Hazel had disclosed to me, out of respect, and the fact that we were both still on fragile ground with each other.

"Thought you didn't like to drink?"

"No, I don't, but today has crushed me, and I just wanted it all to go away," I rationalised, as I began to feel low and glum again.

"Hate to be the one to tell you, but drinking doesn't help. All that's left at a bottom of a bottle is a rather unpleasant hangover." I gave him a look to tell him to shut up. I wasn't in the mood for a lecture, but I did feel a little bit more cheery with Ricky by my side. He then slapped a hand on my shoulder, and tried to set things straight. "Look, we weren't to know that Tank was going to do any of that stuff that he did, but unfortunately the damage has been done, and there is nothing any of us can do to put it right." I rested my head on my hand, then leaned against the bar. "You tried your hardest Grace."

"I'm leaving after all of this is over and done with. I will be gone for good." Ricky stared at me with empty eyes.

"You can't," he told me strictly. "Why? You're the best of the best." It was as if he was trying to reason with me desperately. As if other assassins looked up at me and admired and worshipped my gutsiness and dedication, yet I wasn't interested anymore.

"Ricky there is a big world out there, and I have missed out on so much. I don't care anymore, I don't have the same love for this as I used to."

"But why? I still do."

"I don't. I've reached the top. Where else can I go?" Ricky looked away and didn't say another word.

No more was discussed about that subject. I had got myself another bottle of wine and Ricky was drinking whiskey as usual. The warmth and the fruitiness of the wine exploded in my mouth, as I could feel the liquor trickle down my throat and rest in my stomach. Another three hours had passed, and a lot of alcohol had been drunk by Ricky and I, and many laughs had been had.

"Anyways Ms-s-s-s-s Ace!" Ricky drunkenly slurred. "How did a lovely lady like you end up in a place like this?"

"Hmmm..... it's a long story," I answered him, half giggling to myself, but trying to avoid answering his question. It was always a question that I loathed being asked. *'How did I become an assassin?'*

"Yeah, well get on with it then!" He sloppily sighed. "Mine is fast, look.... see..." He mumbled, whilst not making a lot of sense. He kept fidgeting around drunkenly in his chair in an attempt to straighten up. "I was brought up in a family of killers, and they knew Edward very well. I remember him when I was very, very, very, very, very young!" Ricky then tried to pour whiskey into his glass and randomly went, "Fuck it!" He then shoved the bottle into his mouth taking mouthfuls of whiskey, after failing the attempt of pouring the drink into his glass. He reminded me of a tramp. It did make me cringe how he could drink such a strong alcoholic drink without flinching, or screwing up his face, but I couldn't help but laugh at Ricky's drunkenness. I found it rather amusing. "Anyways.... what was I saying?"

"You knew Edward since you were very, very, very, very young," I recited sarcastically in a dramatic voice.

"Oh yeah.... he was like an uncle to me. Always there in the background of my life.... he offered to train me up, my parents said yes, and here I am." I wished so much that the reason how I got into this profession was as nice as Ricky's. The fact was I never really spoke about why I ended up being an assassin, and I didn't much care for thinking about it either. "Well, come on then! How did the world's best assassin become an assassin in the first place?" Ricky pressured. I couldn't see a way out of answering his question, and I knew that he'd only keep nagging me to tell him. I'd rather say my story in private then let the others know about my past though. So I decided to tell him now before he brought up the topic another day, which could capture other people's attention.

"Fine!" Grumpily I huffed and unwillingly gave up. I took a quick swig of wine for Dutch courage and got on with my story. "I was 11 years old," I reluctantly began, feeling dread course through me. "I was walking back home from school; I only lived about five minutes away from my old school." I paused as detailed images grew fresh in my mind. It was as if I was transported back to that moment in time once again. "I was at the top of my road where I used to live, when I noticed a lot of flashing blue lights, and a thick cloud of black smoke floating and filling the air. When I walked further down my road, to my horror, I saw that my house had caught fire." Ricky gulped loudly, and leant in closure as he began to become more intrigued about what I had to say. "I couldn't help but walk up to my home, and stand there watching flames as big as tidal waves engulf the house. It destroyed everything." I started to feel myself choke up, but I drank more wine, toughened up, and carried on telling my story. "I remember I cried so much, as I couldn't see my mother or father anywhere, or my little brother. I felt so alone, and lost. I didn't know what was going on. The flashing lights of the fire engines and ambulances disorientated me. The loud noises spooked me, and people shouting at the top of the voices only made me more frightened." I then stopped.

I found it almost impossible to carry on. I shut my eyes, and swallowed my tears. I felt Ricky's hand touch mine as he calmly and kindly offered a way out of finishing my tale of sorrow and sadness.

"You don't have to carry on if you don't want to, I didn't mean to make you upset." I shook my head side to side and told him bluntly,

"You have heard the start of it; you might as well hear the end." Ricky then removed his hand and carried on listening to me. "A police man came up to me, then told me to move on and to stop looking on, to which I replied with the fact that I lived there. I remember the look on his face. It was so ghastly and depressed looking. He pulled me away to one side, away from the hectic chaos. He then... he then..."

"Told you that your family didn't survive?"

"Yeah, that." A tear trickled down my cheek slowly. "I don't know what possessed me to do what I did next."

"What did you do?" It was as if he was listening to a ghost story. He had the same tone of nervousness paired up with being intrigued.

"I ran. I ran as fast as I could and as far as I could. Till this day I never understood why I did it, it just felt like the natural thing to do."

"Maybe that's why till this day, when you feel like things are getting too much for you, you just go and hide somewhere and think by yourself." It was a thought that never crossed my mind before. In fact I was never fully aware that I acted like that. It was an interesting comparison and conclusion.

"Anyway," I carried on. "I ended up living on the streets for about a year, I had nowhere to go, and I didn't know who I could turn to for help at that age. I had heard that the police tried to track me down, but I just remained hidden. Then one day just by luck, Edward found me, and took care of me, he almost became a father figure in my life." Nothing was said for a moment or two. I could tell Ricky was trying to process the horrors I had battled with as a child. He finally managed to say a few simple words, but it meant the world to me as no one had ever said them before.

"I'm so sorry for your loss." My manically depressed, tear filled eyes looked heavily at him. I took some comfort from those words. No one had ever said that they were sorry for my loss; it was as if someone cared about the problems I had to face. "Maybe that's why you had such a bad reaction to the death of Mr Brown's family. Maybe it's because you know how that little girl feels." A draining sigh escaped my mouth as I just nodded.

"That girl will grow up so damaged, no matter if she lives with another family who loves her ten times more than her previous one. She will never be the same again." It was the cold, hard truth of the matter.

I then noticed that Ricky looked like he was welling up. I had never seen him look so emotionally weakened before, but Ricky being Ricky 'the macho man' wouldn't ever cry in front of me. He just jumped to his feet and said, "Think we should get some sleep." I agreed.

However, as I got to my feet I couldn't feel my legs. It was as if they had gone. I drunkenly stumbled forward and Ricky, luckily, managed to catch me in the nick of time, otherwise I would have face-planted the floor! I started to laugh in humiliation. I then giggled.

"I think I have had far too much to drink."

"You don't say!" Ricky joked whilst rolling his eyes. He hooked his arm around my waist and lifted one of my arms around his shoulders. His skin felt delightfully smooth, like silk. Ricky was practically dragging me about. My feet were scuffing hopelessly along the floor, as I had lost the capability of using my legs to walk. All sense of co-ordination had gone on holiday. Only problem was two drunks can't balance on one another. It was like the blind leading the blind! It took about five minutes just to leave the room, but no matter. We both found it humorous.

After the massive struggle of climbing up the stairs, which felt like climbing a mountain of never ending steps, we had reached the corridor heading towards my bedroom.

"S-h-h-h-h-h-h-h!" I half whispered and half laughed, "We have to make sure we don't wake up Gizmo as we walk past his room."

"Okay!" Ricky muttered back. Now, I thought we were very quiet, quieter than a church mouse, but within seconds Gizmo's door was furiously flung wide open, and Gizmo didn't look pleased to see us both. His thick framed glasses were slightly wonky on one side of his face, as he had obviously just chucked them on in a rush, and his hair was stuck up at all angles, looking slightly knotted. I couldn't help but laugh, or keep a straight face; he looked a right state, but probably not as bad as me or Ricky appeared.

"What are you two doing!?!" Gizmo barked in an aggravated voice. Ricky then let go of me, half propped me up against the wall behind us and proceeded to apologise to Gizmo.

"Sorry Gizmo, we have had a few to drink." Gizmo scrolled his eyes up and down at us both in a repelled way.

"Yes, I can see that." He sounded snotty and snobbish. Like a stuck up, posh, school boy.

"I'm helping Grace to her bedroom. She is legless!" As soon as Ricky told Gizmo that, I could feel myself gradually slipping down the wall. I tried very hard to keep myself up right. I must have looked so retarded kicking my legs about, stretching out my arms upwards I have no idea why I thought that would help me stay upright! My legs felt numb and within seconds I fell to the floor with a loud thud.

"HAHAHAHAHA!" I burst out; rolling on the floor in fits of laughter thinking this was the funniest thing in the world. I could hear Ricky chuckling, and I was sure Gizmo even let a little smirk creep onto his drowsy face.

"Come on, I haven't got all day... night... whatever it is!" I yelled, suddenly getting impatient for no reason what so ever. I guess I just longed for my bed and for some sleep. I think my mind was trying to tell me to sleep the alcohol off. I pushed myself up on my hands and knees, and attempted to stand up, but no luck. So I gave up, and decided to start crawling, it was so much easier, and safer for me.

I heard Ricky then ask, "Don't suppose you fancy giving me a hand putting her to bed do you?"

"No way, you're on your own!" Gizmo replied.

After crawling like a three legged donkey, I finally reached my bedroom door. Ricky unfortunately was left with the task of picking me up off the floor, and when he did he opened the bedroom door and led me to my bed. He carefully placed me down on it and then threw a cover over me.

"Right, I'm off now. Good night Grace."

"Wait." I found myself shouting. Ricky span round on his feet and peeped at me. I patted the bed as an indication that I wanted him to sit down next to me. He did what I asked him to do. "Can I ask you not to tell the others about my past please? I don't want to be constantly reminded of it."

"I promise you. A word won't pass these lips."

"You know," I yawned noisily as I started to feel sleepy, "You're not so much of an arse-hole!" Ricky gawped at me in slight bemusement and chuckled,

"Thanks. I'm glad you think that. You're not too bad yourself!"

I let out a relaxing sigh, as cheekily Ricky's smile grew across his face. He watched me get comfortable beneath the duvet, which he had compassionately placed over me, for which I was grateful. I couldn't help but become transfixed on his lips. His smiles were always so wholesome and pure. Then our eyes met. The intent look grew intense between us, but this time I treasured it. I was content just to be in his company, admiring the deep, dark mysteriousness of his eyes.

Gradually, Ricky begun to lean in towards me, not breaking the powerfully solid eye contact we had developed. I had noticed his breathing grew slightly heavier than normal. I too found myself moving in closer, and before I knew it, Ricky's supple, tender lips were on mine. His kissing was madly passionate but gentle. I could feel my cheeks burn up, as desire and lust overwhelmed me, making my body ache for his. I couldn't control myself, as my basic animalistic instincts took over. Everything felt so right, so mind-blowing. I embraced Ricky tighter, pulling him in towards me, so my chest was firmly pressed against his, as we carried on kissing lovingly.

He delicately encouraged me to lie back down, as he proceeded to slip under the covers to join me, our bodies still remaining inseparable. The warmth and touch of his body covering mine avidly, sent my blood racing, and my chest pounding. It wasn't till now that I realised how much we longed and craved for one another's sweet, fierce embrace. Each fondle and caress drove me wild and sent me into ecstasy. He made me feel so womanly and wanted. Our bodies were finally united as one, in sensuality, euphoria and bliss.

The next morning I awoke feeling like death warmed up! However I was quickly distracted from the beginning of my dreadful hangover, as I could feel something warm next to me, and hear and feel heavy, hot breathing on the back of my neck. I screwed my face up feeling puzzled. I couldn't figure out what the heck it was that crawled into bed with me last night. As I coyly turned over in bed, Ricky's face was right next to mine. *'Oh yeah, I remember now!'* I thought to myself. Part of mine and Ricky's passion-fuelled love feast came back into my mind, only to arouse me once again.

I admired Ricky when he was asleep. He looked so peaceful and adorable, and more handsome than ever. I didn't know why, but I certainly found him irresistibly attractive that morning. A silly, great, big grin crept up on my face as I felt so elated with myself. Finally it happened. It wasn't the time that I wanted him to find out how I felt about him; I was planning to do it after the poison had been cleared from our bodies. That way I knew that Ricky would be worth going for, and that we would have a shot of making this relationship amazing, long, and full of memories. Then I realised something. I didn't tell him how I felt. I just jumped into bed with Ricky!

"Oh-my-god" I whispered to myself in annoyance. I felt so peeved with myself it was stupid! I had realised that Ricky may think it was just me being drunk, and that I just wanted sex off him.

Before I could torture myself any more I saw a big pair of eyes looking straight at me.

"Morning," he yawned whilst carelessly stretching himself out underneath the covers. I sat up right slightly, holding the blanket close to me, to cover myself up. Ricky then looked up at me, and immediately asked me, "Are you okay?"

"Yeah great... well, actually... erm..."

"Oh no." Ricky dropped his head, "You regret having sex with me, don't you?"

"No, no.... of course I don't." I bit my lip, and tried to think of a way to explain what I was feeling, but I couldn't. My head was starting to pound away, and the need for water was immense. I felt seriously dehydrated to the point that my tongue was stuck to the roof of my mouth. Plus to make matters worse I could taste stale, old alcohol in my mouth from the night before, which only made me feel ill.

"Then what's up?" Ricky started to sound anxious. It was as if he thought he had done something wrong, which of course he hadn't.

"I'm massively hung over." I grumbled, half slouched over, still keeping the blanket close to my chest. I felt so sorry for myself!

"I told you last night that you won't solve anything by drinking, and at the bottom of a bottle there's a..."

"Hang over," I cut in rudely. "I know. I remember, and yes you are right!" I buried my head deep into my covers.

"Hold on, I'll get you some water." Ricky rushed up and into the bathroom. Again I lost control of my actions and found myself staring helplessly at his naked body. He then came back with some water for me.

"Thank you," I mumbled. My voice sounded incredibly rough, almost manly. The pint of cool, refreshing water was so easy to drink. All of it went in less than ten seconds.

"Wow.... you really weren't lying when you said you were hung over!" Ricky found it amusing but I didn't. Memories of the night before were starting to pop back into my mind. Memories such as, waking up Gizmo, not being able to walk properly, making peace with Hazel, and of course the sex.

"Ricky, I want to tell you that... well.... I hope you don't think that.... don't take this the wrong way but," I found it impossible to complete one sentence. My mind was as dead as a dodo!

"Come on girl, spit it out!"

"Okay!" I groaned grouchily. Without thinking, and without me realising me doing so, I heard these words come out of my mouth.

"I hope you don't think last night was a drunken fling. I really like you Ricky." I clapped my hands over my mouth straight away after I had finished talking. I couldn't believe I just came out with it. It was as if I was on autopilot.

"I know that sweetie." He had a crooked smile on his gorgeous face. I was so relieved that my comment didn't back fire on me in any way. He removed a piece of my hair that was dangling in the middle of my face, and pinned it back behind my ear caringly. I was so relieved, and so happy. I just wanted to jump around on the bed or run around naked! On the other hand, what Ricky said to me next just made my heart melt? "I have always liked you for years, but when I first saw you here, when we arrived at the manner, I just fell for you." He grabbed one of my hands gently, and placed it between his hands, whilst rubbing his thumbs on either side of mine. "I never meant to hurt you, or humiliate you, especially with the situation between us and Hazel. You have no idea how much I have beaten myself up over that. You make me happy, and I think you're the most beautiful girl in the world because of that, and no other woman can ever compare to you."

I was speechless. My mouth dropped wide open, as I felt emotional but in a good way. My heart was doing summersaults, and I was brimming with excitement. I also felt so flattered and slightly bashful from the touching speech he gave me. I was unable to talk, but I was more than capable of giving him a great big kiss. His lips were sweet, and felt so good to smooch. I then collapsed into his arms. I snuggled close to him, feeling so warm and secure. I was sure that that moment in time was the happiest I had ever felt in my life. I never wanted that one single moment to end. I could have died feeling ecstatic; lying there next to him, with my head was resting on his strong, slightly muscular chest, listening to his heartbeat. I was honestly and truly was luckiest woman in the world!

CHAPTER 7

LEO BLAKE

As RICKY AND I got dressed, and were making our way down to the kitchen to grab a bit to eat, or in my case eat something to sober myself up a little bit, not a lot was said between us. However, not much had to be said. I was perfectly over the moon with him being next to me. I could feel my cheeks burning red not from embarrassment, but from the fact that I was just simply ecstatic, and slightly bashful. I assumed the only reason I became slightly shy towards Ricky was the fact I couldn't believe that we finally admitted our feelings to one another. Plus, I didn't want to open my mouth and say something stupid that could have spoiled the moment.

The blissful, cheery silence was broken when Ricky asked me something,

"How are we going to play this?" He questioned me in a way which made it sound like a delicate subject. I frowned slightly looking up at him; even now his eyes and handsome features were tugging at my heart strings. "Do you want to keep this quiet and between us for now, or are we going to let the others know?" I didn't know how to react to this as I didn't consider the others a part of our relationship.

"I'm not sure. I haven't really thought about it." I did try to think about it quickly and on the spot, right there and then, but I couldn't. My mind felt blunt as a rusty spoon thanks to the wonderful hang over! Before we could even come to a conclusion, we were greeted by everyone sitting in the kitchen. *Just wing it'* I thought to myself at the time *'go with the flow, they might not even notice that we spent the night together.'*

Hazel, Tank, and Gizmo were all sitting around the rickety kitchen table, still staring at us both. Their stares felt like they were burning holes into my body. Somehow, by entering the room, I had made them all stop dead in the middle of their conversation, and even Tank held his spoon mid-air, before shoving food into his giant gob. I felt as if I was an elephant in the room. I began to grow slightly uncomfortable, and wasn't sure what to do with myself. I wanted to simply act normal, but I then realised I wasn't sure how to act normal anymore. *'Should I sit? Should I get a glass of water? Should I say hello to everyone?'* I kept tossing the questions around in my head. By now I knew I didn't look normal, or was acting right, as usually I was a sharp minded, decisive person. I then saw at the corner of my eye a sly smile creep onto Hazel's face, indicating that she knew what had happened between me and Ricky.

"I knew it!" Hazel blurted out sounding excited whilst leaping up from her chair. Gizmo jumped with fright from Hazel's enthusiastic reaction, and managed to throw a biscuit into the air that he was about to munch on. "I knew it was only a matter of time, until you two got back together again!" She clapped joyfully.

"Are you both back together again? Really?" Gizmo sounded shockingly surprised, whilst quickly snatching another biscuit from a little white plate, which was in the middle of the table. He clutched tightly onto this biscuit and immediately took a bite from it. Ricky and I just looked at one another, and awkwardly shrugged. We then spontaneously nodded to everyone, as we came clean and told everybody with big smiles on our faces that our old relationship had been renewed.

"How wonderful darlings!" Hazel then rushed over to us with big open arms, and gave us a huge, warming hug. Hazel seemed more cheery and happy than I did! I did feel slightly confused as to why Hazel was so pleased for us, as I could remember the bitterness she showed towards me when she tried to possess Ricky, and keep him to herself. I wasn't going to question it for long though. If she was fine with it, then there was no reason to worry myself over something that was in the past.

"Darling you look awful today though," Hazel was quick off the mark to point out as she took a step back and gazed at me.

"I know, I had too much to drink last night, and now I feel hung over." My mind was still thudding, and I had cotton mouth. It felt horrible! All I wanted to do was sit down and drink gallons of water until I exploded like a water balloon. I then dragged my feet along the floor and sat down next to Gizmo. He was looking at me in an odd way. He had one raised eye brow, a crooked, sarcastic grin on his square head, and was looking over the top rim of his chunky glasses, in a slightly scowling manner. "What?" I barked, as I wasn't feeling very well, and I certainly wasn't in the mood for any joking around.

"Nothing!" He started to chuckle to himself.

"NO go on; tell me, what's so funny?"

"You last night," Gizmo sniggered, "you were a right mess."

"I know. I remember parts of last night," I grumbled feeling sorry for myself.

"It's self-inflicted," Ricky playfully joked whilst sitting close to me, and holding my hand. "You don't get any sympathy if it's self-inflicted." I couldn't be bothered to talk back anymore, so I cheekily stuck my tongue out at him.

With all the cheeriness and the pleasantries being passed around I had completely forgotten about Tank. He seemed to have merged into the background. He had nothing to say to me. In fact it was as if he couldn't even bring himself to look at me. I wasn't going to say anything to him either. I thought I'd give him time and let him stew for a bit. Plus I didn't want to anger him anymore. I knew what Tank was like when he became pumped up on rage and lost his temper, and I can safely say it was more than a little bit scary! It was like having a volcano erupt in your face! It's terrifying, loud, and extremely painful!

After breakfast, we all made our way to the study. The study started to feel like a home within a home. It seemed to be the place were we spent an awful amount of time. Some days I didn't mind being in the study, thinking, planning, discussing, etc, but on the other hand, there were days were I would have rather bashed my head against the wall, set fire to my hair, and stuck nails through my eyes, than sit in there for hours on end. Today felt like one of those days. I could barely keep my eyes open, let alone concentrate, or focus for five seconds. Mind you, I did deserve this murderous hang over. What was I thinking, being able to drink bottles, and bottles of wine and not suffer the next day for it!?! Idiot!

"Here we go then." Ricky planted the next case file in front of us all, in the centre of the table.

Gizmo's short, stubby arms reached out, and snatched the file, then moved it closer to himself. He flipped open the folder, and started to read out our next victim's name. "We are going after a... Mr Leo Blake." I saw at the corner of my eye that Hazel suddenly started to fidgeted nervously. I immediately knew that something wasn't right, and it became apparent to me that Hazel had become very anxious. Something was up!

"Are you alright?" I whispered to her, as she began to look more uneasy by the second.

"Me and... Leo go back a long time ago," she growled unpleasantly. Even when she pronounced Leo's name it sounded like she spat it out, more than spoke it. As if the name left a bad taste in her mouth.

"Oh really, how do you know him?" I asked curiously, but as soon as I asked, Gizmo started to read.

"He's an owner of a strip club. It's very well-known to the rich, dirty, old gits. It seems as if Leo milks every last penny out of these men, just so they can get their jollies." My mouth dropped wide up in horror. The penny suddenly dropped.

"You were a stripper!?!" I gasped uncontrollably without me realising how loud I had blurted that information out. The others turned round with bizarre expressions on their faces, as Hazel started to shrivel like a shrinking violet, or a dying weed.

"It's true, yes." She sounded ashamed of herself for a brief moment, but then she perked up. "I was amazing at it too. It was so exhilarating and exciting, and I loved the way men couldn't take their eyes off me. I knew that each one of them wanted me, but they couldn't touch me, even if they wanted to. I enjoyed it a lot." The way that Hazel was talking was strange. Her voice was a mixture of all sorts of emotions. She spoke as if she had a great time being a stripper, but listening to her much more carefully I could hear the bitterness and regret lurking behind her words. I could tell there was much more to this story than Hazel just being a stripper for Leo Blake. On the other hand it certainly explained why Hazel was the way she was. She was such a flirty, charming woman, always used to getting attention from men. It struck me that she had always depended on her looks even before she became an assassin to make money. I couldn't help but think it was a shallow way of living life.

"How old were you when you started?" I asked reluctantly hoping that she was a decent age when she started this type of work.

"Fifteen," Hazel mumbled not sounding too happy with herself. It was as if with hindsight she wished she had never started at that age, or at all. The fact that we all looked so gob-smacked probably didn't help the way she felt either. *A fifteen year old shouldn't be doing strip teases, and taking their clothes off to make money. It was disgusting. How could Leo have agreed to this!?!'* I thought to myself. *'Shows how much of a money-grabbing bastard he is, and the fact he has no morals.'*

Hazel carried on explaining. I guess she didn't want to make herself sound bad, or sound like a whore and leave us with a bad impression of herself.

"I had walked out from home, because my mother was a drunk. She couldn't cope with reality after my dad left her for the Spanish house keeper we had working for us for over ten years. I couldn't put up with my mother's bad drinking habits. I told her time and time again that she needed to stop, and that it would be the death of her, but what made things worse was the fact that she was a violent drunk… an abusive drunk… all in all, a nasty bitch!" I watched Hazel closely as I could see the hurtful memories come flooding back to her. "I had managed to find a rough, little annex for myself to live in. It was all I could afford, but soon I realised I couldn't go to school, and finish my education. I had to make money, and find work. I had to make money to survive, but I didn't know how. I knew I was a very pretty girl, and I had heard so many woman talking about how great it would be to just make money by the way they looked." Hazel began to fiddle, and play with her slim fingers and thumbs frantically. I think she felt so stupid looking back on her life now, and regretted it all. "So I became a stripper, it was easy money, and I didn't have to have any qualification to become one. In a way my body was my grade A. After a while Leo, my boss at the time, noticed that I tended to be the gentlemen's favourite dancer, so one night he told me..." She stopped talking. Hazel took in a sharp intake of breathe. I could feel the pressure pushing down on her, but she still soldiered on. I began to feel increasingly sorry for her, as I found it hard enough to talk about my own past to just one person, let alone in front of everyone.

"He told me I had to whore myself out to the rich men. I told him that I had never had sex before, and that I was still a virgin, but he didn't care... instead he did the unspeakable... he raped me." My heart sank deep into the pit of my stomach, and burned up in the acid. I felt physically sick. I couldn't imagine going through something as horrific as rape, especially at such a young age. It was loathsome, and any person that was capable of doing such a disgusting, evil crime deserved to be shot point blank, or even deserved to be tortured forever and more. Leo had taken the one little bit of innocence that was left in Hazel's life.

My breathing became heavier and erratic as I couldn't help but think more and more about the horrors of rape. Hazel carried on painting a vivid nightmare; her voice started to shake. "I remember I was so terrified, and so frightened. The pain was awful. He wasn't gentle, or caring. He just prised my leg open, and tore right through me. I tried to struggle out of his grasp at first, but he was too strong. I gave up, and became too tired to fight back. I had no choice but to let him carry on, and finish his business. I cried for nights after that. In fact sometimes I still do cry."

"Why didn't you leave, or go to the police?" Gizmo enquired sharply, but softly, having a sense of urgency about him.

"The money was too good." Hazel began to grind her teeth together as she then said, "I was scared that I might not find another job, or any type of work, and as long as I was working there, the longer I could live away from my mother. I was also so young, I didn't know what to do, or who to turn to. I didn't know any better." Everyone was silent, no one could think of anything to say to Hazel. What can you say to help, or comfort someone who had been through such a traumatic experience? Everyone's minds were purely focused on how Hazel must have felt.

I started to feel guilty for hating her so much at the very beginning. She never meant to turn out the way she had. It had become a way of life for her, and the only way she knew how to live. I then saw Tank look at me, as if to say he was right. It was almost as if he knew about Hazel's past, but wanted me to find out for myself. Hazel then looked away from all of us.

"I had to sleep with all the creepy, perverted, sick men otherwise if then I was beaten, or I wasn't paid, or Leo would rape me."

"That's... that's the most heart-rending thing I have ever heard Hazel," I told her whilst placing a hand on her shoulder. I couldn't picture anything like that happening to me. She had had such a tough life.

"It's in the past, and to be honest, I'm glad I get to nail this bastard for the last time." The twisted anger filled her voice, and rage covered her eyes. This man deserved to suffer.

"We best get planning so we can put an end to his heartless ways." Hazel then perked up a little bit. It was almost like the thought of this man dying at her hands, had always been a guilty pleasure of hers.

Hazel was keener than ever with the planning process. I could see it in her eyes that this was something she had been waiting for a long time. This was a personal vendetta, but I had to remind her, not to allow her emotions to get in the way and not make this to personal. I felt like I was asking for the impossible, but we couldn't afford anything to go wrong. On the other hand, as we dived deeper into Leo's past, it seemed that Hazel wasn't the only young woman who had to suffered and endured Leo's sadistic vile ways. It only encouraged Hazel even more to push on with the planning. She became a slave driver.

Just over a week had passed. The normal planning procedure had been completed. Blue prints of the strip club gave us a clear idea of what the place looked like, and where Leo could be inside the building. Hazel was able to donate a lot of information towards the blueprints. We knew how we were going to enter the club, how we were going to kill this man, and this time we made sure that Leo would be able to read the coded note that was left for him, unlike the last killing with Oscar.

The notes still had me puzzled and kept me wondering what it could all possibly be about. I still stuck to my original thought that somehow, Edward had a personal hatred, or problem with these people, and was getting us to do his dirty work. But why would the notes be coded?

After we had all geared up, and got ourselves ready for this assassination, I saw Tank sitting on a step on the staircase in the grand entrance to the manor. He looked lifeless, and was just staring through the front door that had been left slightly open, which provided a glimpse of the long gravelled driveway. I thought it was about time that we should say something to each other and clear the air. After all it had been a while since that unpleasant, indescribable mass slaughtering insistent, but I knew I couldn't forgive him for what he had done, but I felt like I should do something to try and rebuild our year's worth of friendship. I also didn't enjoy giving Tank the cold shoulder. If anything it made me feel silly and pathetic. It was child's play. We were both adults, and Tank had grown up considerably. We should be able to talk to one another openly, to try and patch thing up again.

I made my way towards Tank, sat myself alongside him, then looked at his drained face. He didn't look at me. Tank still seemed furious about the situation and clearly didn't want to talk, but I was determined for him to at least say something to me.

"Hi," I began with, not really knowing what I should say. I certainly wasn't going to apologise to him, and I was one hundred percent sticking to it too. Tank didn't say a word. So I tried making casual conversation in an attempt to get things kick started. "So, how have you been?" Tank lazily shrugged, still not making any eye contact, but at least I got a little reaction from him. At least I knew that he hadn't gone deaf! I was slowly getting wound up, but I wasn't going to show it, and I was determined to rise above Tank's annoying, stubborn attitude. So I did what I could only do, and kept talking in hope he may say something back to me at some stage. "You ready for this assassination? Have you got everything with you? Do you understand the plan? I'm looking forward to this one." Suddenly Tank just sighed heavily, and stood up, and walked away. I watched, my mouth opened wide, as he started to head towards the massive front doors.

I felt rather insulted. I was amazed at what he had just done. Tank was either fed up with me, or he just couldn't stand me anymore. Well, at least he walked off; I'd rather that than be thumped in the face. I'm sure a hit from Tank would feel like a piano falling on top of you! I felt a little hurt that he just didn't seem to care anymore. It was as if we were strangers to one another, not a couple of people who have practically grown up side by side. I started to wonder whether we would ever talk properly again, or go back to our old ways. It was then that I realised I was starting to miss him.

'Fine' I simply thought to myself. 'If he can't be bothered to make an effort, then I can't. He can remain alone by himself.'

"Grace?" Ricky's voice broke my train of thought. "Are you alright?" he asked looking at me, and then his eyes began to watch Tank, as Tank stood slouched against the side of one of the front doors, blocking the view of the driveway. He still seemed fairly lifeless, blankly gazing in front of him. It was as if he had been turned into a zombie.

"Yes, I'm completely fine," I replied, as Ricky helped me off the step. "It's just...Oh it doesn't matter." I decided not to divulge to Ricky what I was thinking at a time like this. I wanted to remain focused. "Where are Hazel and Gizmo? Are they nearly ready?"

"Yeah, they are just coming. Should we wait in the car?"

"Not a bad idea." As I was just about to walk over to the car, Ricky randomly grabbed my hand, and squeezed it tighter than ever.

"Stay safe." He then ordered me in a concerned way. I just nodded and got into the car. This wasn't the time for romantic pep talks, although I could feel my heart race with joy. 'He really cares about me.' I smiled to myself. It made me feel all hot and fuzzy.

Everything turned very serious though when we were all in the car. Hazel was determined to get this man. She kept running through the plan, time and time again. In fact the atmosphere was so intense, and adrenaline pumped I had forgotten all about Ricky, and my loved-up emotion towards him, and the same went for Tank. I had forgotten he was with me as well; the frustration that he had been causing me seemed to have faded into the back ground. Hazel was revving us up, telling us more horrific things that this man did to her. Such as having thugs go round to where she lived to beat her up, breaking up her first true relationship, because it wouldn't look good for business, and all the immoral, blunt-minded, creepy men she had to sleep with. I started to feel like this was personal for me too. Not only because I was a woman, but because Hazel felt more of a friend to me now. I wasn't allowing this man to carry on his reign of terror over woman.

We pulled outside the club at 4:30am, just like we had planned. The idea was that every employee and punter would have gone home by now, which would leave Leo all alone in the club. Easy pickings, and one that Hazel was more than happy to have. She had told us that there would be no bouncers, or anything like that around. Leo always thought of himself as a tough man and because of that he had always believed that he could take care of himself. Even though Leo had aged, he still looked mighty strong and powerful. He was almost the same size, and build of Tank, and possibly just as strong, judging by the photo in his case file.

Ricky and I got out of the car with Hazel. We were going to go along with Hazel when she entered the building more for her own safety, and so she had extra protection, just in case there was more than one person in the club, or just in case something else might have gone wrong, at least she would have extra back up. I felt like bouncing about. I was so pumped, and I reckoned that Hazel felt the same way as well. How could she not be? She must have dreamt about this moment in time for so many years and I figured that she was going to make the most of this. Gizmo was walking close behind me. We needed him, as he had a gadget to crack open the security lock for the front door, which was inside the building by the front door, so all three of us could gain access quietly and not look too suspicious. Tank remained in the car and was our eyes from the outside on this task.

As we got to the front door we saw that the electric security lock wasn't on the outside. Hazel had told us it had always been on the inside, so we were glad that the building clearly hadn't changed that much since she worked here. I was glad, because it gave me more faith in the blueprints that Gizmo and Hazel had drawn up for us. Hazel then silently guided us around the corner from the door to the side of the building where there was a little square window. Ricky crouched down, then Gizmo climbed on top of Ricky's shoulder. As Ricky began to stand up, with Gizmo precariously balanced on his shoulder, he wobbled a little.

"Keep it steady," Gizmo barked down as he began to try and gain entry through the window.

Gizmo stuck his arm out at a funny angle, then placed his wrist near the small glass window. With the other hand he pressed a button on what looked like a normal wrist watch, but it wasn't a normal watch. A sudden, bright beam of red light shone out of it and started to penetrate the glass. There was a slight hissing noise as the laser from the watch started to cut effortlessly through the glass. Within moments the glass became loose and Gizmo managed to gently capture the sheet of glass in his hands. As the sharp-edged glass lay in his hands, he passed it down to me. I couldn't help but admire Gizmo's handy work.

Ricky then had to help Gizmo pass through the small hole where the glass once sat. It was useful, and good news, that Gizmo's small, skinny body could fit through the tiny hole. Otherwise we would have been stuck!

We all watched with concerned expressions on our faces as Ricky stood back. I found it slightly amusing watching Gizmo's little legs kick around in the air, as he managed to wriggle his way through, down and inside the building with great success.

"Are you alright Gizmo?" I asked, making sure that there weren't any shards of glass left behind by his laser cutting skills, or that he had had a bad landing onto the club's floor.

"Yep, all good," a little squeaky voice whispered back, I smiled knowing that this mission felt like it was going well and that we were already doing a good job. As I looked round I could see that Hazel's smile was even bigger than mine. She looked as if she could have burst with anticipation and excitement.

Now it was the case of playing a little waiting game. As Gizmo was inside the club, we knew right then that he would be working as fast as he could, to crack the pin coded lock from the inside. Again he was using a special gadget to do that. I couldn't help but think to myself, *'If Gizmo wasn't an assassin; he would have made a brilliant bank robber, or safe cracker.'* It took about a minute for Gizmo to finish his part of the mission. Then finally we heard the clicking of the front door being opened. We poked our heads round the corner to make sure it was Gizmo standing in the entrance of the club, and not someone else, but sure thing, there he was.

"It's all clear," Gizmo told us in a hushed voice. "But there is definitely someone inside. I could hear someone moving around. So be quick." Hazel then jumped to an assumption.

"It will be Leo. I know it!"

"It's a good possibility it is," I muttered silently, "but we will have to check it out just to be sure." Hazel knew I was right. I didn't want a repeat of the last mission where more than one life was lost for no reason. Plus we didn't want to get the wrong person, simply because Leo would then for certain know that someone could be after him. Assassination is like hunting.

Gizmo quickly dashed off back to the car to join Tank, as the three of us made our entry into the building. As we got inside, my heart started to race, palms became sweaty, my mouth was dry, but I managed to keep myself at bay and engaged. We began to creep up through the entrance. The entrance was almost like a separate room from the main room, where all the strippers would have been. The only thing that divided us from the main part of the building was two large pieces of frosted glass that seemed to make everything look deformed and deranged. Luckily for us though, the entrance to the building was very dark. Up ahead there was dim lighting and the clattering of a glass banging against the surface of a table.

We crouched up close to the frosted glass. Ricky and I were hidden behind one piece, and Hazel was concealed by the other. We allowed Hazel to look around the corner of her half of the frosted glass, to see if the lonely man in the club was our target. Her eyes glared, and then she took a rather surprising sharp intake of breathe. She gave a subtle nod. I could only assume that seeing Leo once again after all these years must be daunting for her. The old emotions, and the pure fear of this man that she had suffered from must have resurfaced again. His face seemed to be haunting her as her eyes seemed to have glazed over.

I then made a number of hand gestures towards Hazel asking whether she was okay, to which she replied with her thumb sticking upwards. I was pleased she was keeping herself under control. The last thing we needed now was Hazel to lose her nerve, and have a mental break down, or something along those lines.

I wanted to see this man for myself, plus try and check out the area off the club to double check no one else was around. The strip club looked like any other strip club. A big, long, bulky bar lined the left hand wall, with endless amounts of glasses and bottles piled behind it on glass shelves. Four silver metal poles, with little circular stages surrounding them, were placed almost in each corner of the room. There was a large glamorous looking stage, which had a catwalk running from the main stage down the centre of the room. I could only think about the women who would parade up and down that aisle with barely anything on, and being scared or worried about what could, or would, happen to them later on that night. There were plenty of chairs and tables that were scattered about, and to the far right hand side there were little private booths.

Leo was slouched over one of the tables and he began to sing. I couldn't understand what he was singing; he seemed to be very drunk. All his words were slurred together, and jumbled up. He had no rhythm or beat to the song he was trying to sing. It was almost like he was possessed by an alien species, and speaking a strange foreign language! I loved the fact that he had no idea what was about to happen to him. I adored the fact that we were sitting there, ready and poised, and just watching him making an idiot out of himself before he died. I embraced the fact that this man would be dead in a short amount of time. It was strange to think that his last few moments on earth he spent drunk, alone, and acting like a fool, but even so, Leo was a very intimidating, thuggish looking character. Big build, tall, with aggressively spiked grey hair. On the photo that came with his file Leo had a tattoo of a snake wrapped around his neck and the snake head was on his cheek. It gave me the impression that one, this man is mad, and two he doesn't mind pain. We then decided to creep up on him as his back was towards us. The plan was that we would confront him, hold him down, make him read the coded note, then kill him right there and then.

I then gave the signal to move forward, and towards Leo, so we began to slyly sneak up on him. Each step I took matched the rhythm of my heavy pounding heartbeat. I pulled out my pistol, preparing myself to fire it at any moment. Suddenly, to all of our horrors, the floor board creaked underneath us. The loud squeak of the floor board echoed through the empty room. Leo stopped singing. My heart came to a sudden, violent halt, and I started to tingle with nerves. *'Please tell me you didn't hear that!'* I desperately thought to myself. My eyes then darted at Ricky as he stared back at me. He looked just as anxious as I did. When I rapidly took a look at Hazel, her eyes didn't move off her victim. She was fixed on him, like a lion stalking its prey. Nothing was going to faze her, nor distract her.

Leo then spun round as fast as lightening. His eyes shot wide open. No one moved or said anything until Hazel spoke with an evil sounding voice.

"It's been a long time Leo." She then casually walked over to him. She kept her gun grasped tight in her hand, but lowered it slightly. Leo rose to his feet, swaying slightly from side to side.

"Do I know you?" He shouted out sounding extremely edgy.

"You sure do," She snidely replied. As Hazel was distracting Leo, Ricky spoke into his headset, warning Tank and Gizmo that we had all been spotted by the target. "Does the name Hazel mean anything to you? Or Ms Roxy who's so foxy!?! It should jog a few memories." Leo screwed his eyes up tight as he examined her.

"Oh my dear lord!" Leo gasped. "Hazel, are you serious? Is that really you?" He seemed to be completely speechless almost, but the way he spoke made Hazel sound like an old friend he hadn't seen for a long time.

"It sure is darling." Hazel then got closer, and closer to him.

"What are you doing here?"

"I'm here on business."

"Right, and what business would that be? Women like you wouldn't have a clue about any type of business." I couldn't believe his cold sexist remark, but it was okay. Hazel knew what he was going to receive by the end of the night.

All at once, Hazel grabbed hold of Leo, and shoved him against the table. Leo stumbled backwards, smacking the back of his head on the table surface. I jumped, unaware that Hazel was going to get so hands on. She shoved her face into his face, their foreheads pressed up against one another's.

"You wrecked me, and now it's time to get my own back," Hazel mumbled in a low pitched tone. She sounded deadly threatening. To my surprise Leo started to heartlessly laugh aloud. Hazel slapped him hard round the face, causing Leo's head to viciously jerk to one side. The slap was so fierce it even made my face felt like it was stinging. "I come with a message from Lord Edward Hamston as well." The room fell silent. Leo lay still. It was as if he stopped breathing.

"No... no..." Leo kept repeating in a spine twisting terrified way.

All of a sudden Leo flung one arm into the air, swiping Hazel. It was if he was swatting flies. Hazel flew backwards, and plummeted to the ground. Leo jumped up, and started to run and make a rapid get away. Ricky chased after him immediately. They both moved faster than a bullet. I quickly grabbed hold of Hazel and dragged her off the floor. She took a brief second to sort herself out, then we both joined the chase. I was so full of adrenaline I felt like I could explode.

"He is heading for the backdoor exit," Hazel shouted into her head set. My legs were pumping away. I was moving them as fast as I could. My heart rate increased dramatically to the point as if it felt as if my heart could have leapt out of my mouth.

Hazel heard a loud bang. It sounded as if the back door had been thrown wide open, and it crashed against something. Then I could hear gun shots.

"Oh my god, no!" I screamed as I thought the worst. I had had a horrid thought that Ricky had been shot and I could imagine him lying on the ground bleeding helplessly to death. This only made me run faster. I overtook Hazel, and pushed past. I reached the back door that was left wide open. To my relief Ricky was half crouched in a narrow alley way firing his gun at Leo. To my amazement Leo had clambered onto a motorbike and was speeding down a dark, desolate alley way.

"KILL HIM!" Hazel bellowed at the top of her voice. She then yanked out her gun, and was firing aimlessly towards his direction. I was shocked that Ricky hadn't been able to stick a bullet in Leo yet. Normally by now Ricky would have put about five bullets into someone like Leo.

"Leo is on a motorbike, he's getting away." I said down my head set in a panic, I watched hopelessly as Leo started to get away down the long alley way. "Quick do something now, do anything?" I blurted out. As the loud roar of the motorbike engines began to get quieter I began to lose hope.

Quicker than a blink of an eye, Gizmo and Tank pulled up, blocking the exit of the alley way with the BMW. I looked on intensely as I began to feel violently ill. Would this stop Leo? I began to run towards the car. The more I ran towards the car the better I could see the motorbike. I watched, whilst running, Leo smashing into the front of the car. The bike rebounded backwards flying back down the alley way, bashing off both brick walls on either side of us. Leo was harshly thrown into the air, like a pancake being flipped, and landed on the bonnet of the car with an almighty thud. I heard the crunch of the metal being dented by Leo's hulking body. I ran faster and faster towards the chaos. I wanted to make sure that Leo didn't get away. Also I wanted to make sure that Gizmo and Tank were safe and well.

As I dashed up to the car, Gizmo stuck his thumb up to sign that he and Tank were okay. I was relieved. There were shards of pointy, broken glass scattered over the floor, and on their Gizmo's and Tank's laps. The force of the shunt of the motorbike was so great it managed to break the driver's window. There was a long painful groan that flooded out of Leo. His body looked mangled, and disgustingly knotted. Blood was pouring and leaving his body like water being poured from a bottle. He tried to move but couldn't. I took a closer look at him, and saw that his femur on both legs had snapped in half and torn through his bloody flesh, and ripped through his muscles. His arm lay limply off the side of the car bonnet, because he had gruesomely lodged his shoulder out of place. He was a mess. Just a bag of broken bones and thick, red blood.

Tank got out of the smashed up car, then walked around from the back. Whilst he came closer to me I could hear the footsteps of Hazel and Ricky rapidly getting louder behind me.

"Wow," I heard Ricky gasp from behind me. Leo wasn't a sight for the faint hearted.

"Help," grumbled Leo as he lay helplessly on the bonnet. "Please help me." He started to beg, plea and whine painfully like a dog howling. It was hard to hear what he was trying to say though. It was as if he had bitten off his tongue.

"No bloody way," Hazel blurted out. She then approached Leo with force. She grabbed hold of him by his shirt collar, and violently threw him off the car bonnet. "You deserve every second of this," she yelled in Leo's face, as Leo hit the uncomfortable ground, and bashed his head once again, against the thick brick wall. His head looked like a deflated ball, all deformed, with parts caved in.

"Please," Leo carried on begging. I could see the pain in his eyes as they started to flood with tears. I couldn't imagine how much agony he must have felt at that time. Hazel didn't ease up on him though.

"NO!" She spat angrily. "You don't deserve help. Think of all the women you put through hell, they all wanted help didn't they!?!" Leo didn't reply. He lay slouched against the wall just staring at her.

Leo's face was cut up, and swelling badly. I then noticed that half of his face was dropping lower than the other half. He had disconnected his jaw; it just hung there.

"I hope you're in pain Leo, and I am so glad to see it too."

"Help me please.... I'm sorry." I saw that Leo had crushed, shattered, and lost most of his white pearly teeth from his mouth. It made mine stand on edge!

Hazel showed no mercy. We all watched as she slapped Leo with full force and screamed, "NOOO!" Leo let out a loud, long groan as Hazel's hand made contact with his face. I saw the dislocated jaw take full force of the blow. As the jaw took the shunt of the hit, it moved to the left hand side of his face and remained there. "I will be the one to put you out of your misery Leo." Leo then started to cry and whimper.

The realisation kicked him in the guts. He was either going to be left in this painful state of affairs, or the more likely of the two, be killed and lose his life. I felt horrible watching this man suffer like this, but I kept reminding myself of all the devilish evil actions he had inflicted onto Hazel, and other woman. I then felt a hand slide into mine quickly. I looked around and Ricky was there. He was holding my hand, obviously because he could see that I did not like this. It felt like we were bullying him, and we had an unfair advantage, but once again he did deserve it.

"But first read this." Hazel shoved the coded note right in front of his eye line. He tried to ignore her, and just carried on making eye contact with Hazel. "I said fucking read it!" She grabbed the top of his bloody head, and brutally forced him forward. Her hands were shaking with anger and rage. We watched as the dead man's eyes scrolled along the note. It was hard to figure out what his facial expression was after finishing reading the note, but by his eyes he seemed just as scared as Gabriel did when he read it. Hazel then crouched down in front of him, so she was standing over him looking intimidating. She let go of the note and it fell into his crippled lap. "I will see you in hell darling!" The words she spoke were so cold it would have frozen his soul. She placed both of her hands on each side of his face. Then, suddenly, she cranked his head round with such a force that caused a hair-standing crunch and cracking sound.

She stood up, and took a couple of steps backwards. She looked at Leo's dead body as his head hung loosely from his shoulder, just like his jaw did. He looked slightly like a chicken which had had its neck wrung.

"Thought you were going to stick a bullet in him?" Gizmo piped up admiring her handy work.

"No." She spoke quietly still gazing at the twisted, distorted body. "I killed him like that because it looks like he died in a motorbike accident. Like a hit and run. That way we don't have to waste any more of our precious time cleaning up this scum-bag's body. He can be found by a random stranger from off the street, or even better some poor woman that works for this monster. That would put a smile on anyone's face!" Hazel then casually walked off and climbed into the back of the dented, badly smashed up car. I took one final look at this man; well a pathetic excuse for one anyway. I think Hazel felt like the weight of the world had been lifted off her shoulders. She knew that other women who had suffered Leo's ways were now free to do what they wanted. She must have been full of pride; and she had her dignity back.

CHAPTER 8

THE DESTROYER DESTROYED

As WE RETURNED TO the manor, and ditched the smashed up BMW on the driveway, I noticed that curiously everyone was chatty, and felt much more enlightened. I suppose that was because the ever so sweet antidote felt closer than ever. A task that was put in front of us all, that we didn't think would be possible to complete, suddenly became something of a memory. We were doing so well! Everyone felt great and in good spirits, apart from Hazel. I safely assumed that she was just taking in the bare fact that she had just achieved what she wanted to do for so many years. She had finally killed the man that turned her life upside down. I didn't blame her for being so quiet, after all I think if I was in her shoes I would be replaying that memory time after time in my mind, especially concentrating on his bloody, crushed up corpse lying still in the cold dead of night.

"What are we going to do about the car?" Gizmo enquired whilst taking a last look at it as he slammed the heavy, oversized front door shut.

"I wouldn't worry," Ricky remarked confidently. "Edward probably has hundreds of cars lying about over the estate. It's not like he was short of money or anything. Plus Edward left us that car to use, because it was probably one of the most practical cars he had for the job."

"Strange to think that in a kind of way he was helping us out, and leaving us all those case files, all neatly prepared. It's almost as if he didn't want to poison us." I said sarcastically.

"You believe what you want to believe. He is still a bastard for poisoning us in the first place!" Gizmo snorted, and then everyone found themselves unanimously agreeing to his comment. "And on that note," Gizmo carried on speaking, "I'm off to bed. Good night all." His stubby legs carried his tiny body past us, then he started to climb the staircase.

Ricky then leant in closer to me, and whispered in my ear saucily, "I think we should go to bed too!" I looked round with a smile tugging at the corner of my mouth, as he naughtily winked at me. My body started to tingle with excitement, and my mind automatically flashed back to the last time Ricky and I made love. My face blushed slightly, as my heart begun to race. We both sprinted to my bedroom, as I couldn't wait to be ravished by him!

Later that night, I was fast asleep alongside Ricky. I was lying in his arms, all warm, and cuddled up. My head was pressed up against his chest, and our legs were knotted together. The quiet, peaceful serenity was shortly interrupted by a hugely loud, BANG!!! I shot upright. My chest was pounding and my heart felt like it had skipped a few beats with fright and fear. I quickly gazed down at Ricky, to see that his eyes were wide open and startled like mine.

"You heard that right?" Ricky asked making sure he hadn't gone mad.

"Yeah," I gulped anxiously. "It sounded like a gun shot." I added nervously. I gingerly started to get out of bed, deliberately trying to remain as silent as possible. I begun to feel sick, as there should not be a gunshot sound for miles around this place. *Has someone turned against us? Has someone found out a bunch of assassins are staying here?'* Questions took over my mind, but then a hair raising scream cut my thoughts.

"AHHHHHHHH!!!"

I turned round to look at Ricky and in a panic said, "That sounded like Hazel!"

We both threw on any item of clothing in a mad dash, snatched our guns and held them in a tight clasp. An assassin is never far from a weapon! As we were about to exit the room, I could hear footsteps moving closer towards my door. The steps sounded incredibly fast, as if someone was running towards us. Ricky was about to open my bedroom door, but I swung out my arm out, and grabbed hold of his. I shook my head side to side, and pointed to my ear as an indication to tell him to listen. The last thing I wanted was to give away our hiding spot, if there was anything dangerous going on beyond my bedroom door. He paused for a moment and heard the steps too. The steps were about a metre away from my door. My mind was fuzzy; I couldn't plan nor think, as the adrenaline whooshed around my body. I begun to shake as the adrenaline became too much, but luckily my killer instincts told me what to do.

I found myself waiting on one side of my door and Ricky was on the other side. Our backs were flat against the wall, like an iron on a piece of clothing. Within the next couple of seconds the bedroom door was flung wide open. The door had blocked my view, as it had swung so far open it nearly hit me in the face. I jumped out rapidly from behind the open door, and held out my pistol about head height. I was then faced with Ricky having a tight grasp around someone. Ricky's hands had someone's arms pinned behind their back, and he managed to kick the person's legs apart, making it much harder for the person to make a getaway. I couldn't see who the struggling person was, only a silhouette.

"It's been a long time since you've been so rough with me darling!" Joked a voice.

"Hazel?" I suddenly felt very confused. Hazel shrugged Ricky off her harshly and began to pant, as she attempted to catch her breath. My eyes then started to adjust to the darkness. She was wearing a strappy white top, with loose, baggy, white pyjama bottoms. Her hair was all over the place, sticking out at all sort of different angles. She suddenly spun round and shut the door behind her with a sense of urgency. "What are you..." I started to say.

"No time, we have to hide!" Hazel blurted out. I couldn't help but frown, but in a frenzy we found ourselves climbing up my thick, strong, sturdy curtains, and hiding at the very top of them. We held on tight. Hazel and I were up one set of curtains, and Ricky on the other.

"What the hell is going on?" I whispered at Hazel, trying to make some sense out of why I was up a pair of curtains.

"Gizmo's been shot dead!" Hazel huffed back in horror. I gasped in pure disbelief. *'Gizmo...dead...no!'* I remember thinking to myself, as my heart sank to the deep dark pits of my guts. I felt cold and numb with sadness, but then my worst fear had come true. Someone was after us.

"What? But, why? How?" Ricky bellowed. He was just as shocked as I was about the tragic news. Hazel then bit her lip and looked away. I watched her facial expressions change from sorrow to complete panic.

"It's Tank," Hazel admitted. "He's lost it. He's gone mad. He shot Gizmo whilst he was in bed."

"Wait, what!?!" I couldn't believe my ears. I didn't want to believe them. *'Why would Tank do something like this?'* I thought to myself. *'How could he turn on us?'* Even more questions started to drown my mind in the mist of confusion. I didn't want to accept the fact that Tank could be doing something as crazy as this. My judgement was clouded by all the years we had spent together, and growing up with one another. He was like a brother! Then a thought crossed my mind. "Wait, how do you know that Tank shot Gizmo?"

"I heard the gun shot, and I knew it was very close to my room." She puffed. Hazel was still trying to catch her breath. "I went to have a look to see what was happening, and then I could hear movement from Gizmo's bedroom. I slightly opened the door, and there he was. Tank standing over Gizmo, with a double-barrel shot gun!"

"Jesus-Christ!" Ricky shuddered. "Poor Gizmo, he never stood a chance."

"I know." Hazel muttered in a disgusted voice. "Tank saw me, then started to chase me. I think he's coming for all of us."

I hated the thought that Tank could put an end to my life, and I was still in denial about it all. It just didn't feel right. Something was majorly wrong, but before anyone could say anything else I heard the bedroom door open. My fingers and toes started to burn and ache while clinging onto the curtain for dear life. We all listened carefully. It was definitely Tank who had entered my room. His breathing was heavy and loud and his footsteps were clumsy and clunky. It was almost like he wasn't even trying hard to '*kill*' us all. I couldn't help but think there must be a mistake, or a misunderstanding. Even though, it did sound like Tank was checking every corner of the room we were hiding in. I could see Hazel's face shining in the moon light. I saw her biting her lip nervously, and she had her eyes tightly shut, as if she was wishing she was anywhere else but here.

Then, down below I felt a slight tugging movement on the curtains. I precariously peered down, and Tank was standing underneath us. I held my breath as I didn't want to draw any attention to us. I wanted to blend into the darkness. Tank, thank my lucky stars, hadn't noticed us above him, but for sure, there was a shot gun tightly grasped in his massive hands. He just stood there for a moment staring out of the window. I guess he was double-checking that we hadn't run outside in an attempt to escape from him. He then turned round casually, and walked off normally. It was as if he didn't realise he was killing people; as if he was sleep walking, or drugged, or under some weird mind control!

We slid down the curtain and landed on the floor delicately as we heard the subtle noise of the door being shut. A loud sigh erupted from Ricky and Hazel. My toes and fingers were seriously achy. I tried to stretch them out and shake off the pain but it didn't work.

"We have to do something," Ricky ordered sharply.

"Yeah, but what?" Hazel grumpily sighed in exhaustion.

"Couldn't we just talk to him, or something?" Desperately and in a lot of hope, I then pleaded. Ricky and Hazel just stared at me as if I had gone stark-raving mad!

"You are kidding, right?!?" Ricky half laughed and gasped. "You want to go and talk to a man three times the size of you, who has lost his mind, and has got a shot gun, and has decided to go on a casual killing spree!" He vigorously crossed his arms and stamped his foot, whilst telling me in a strict tone, "No bloody way."

"I think that," Hazel began to speak, but I spoke over her. I didn't like Ricky's macho attitude. He stood there looking controlling. There was no way I was going to tolerate that from a man!

"Who says you can tell me what I can and can't do?" I growled at him.

"I do!" he spat, "especially when you'll end up with a shot gun pointing in your face!"

"This is Tank though, he wouldn't shoot me."

"HA!" Ricky blurted out, sounding mean and cold. "I can't believe you're saying this! Are you stupid or something?" Ricky then started to move closer towards me until he was standing on top of me. "If you're thinking I'm letting you go out there to 'talk' to him you have another think coming." I gritted my teeth together, and clenched up my fists. I didn't want Tank to end up dead by the end of the night, and yes we had recently fallen out, but it seemed so cruel and unfair just to shoot him down. There had to be a reason as to why he had flipped like that.

"He won't shoot me, I'm sure of it. I and he go..."

"Way back, yeah I know all that!" Ricky finished my sentence, and carried on by saying, "But don't forget he has just killed Gizmo in cold blood. It's like the repeat of Oscar Browns family again. He killed them for no reason too. THE MAN IS CRAZY!"

"No," I simply said. I couldn't accept that fact. All I could think about were the years spent together, and through all those years Tank never showed one sign of weakness mentally or physically. I just couldn't bring myself to face it. "I'm not going to let you kill him." I stood still, and firm and remained in my place. The room fell silent. Ricky at this point was practically leaning over me with frustration, fear, and anger. I didn't understand why, but I didn't fear Tank. Yes, he made me feel nervous and worried, but I wasn't scared. Not like Hazel and Ricky were. I truly believe in our friendship. I felt I could reach out and help him.

Without saying anything, I turned on my feet and marched out of the bedroom.

"Grace, NO!" Hazel screamed out from behind me,

"DONT BE DAFT!" Ricky added. For some reason this only fuelled me even more. I began to sprint down the corridor in an attempt to find Tank, and reach him before Ricky and Hazel could grab me, or get to him first. I couldn't bear to think of his huge body, lying lifelessly and dead on the floor. I was so full of determination, and was so sure of myself I felt indestructible. It was almost as if I was a bulldozer, and nothing was going to stand in my way.

My legs were moving quickly. My breathing became erratic and short. My heart was thumping. I squealed round a corner and was faced with Tank's back.

"Tank?" I softly whispered whilst abruptly coming to a halt. At first Tank didn't move a muscle. It was as if he was processing the voice to figure out who was talking to him. He then began to turn very slowly, at which point Hazel and Ricky had caught up with me. They stood behind me, and watched. I felt as if I had a point to prove, and started to feel the pressure all of a sudden. As Tank fully turned round he had a deranged look on his face. His skin was pale, whiter than a ghost. His eyes were wide open, and he barely blinked. They looked sore and blood shot. His lips were slightly apart, where he was breathing just as heavy as I was, even though I knew he had done no running. He clutched the double barrelled shot gun close to his chest, as if he thought someone was going to snatch it away from him. The most blood curdling part of him was the haunting sight of Gismo's blood, splattered over him. Tank had made no attempt of clear up the blood. He was wearing Gismo's blood as if it was a statement. I began to shudder, as the daunting thoughts, and doubts started to run in my mind.

I finally managed to bring myself to repeat his name again, but he didn't reply. He just looked at me with such intensity, it was as if he was staring straight through me, as if I was invisible. His eyes looked dead, like he had no soul.

"Fuck this!" Ricky foolishly shouted out, and yanked out his gun then held it high with a steady hand. It struck me then that he had no problem shooting Tank dead there and then. The steadiness of his hand showed he had neither any emotional attachment nor connection to him. I frantically grabbed hold of Ricky's arm, and shoved it back down again, pointing the gun at the floor. I wasn't going to let Ricky stick a bullet through Tank's muscular body.

Ricky's rash actions made the situation much worse. As I rapidly looked back round at Tank, he had automatically aimed the gun at Ricky.

"Tank." I spoke with a much stronger, clearer voice. "I don't want them to hurt you in any way." I told him, but still there was no reaction from him. "Look, I'm putting my gun on the floor, okay." I spoke slowly, and precisely so there was no confusion, and also in an attempt to calm the dramatic, spin-chilling situation down. I carefully bent over, and meticulously placed my pistol on the floor. I didn't break eye contact with Tank all the time. I didn't want to look away just in case he did something unexpected, or bold. As I began to gradually stand up straight again, I noticed that he was still aiming the gun at Ricky. I assumed that Tank now thought Ricky was the biggest threat amongst us. I stuck my hands up into the air and said to Tank smoothly, "Please put the gun down. No one wants any more trouble." Once again there was nothing from Tank. So I made a brave decision, and took a pace towards him. As soon as I began to move myself forward, he shoved the barrel of his gun my direction, before I had barely placed my left foot flat on the floor.

The nerves and fear now started to kick in, and my heart began to race so much I could feel my pulse in my throat, chest and finger tips.

"I'm not going to do anything bad Tank." I told him, as I carried on warily re-starting to take steps towards him. He still kept the gun aimed at me, and I could sense that Ricky's trigger finger was itching. "I just want to talk to you." I carried on, talking to him tenderly. "You know I wouldn't hurt you, and I hope you would do the same for me. You are like a brother. I can't stand the thought of you doing something stupid." I was now standing at the tip of the shot gun. It was an inch away from my stomach. I couldn't tell at the time whether I was being brave, or just darn right stupid! If this was going to go wrong, it really was going to go wrong in a big style!

"I'm sorry if I have been too hard on you, and I'm sorry for anything I may have done to upset you." It was only when I was close up to Tank that I could tell he was just as frightened as I was. I could feel the distress from him. "I want to help you." I know Tank was listening, and taking in every word I was saying, but it was horrifying to think that I could accidently say something wrong, and he'd pull the trigger. My guts would be scattered all over the place. My voice shook a little as I then told him, "Please put down the gun." I noticed it wasn't just my voice that started to shake; my legs had turned to jelly as well. "I just want to talk, please put it down, before you make a mistake." Then Tank spoke, his voice almost made me jump. He sounded dreadful, as if he had swallowed battery acid. He sounded rough, tired, and fed up.

"I have already made a mistake." I guessed that he was talking about Gizmo, but the way he spoke concerned me. It was as if he knew he was going to do something insane again. I didn't say anything, and everyone was silent.

Within the next split second Tank flipped, and freaked out. Without warning, he pressed the barrel of the gun against my throat, and forcefully shoved me against the wall. He did it so fast I didn't have any time to react. He began to choke me. I kicked Tank, time and time again hastily, in an attempt to push him off me, or inflict some sort of pain that he wouldn't be able to with stand. No matter how hard I kicked, Tank carried on pressing the gun harder against my throat. I started to feel the pressure of the force he was placing on my neck. I shoved my tongue on the roof of my mouth in an attempt to strengthen my airways, but it didn't seem to work. He was crushing my windpipe, and I was feeling the full effect of it.

The next thing I knew, Hazel jumped onto the back of Tank. I saw her dig her roughly long pointy nails into Tanks fleshy cheeks. She then dragged her nails back, leaving deep, bloody cuts across his face; it was almost like Hazel's fingers acted like a rake scraping and tearing his skin from his very bones. Whilst doing that, she bit his ear. She bit it to such an extent that blood started to dribble out, and into her mouth. It still didn't work. Tank was a man possessed, and on his own personal mission. Nothing felt like anything could help me. I carried on desperately gasping for air, like a fish out of water. My face felt like it was on fire, and I began to start feeling weak and tired. I tried so hard to get some oxygen back into my lungs, but my lungs began to feel like they were aching and straining. I was in agony. The pain only sapped more energy from me, and it was energy I seriously needed to pushed Tank off and escape.

Then, Hazel locked her arm around Tank's throat, and gave him a piece of his medicine. She leant back and put a massive amount of strain on Tank's neck. Tank then let go of one side of the gun, still being able to hold me against the wall with just one hand. With his free murderous hand, he grabbed hold of Hazel's hair. He managed to grab a big hand full of her tangled hair and tugged so hard, Hazel flew off his back. She was thrown by her hair, and had hit the wall behind her with such a force; she had smashed her head, and lay on the floor unconscious. Her body lay still and helpless.

Tank quickly placed his other hand back on the gun and was even angrier than before. He begun to slide me up the wall. It felt like the barrel of the gun could have cut through my neck. He lifted me so high, I was taller than Tank. My feet kicked about aimlessly, and I tried to push away the gun using my hands. Nothing was good enough though. I started to think that this was it. I was a goner. Hazel and Ricky were right. I was stupid and idiotic to think I could talk sense to a mad man. I honestly thought I was going to die in vain.

"NO!" A powerful voice yelled out. It was Ricky's voice. I was so glad to hear it. At that point, Tank looked up at me and said something that took me by surprise.

"I'm sorry." I couldn't believe what I was hearing. I didn't know whether I was beginning to go insane from lack of oxygen, but I could see it in his eyes; he now knew it was all over. Within a second, Ricky shot Tank. I watched everything happen as if it was in slow motion. At the corner of my eye I could see Ricky hold his gun up, and then a loud bang echoed through the corridor. A bullet entered Tank's head. Ricky had managed to hit the temple on the top side of his head. It tore through Tank, like scissors cutting paper. Tank then hit the floor with a loud thud, and I fell down with him.

I took one almighty gulp of air, as soon as I collapsed to the ground. Air had never felt so amazing before. Each lung-full I greedily sucked up, felt like I was inflating my lungs again. The force of the gun being held against my throat made my neck feel bizarre and painful. Even though I knew I wasn't being held up by the gun against the wall, the sensation was still there. I could still feel the pressure on my throat. Ricky ran to my side, and crouched down beside me.

"Are you okay?" he manically asked me. I didn't speak at first. I slowly sat up.

"Yeah, I think so." I couldn't stop rubbing my throat. I couldn't believe I was still alive. Then my eyes fell on Tanks body. He had fallen on his side, then rolled over onto his back. His eyes were still wide open, and deranged looking. Even though Tank tried to kill me, I couldn't help but get emotional. A hard lump formed in my throat, and tears began to fill my saddening eyes.

Then there was a low groaning sound as Hazel rolled over and sat up right.

"My head!" She moaned grabbing the back of it, and wiping Tanks blood off the corner of her mouth. She looked like a vampire.

"Are you alright?" Ricky asked Hazel, whilst he wrapped his warm arms around me. The way that Ricky held me showed me that he was terrified of losing me. I was expecting him to make a snide remark, or say something along the lines of *I told you so.'* But he didn't. He dealt with the situation sensitively and delicately. Hazel didn't answer Ricky, she just sat still, and looked just as shocked at Tank's dead body, lying limp on the floor.

"What happened?" Hazel questioned still sounding groggy as she gathered her bearings.

"You were knocked out." Ricky explained. "He chucked you off his back, and you bashed your head against the wall. Before Tank could do any more harm to anyone else, I... shot him." He whispered the last part as if he didn't want me to hear what he had done. I didn't understand why. I witnessed everything.

Then Tank's last words came to me. They swirled round my mind like a vortex of destruction. *I'm sorry. I'm sorry. I'm sorry.'* It was maddening. I could hear the sincerity in his voice, and the fact he knew he had done wrong.

"I'm sorry." I repeated them out aloud so Hazel and Ricky could hear it.

"What darling?" Hazel asked. I finally managed to pull my eyes away from Tank's body, and looked across at Hazel. She seemed worried.

"He said he was sorry. Just before he was shot. It was as if he knew he was going to die soon," I explained. "I don't think he wanted me to hate him for all his awful actions."

"But he tried to kill you, which is a good reason to hate anyone."

"Yes, but I put myself in that situation. I was stupid enough to think I could somehow talk to him. You were right; it was a silly idea, and it lead to Tank having an undignified death." I started to beat myself up about.

"Look," Ricky sighed whilst comfortingly rubbing my back, "You believed in him, and your friendship." I gazed up at him, into his dark eyes, and I could tell that he wasn't talking for the sake of trying to make me feel better. He meant every word that came out of his mouth. "There are not many people who would stand by their friends after something like murder, or going crazy, or anything like that. What you did was a true act of friendship. You were trying to protect him, and give him another chance. Hazel and I understand that. Don't be hard on yourself over this." I couldn't think of any words to say. My mind was all in a jumble. "I'm sorry that I shot him, but I hope you understand that it had to be done." Ricky carried on explaining, it was as if he felt he had to justify himself. I just simply nodded. So many thought and emotions were running a riot inside of me.

I reached out my hand and held Tank's. It was still warm, as if he was still alive. I held onto it tightly as I then cried out, "Why Tank? Why did it have to end like this?" Tears exploded from my eyes as I sobbed like a little baby. "I hate the fact that Tank and I had fallen out over the past few days, and that it had to end like this. Why?" I just longed for answer to my questions. I felt so lost and lonely.

As I squeezed Tanks hand even tighter, I felt something in it. I whipped away my tears quickly, as I turned his dead hand over. There was the photograph of the Mr Browns little girl.

"Oh my god," I gasped in shock.

"What is it?" Hazel enquired as she slowly brought herself to stand on her feet. I took the photo of the little girl out of Tanks hand, and showed Ricky and Hazel it. They looked disturbed.

"I did this to him." I truly believed I was the cause of Tank's madness and death. "I screamed at him for killing that innocent family, and destroying the girl's life, and I threw the picture at him. He must have kept it. He must have felt so guilt ridden. The guilt must have eaten him up." Ricky then firmly grabbed hold of me, and forced me to look at him instead of Tank.

"You didn't kill him."

"But the photo... that was my fault."

"Yes, but he would have shot that child anyway. If I am being honest here, I think Tank was slowly losing it from the beginning." Ricky desperately tried to reason with me, and tried to show me that his death wasn't my fault. "He didn't have to kill that little boy, but he did, exactly the same goes for Gizmo too. Poor Gizmo didn't do anything to Tank, same as the child and the wife, but Tank still killed them all. His mood was changing, and he changed as well Grace. You have to see and understand that. Tank was a sick man, and there was nothing none of us could have done, even if we wanted to."

"Ricky's right Grace." Hazel said to me, as she was still looking at Tank's body. "We are assassins, but we are not crazy murderers. I guess it's an easy path to go down though."

I couldn't bring myself to say anything once again. I just threw myself into Ricky's chest, and held him, as I wept.

"We will throw a service for Tank, and Gizmo. We can bury them in the estate. Somewhere peaceful and quiet," suggested Hazel nicely.

"Next to one another? "Ricky frowned at her.

"They were comrades. We are all in this together. Gizmo wouldn't have known what had happened to him. Tank killed him quickly. I think if Gizmo was still here he would understand, and would have said the same thing, if it was any of us that was killed instead of him."

"Very well," Ricky agreed. My mind kept flashing back to times when Gizmo and Tank would either be simply sitting by one another, or exchanging comments between each other. Both of them together worked well. The brawn and the brain. I could never have imagined that Tank would be the cause of that brilliant, genius man's death. Ricky then told me that I should probably head back to my room, and try and get some rest. I think he was telling me to get out of the way politely, as the bodies would have to be removed and put somewhere for the time being.

I fell backwards, flat on my bed when I got to my room. I just couldn't stop playing what had happened over and over again in my mind. It was almost like I was torturing myself with it, but I think deep down I was only searching for answers. My eyes felt sore and puffy from where I had been crying so much, and trying to stop the tears, and clumsily wiping my eyes. Then, to make matters worse the thought of completing the final mission with two men down almost killed me. Lord Edward Hamston, had chosen us five for a reason, and now we were missing two people. It made me think that the final mission was going to be made ten times harder, especially as I was the person who suggested saving the hardest assassination till last. I then started to receive my defeatist attitude again. I just had a horrible gut aching feeling that we were either going to die trying to assassinate the last person, or fail and we would all die from the poison. If I was being honest, I felt like dying right there and then, even though I had been staring death in the face only moments before hand.

CHAPTER 9

THE BURIAL

I T WAS A CLOUDY, cold day. The miserable, bitter weather matched my mood. Hazel, Ricky and I were standing outside. The brisk crisp wind penetrated my skin, and made me shiver, but I didn't care. I was stood in front of two graves that Ricky had made for Tank and Gizmo. I had picked some wild flowers that were strikingly beautiful, and laid them on top of the graves. It didn't feel right just sticking them in the ground, and forgetting about them both. How could you turn a blind eye to something so tragic? The small grave that Gizmo would be resting in peace in, was maniacal compared to Tanks. It did look a little odd, but I felt good that they both had a decent burial, and that their final resting place was by the little river that ran through the estate. It was a tranquil area. I could hear the sweet bird songs in the background, along with the rustling of the leaves in the tree that surrounded us.

Hazel had offered to say a few words. She spoke in a gentle tone, but she also had a voice that sounded like she was proud of these two men, and grateful for their hard work and dedication into saving our lives.

"Today, we are here to say our final farewells to two brave men, Gizmo and Tank." The thought of this being the last, and final time all five of us would be together was a disheartening thought in itself. "These men gave us hope, and something to be proud of. It is an honour to have met and known them. They helped us through difficult times, and gave it their best efforts to save us, and we thank you for that. We hope that Gizmo is resting in a good place, and the same goes for Tank."

My tears started to prick my eyes again, but I remained strong. I remember all the times that I would cry, and Tank would be there to keep me strong, as he hated to see me crying.

"But this is not a final goodbye," Hazel announced holding her pretty head up high. "The ones we love, and truly care about will live on in our hearts and minds. They truly made an impact on our lives, and have left us some great memories as we had the privilege to spend their last few moment in life with us." Hazel then stood back from the graves, signalling that she had no more to say. I heard her whisper in a shaky voice to the graves, "Rest in peace darlings."

With that she turned away and walked back towards the manor. Ricky then held my hand and said, "Are you coming back with us now?"

"Not right now," I told him. I didn't make any eye contact with him. "I want a little time alone. I'll see you a little later okay?"

"Okay," he replied in an understanding voice. I then found myself standing alone faced with two dead bodies closely linked to one another. I just stood there, and thought about the good times that I was a part of. They both had played a significant part in my life. I felt like a part of me had died with them. I think we all felt like that. In the situation we were placed in we had to depend on one another, and that allowed us to get close, and attached to each other. It wasn't a bad thing, but it sure did hurt now.

"We might be seeing you guys shortly," I joked to the ground. "If we don't pull off this last mission we will be lying along side you guys." I don't know why I thought talking to the muddy mounds of dirt would help me. I assumed, I just thought if they could hear me, then maybe they could help in some way, or protect us from up above, or where ever they may be. I doubt they could though, but it was a pleasant thought. I hoped that the small simple service that we gave them was enough for them as well. Hazel's words were beautiful, and well chosen. "I'm sure we will cross paths soon. Good luck, and rest in peace," I said as I managed to yanked myself away from the graves.

I felt lonesome as I strolled through the empty corridors; I couldn't help but feel a sense of sorrow and anguish. My emotions were only made worse when I walked past Gizmo's room. The door was tightly shut. It was as if the door was rubbing in the fact that Gizmo was gone. I attempted to try and think positively in a hope that it may raise my mood slightly.

"One door shuts, another one opens," I quietly told myself, and as I did I noticed that Tank's door wasn't shut. '*Odd*' I remember thinking to myself, as I walked closer to it. The door was slightly ajar. I carefully pushed Tank's door open and found myself feeling curious.

As I entered Tank's room there were piles and scraps of paper scattered randomly across his bed. I took a closer look, wondering why Tank would leave so much stuff lying across his bedding. As I started to examine the pieces of paper it became very apparent that Tank was trying to find out who his biological parents were. I couldn't understand why though. I knew he had always hoped that his parents would have been good, honest people, and had a decent reason to give him away at birth. I presumed that thought for Tank was something that kept him motoring on.

As I sieved through all of the paper work I was making a disturbing discovery. Tank wasn't given up for adoption, he was stolen from his parents. I came across letters from Tank's parents to him. Tank had obviously somehow managed to track them down and made contact with them. I found the letter that must have sent Tank into a downwards spiral. The letter read:

> *My Dear much missed son. How I have longed to hear from you. I am so proud of you for being able to track us down, although you doing so may have put myself and your father's lives at risk, but it is worth it to hear from you once*

again. There isn't a day that goes by when I don't think about you.

The reason why I say our lives could be in danger, is because your boss, Lord Edward Hamston, stole you from us. He thought he had got away with it, but he was wrong. We found out who he was, and what he was doing, and we discovered that you had been trained and brought up to be an assassin. Edward found out about this, and he sent one of his assassins to our home one night and threatened that if we spoke a word to anyone else about his assassins club, or even made contact with you, we would be killed.

I hope this gives you some closure my darling. We didn't give you away you were cruelly taken from us. Rest assured though, your father and I still love you dearly.

"No-o-o-o-o!" I gasped in dismay. I reread the letter time and time again. I was completely astonished. Thoughts trickled through my mind. *'Why would Edward steal a child? Is this what made Tank finally lose his mind? Has anyone caught wind of this, or did anyone know about Tank contacting his parents?'*

I clasped the letter, and sprinted down stairs into the bar room where I knew Hazel and Ricky would be, enjoying a solemn glass of booze. I burst through the door and was shouting aloud,

"LOOK... LOOK AT THIS!" I made them both jump to such an extent that they all almost fell off their bar stools. I dashed over to them with a sense of urgency, as Ricky and Hazel tried to compose themselves. "This is crazy! Look at it." I spat whilst slamming the letter onto the bar in front of them.

"Calm down darling." Hazel spoke sensitively, whilst patting me on the back.

"NO! Just read it. There's something very wrong." As their eyes started to scan through the letter, I suddenly became overwhelmed with rage and betrayal. How could Edward do such a thing? It was so evil and nasty. I knew he was an unhinged man, but not to go round stealing babies from their loving parents, and even worse to brain wash them into becoming killers and assassins. The thought was sickening. I then started to wonder how many more assassins that Edward had taught were stolen children.

Hazel then sat back with her mouth, inelegantly wide open. She peered down and shook her head, as I could see she was trying to wrap her mind round this particular shocking fact.

"I can't believe it."

"NO neither can I." Ricky looked and sounded just as surprised. They made it very clear that they didn't have a clue that Tank had found his parents.

"I think this is what finally made Tank go mad." I said in a loud strong voice. "Maybe he was going round trying to kill us all, because he couldn't bear the thought of what Edward had done. Maybe he couldn't stand the idea that he was stolen from his parents. Maybe Tank couldn't help but wonder what his life would have been like if he had remained with his parents. He was always one to feel like he had a family of sorts, and I guess I was the person for years to fill that gap."

"You make a good point darling."

"But how did Tank find out where his parents were?" Ricky asked whilst raising one eyebrow, and scratching the top of his head. I stood still and desperately tried to think of the answer, but nothing came to mind.

"It could have been by luck," Hazel suggested. "In all fairness he wasn't the brightest light in the room."

"You can't find people by luck," I said rolling my eyes in exhaustion. "He must have been looking into it for years."

"So why didn't he tell you?" Ricky faintly enquired, whilst adding, "After all you were the closest person to him."

"I don't know. I guess maybe he didn't want to upset me, or make me worry. I'm not sure."

I then roughly dragged a bar stool between Hazel and Ricky and sat down slowly.

"I guess there is one small silver lining." Ricky smiled slightly. Hazel and I looked at him with puzzled expression our faces. "He made contact with his parents before he died." The thought was haunting.

"Yeah," Hazel sadly sighed. My mind couldn't help but flash back to that terrible night. "It all makes sense now. The way his mood changed, his careless behaviour, why he tried to kill us. It was almost as if he was trying to wreck Edwards's reputation, and destroy all of his hard work, and empire."

"Such a sad thought," Ricky stated, as we now all knew that Tank wasn't an insane man to some degree. We had all made that mistake of assuming that he had lost his mind. Tank was just a man fuelled with hatred and revenge. I felt a little relieved in a strange way. I felt good about myself clearing Tank's name, even if he did try and kill us all, but we could all understand Tank's frustration and anger. I prayed at that moment in time that Tank was somehow looking down upon me from where ever he was and smiling. I too, couldn't help but wonder if Gizmo would have understood all this.

CHAPTER 10

THE FINAL PLOT OR
THE FINAL STRAW

AFTER MAKING THE STARTLING discovery about Tank being stolen from his parents, it made me panic and I felt quite distressed. What was Edward thinking, or was he thinking at all? After all Edward was a mad man, but this seemed too much of a rash action even for him. The Lord was renowned for his meticulous planning, sly thoughts, and had a cunning eye for detail. Cruelly snatching a baby from its parents, and then sending thuggish assassins to go to their house and threaten them so they wouldn't say a word to anyone, wasn't Edwards's style. Plus, I was a hundred percent convinced that Lord Edward Hamston, would have no qualms blasting their faces off at point blank range, to make sure that the parents would remain silent forever. Also Edward nearly gave up on Tank through the early stages of his training. If it wasn't for me, Tank would have been a goner. So what was all the effort about? It seemed to have been a completely pointless action.

I then started to expect that there had to be more to this, lurking under the ugly obviousness. In fact everything since day one had only been bitter lies, twisted stories, and heartless betrayals. I found myself longingly wishing that Tank was alive again, as I felt a desperate need to talk to someone in an attempt to clear my mind, and forget my irritating thoughts and anxious emotions. A deep, dark feeling of solitude settled in the pit of my stomach, as the realisation of being alone with my mind was very real. The tough, cold, hard truth was I couldn't bear the thought of not having Tank around me anymore. It was then I discovered how important he was to me, and how sane he made me feel, even though Tank's stupidity was on borderline of insanity!

You never know what you will miss until it is gone. I did ponder whether talking to Ricky would help ease my troubling thoughts, but I had decided against it. Ricky would only tell me to forget about the whole ordeal, and move on as if nothing had happened, which wasn't going to help me much. I needed much more than a few measly, shrugged-off, meaningless words. At the time, I felt like I was searching for closure.

The next day my mood had not improved, neither had Hazel's or Ricky's. We sat round the planning table with blank, gormless expressions on our faces, just staring into oblivion. No one muttered a word, or bat an eyelash. The atmosphere was very morbid and heavy. The room felt empty and lifeless with two team members gone. I was waiting for Gizmo to rush through the doors with a mind-blazingly brilliant idea, or some very interesting, useful information that could be put to good use. Instead I could hear the second hand on the clock slowly clunking around the clock face. It was mind-numbingly annoying.

God, I missed Gizmo's unique, squeaky, snarly voice, blurting out ideas left, right and centre. Then it hit me. I realised that I had been selfish, in the fact that I had taken advantage of Tank's and Gizmo's handy traits. We all had! They had contributed their skills, but the mission had over shadowed their accomplishments and talents. We never had the chance to say *'well-done'* when need be.

Ricky then let out a long, exhausted sigh, and heavily huffed,

"Right." Hazel and I watched him closely as he pulled open the final file and grumpily said, "Sitting around feeling sorry for ourselves won't get us anywhere." His comment seemed rude and insulting at first. I couldn't help but feel a little irate after hearing his opinion after the trauma we all had to endure. As his words sank slowly into my aching mind, I realised that he was making sense. We couldn't afford to mope around, and focus on the past, as the sand of time was trickling through the hour glass. We needed to get a move on to save ourselves.

"The name of our next target is an Ms Alana Willow." Ricky spoke whilst his eyes were firmly fixated on the pieces of paper in his hands. His eyes seemed to have a more intense glare about them than normal.

"Hang on darlings." Hazel squeaked like a little mouse. "I know that name." Immediately my heart sank. I begged and pleaded to myself that this wasn't another personal vendetta she had with someone else. My fears were shortly put to rest as Ricky spoke.

"You probably have. She is a multi-millionaire, and moves around with the very rich and high class type of people, and it looks like she knows some very influential people too." Ricky's eyes scanned back and forth across the page as he then murmured, "We probably have assassinated some of her *friends*, or business partners." He chuckled to himself afterwards, finding it strangely amusing.

"What makes you say that?" I questioned whilst raising an eyebrow. He shrugged,

"I'm not sure, I just have a feeling, oh wait... yeah, she used to know someone by the name of Henry Founder, and he was someone who used to work in her gang. I believe you had the delight of killing him Grace."

"I sure did. Messy sod too!" I bowed my head whilst reminiscing about that particular kill. "But wait... he worked for this woman?"

"That's what it looks like."

"Oh god." I gasped.

Hazel's eyes shot open in worry as she asked, "Why oh god? Why are you oh god-ing darling?" Hazel then began to nervously plump up her luxurious, soft hair, whilst trying to remain and act cool.

"I just hope she doesn't know it's me that assassinated one of her gang members."

"No, it stands to reason that if she did, she would probably have come after you!" Ricky reasoned with me, sounding confident in his assumption. I too agreed, as she seemed to be the type of character who would seek revenge. Not because she cares for her followers, but because she doesn't like being made to look like a fool, or made to look weak, as if someone can just walk over her. She may have thought the killing of one of her men was a message by someone. I didn't question the assassination at the time, although I had an odd feeling that I may come to regret not looking more into Henry Founder's life, before killing him.

Ricky then began to give a download of information on Alana's background to present day. He explained Ms Willow started out as a small time drugs dealer when she was in her early teens. It turned out that Alana had been thrown out of her family's home at a young age. Her family were extremely religious, and strict, and didn't stand for any bad behaviour, or anything bad that may harm their body. Unfortunately Alana's curiosity seemed to have got the better of her, as she began to experimenting with drugs, and became hooked.

Instead of her family trying to help her get off the drugs, and stop her getting her fixes, they threw her out on the street like trash. A story that I had heard many times before, with fellow targets. So instead of trying to get off drugs, and start a new life for herself, she got even more involved with drugs. Almost in spite of her family, and dealing drugs was an easy way of Alana making quick money. It was a saddening thought that many young people such as Alana Willows chose to go down the wrong path in life, and it was odd to think that this path had led her to us putting a dead end to it. Then my mind flashed back to Hazel's teenager life briefly. Maybe she was like Hazel. Didn't have much of a choice in the matter, and desperately needed the money.

After a while of Alana doing some drug dealing, she began to get noticed by local gangs, and petty criminals. Instead of pulling out there and then, and stopping the fact that she was receiving money for feeding people's dirty addictions, she carried on. Before she knew it she had joined a London based gang called the Bolt-Heads. The gang was nothing much when Alana first joined, but when she did, and earned respect from many members of the gang, she pretty much ended up running the joint, and calling the shots.

This gang became more and more threatening, and soon people would whisper *'Bolt-Heads'* in hush anxious tones. They were fierce. At first there was no real reason to why they were called the Bolt-Heads, it was just a name, but Alana gave them a reason to be called that. Her twisted drug-addled mind concocted something most foul and evil, to make the name, Bolt-Heads, stick even more into people's minds! The reason why they remained being called the Bolt-Heads, was because if Alana found out someone had grassed them up to the authorities, or was feeding other gangs or anyone else any information about what the Bolt-Heads were up to, or was even planning to leave or escape the gang, then she had a ruthless, cruel way of dealing with them. They would put the 'traitor' through an expurgating amount of pain until they begged for death.

First of all Alana would order fellow gang members to hammer nails into the traitor's feet. Some nails would spear all the way through the foot, till the sharp tip was piercing out the other side, and others would crunch and crush through bones, or be half nailed into the foot. This was supposed to represent that their body, and soul, belonged to the Bolt-Heads, but mainly belonged to Alana. Depending on what they had done, or how much the traitor had displeased Alana, she would even sometimes order the traitor to try and walk around, or even worse be made to jump! If Alana really hated you, she would personally give the traitor electric shocks, to make them leap up into the air, often resulting with parts of people's feet being ripped apart, and chunks of feet remaining nailed to the floor, leaving great big gaping holes, bleeding relentlessly. It was as if it was a joke to her, all fun and games! Like a kid burning off an ants with a magnify glass.

Afterwards, the traitor's hands were nailed together. The middle and little fingers and thumbs were brutally destroyed, as a nail would rip through the skin and bone, permanently connecting both hands together. The majority of the time, the hammer would shatter, and squish the fingers to a pulp, so they were unrecognisable. Following this angry, violent display, nails then would be hammered harshly in random areas of the body, but these nails were not sharp. The sharp point to the nail had been removed, so the effect would be as if a metal rod was being forced through the skin and muscle. This went on to such an extent that the traitor would look like a life-sized pin cushion. To make things worse the pain would only increase if you moved or fidgeted about. Normally people would vomit aggressively, because of the amount of pain they were in, resulting in more pain to follow.

Then when Alana got bored, she would give the order to finally finish her victim off. A specially adapted nail gun would be pressed against the head of the traitor, in between the eyes, and then would fire a thick bolt that would lodge itself into the brain. Not a good way to go, but hence the gang's name Bolt-Heads. Alana ruled with fear and an iron fist. She seemed to be a blood-thirsty, money-craving, power-obsessed maniac, who seemed to suffer from paranoia! She was a determined, knowing woman. If she wanted something out of life she was going to get it, no matter what the cost may be. I couldn't help but think, if her family had just helped her a little bit, and were more understanding then this monster would have never been created.

"We are dealing with a woman who doesn't care whose blood she spills," Ricky started to sum up. I could hear the nerves rattling around in his voice, and his eyes became dull and disheartened.

"Darlings," Hazel piped up, "I'm pointing out the obvious, but this is going to be one heck of an assassination." She then began to wriggle about in her chair, as if she had ants in her pants, but I knew how she felt. An unsettling discomfort overwhelmed me. Then it hit me, as I spoke confidently.

"This is it, this is our final kill." A smile crept onto my face, as I realised we had made it so far, even though at the beginning we couldn't even dream nor contemplate of getting this far, and be standing where we were. "One more kill, and we are free, for good!" I felt as if we should rejoice, and celebrate. As if a heavy weight had been lifted from my shoulders, but I knew it would be too early to relax, and take things easy. As we all knew, this assassination was going to be the toughest of them all, and as we were two men down it was going to be made considerably harder for us, but still, I couldn't help but feel hopeful and excited. I had never felt more determined in all my life. "One more kill... and I will be free!" I muttered to myself.

The other two peered over at me with intense expressions on their faces. They knew I had had enough of this game. In theory this was to be my last job, ever! It was daunting, as living in the shadows, being invisible, and killing was all I ever knew, and in my mind, all I was ever good at, but at the same time I couldn't help but feel delighted. The thought of no orders, no lurking about, no more of taking people's blood, and destroying lives was bliss. This journey had changed me. If you had asked me a year ago whether I would have ever given up my line of work, I would have laughed at you, and said never! The fact of the matter was I didn't feel pride in what was doing, even if I was classed as top-dog, so what was the point?

Then Hazel's distinctive voice filled my ears, and snapped me out of my little daydream rather abruptly.

"Darling." She then rose from her chair, gingerly walked over, and tentatively held my hand. "I don't blame you." She sounded so sincere and honest. Her heavily made up eyes looked into mine, as I knew she felt the same as myself. The shimmering twinkle in her eyes showed me that she was pleased for myself, and glad for herself too. I understood the fact that Hazel no longer wanted to be an assassin anymore.

Ricky stood aside and watched on, after all he had no idea that Hazel had other plans for her future as well. A part of me wanted her to open up to him, and announce the fact that she too, wanted to live a different life. At the time I assumed the reason why she wouldn't tell Ricky anything, was because she was too proud. After all she had slept with Ricky, so for her to admit to him that she was losing her touch, her looks, and that she was aging, would have crushed her. Not only would she be telling him that she got by in her career on luck and looks alone, but facing up to the fact that her looks were fading. Hazel would never tell a male that, no matter how close she was to him, but she was still a glamorous foxy woman, who knew too well how to strut her stuff.

The stare between Hazel and I was broken by Ricky.

"Hang on... what the hell is this!?!" Eyes darted towards his direction. He carelessly dropped piles of paper onto the table in front of himself, whilst clasping onto one piece of paper tightly in his hands, and there was a complex look upon his face.

"WHAT?" I jumped to my feet to investigate, as the suspense was killing me. I had an awful feeling that something had gone wrong once again! I stormed over to his side, and glared over his shoulder to see what he was examining. My eyes then meet a blue print of a building, with writing roughly scribbled over it. An uneasy feeling started to build up inside of me. It didn't feel right that a blue print with what seemed at first aimless writing all over it, would just be lying in the case file. We had to do the research, and carefully put the plans together from scratch, so why would this file be any different?

"Darlings?" Hazel questioned as she too made her way over to join us. We all ended up huddled together staring at this piece of paper.

"I don't believe it!" Ricky sighed happily.

"What?" Spontaneously I and Hazel asked.

"Gizmo's a bloody genius!"

"What?" We repeated, eyes becoming even wider with anticipation.

"I could kiss him... well I would if he..."

"Ricky for fuck sake!" I exploded and snapped, finally losing my patience. I didn't mean to speak such vulgar words, but I was becoming sick and weary of him talking rubbish. "What in god's name is this about, and how does this have anything to do with Gizmo?"

"This is his work... look." Ricky then gently flopped the paper onto the table, as we lent in to have a closer look in detail. Ricky carried on talking whilst my eyes scanned over the plan. "He had obviously started to work on this assassination, before we even started it as a team."

"But why would he do that without us knowing?" Hazel smartly asked, and it was a question that started to ring alarm bells in my head.

"Knowing Gizmo, the most likely answer is that he was trying to save time for all of us, so we could concentrate on what we needed to do, after all Gizmo was the brains of the project. He may have even done this just in case he did die, as if he is still giving us a helping hand even when he isn't here. God... I love that man!" Ricky looked up into the air with a big, fat smile on his face, whilst Hazel leapt up and down singing,

"Oh, this is brilliant!"

"Hang on," I grunted reluctantly. I didn't want to burst Ricky's bubble, but this wasn't settling down well with me. Something didn't feel right, but I couldn't put my finger on why, or what. I had to voice my concerns anyway, as I had a gut-wrenching feeling that we shouldn't pay any attention to this plan. "We haven't had one bit of good news through this whole journey, and nothing has been made easier for us! How are we so sure that this is Gizmo's work? My instincts are telling me to forget about this."

Hazel's enlightened facial expression had turned sour as she listened intensely. She looked like she was ear-wigging into the conversation, when really she should have felt much more a part of it.

"Grace." Ricky placed a hand on my shoulder lovingly. "I care about you, and I care about how you feel, and what you're thinking, but... there is nothing wrong with this, I don't understand why you are acting like this." His comment irritated me, as I had a feeling that he didn't care, and he was just talking for the sake of talking. I could see in his eyes he was going to be stubborn about this, and he wasn't going to give up, or change his mind in a drop of a hat. I could sense a fight coming over the horizon. He had basically pushed my concerns aside, and wasn't even giving this a second thought. I pushed his hand off my shoulder swiftly, as I felt as if he had a patronising aura about him.

"How do you know that this plan is alright, and safe, and nothing has been missed out? Don't forget as brilliant and talented as Gizmo was, he had made mistakes in the past."

"Look, everyone makes mistakes." He looked down on me, and spoke to me as if I was his three year old daughter, instead of his girlfriend.

"Oh, and I suppose that's okay when we are about to do our final assassination!"

"Look, very few times he had made mistakes, and most of the time he had a backup plan."

"He didn't when we were in the casino. If it weren't for me we would have been toast." My anger started to rise, as I could feel my body tense. "And like I said there is no proof that this is his work." Ricky then slammed his hand onto the table, and swiped the blue prints off it with one quick sharp move, and shoved it in my face, forcing me to take a step back.

"Look," he shouted at me, "This is his hand writing, and this is his style of planning. What more do you want woman?"

"Woman?" I huffed harshly.

"No, I didn't mean to..."

"No, I don't want to hear it." I shook my head in disgust, before I got a long-winded explanation from him. We may have been disagreeing and bickering, but there was no reason to speak to me as if I was dirt. I looked away as I tried to contemplate what my next move would be.

Ricky then placed the hand that I had pushed away onto my cheek. His smooth touch, annoyingly, started to calm me down. He raised my head to make me look at him, as I could feel his thumb softly stroking against my hot skin.

He gently whispered, "Please trust me this time." We just stared at one another, his eyes full of desperation, almost with a hint of pleading, and know-it-all-ism. Mine, empty. I wanted to stand down and give up, as I didn't enjoy fighting like this, and it would only put strain onto the relationship, but I could not shift that awful moaning feeling inside of me. I was taught to live by my instincts, and this was what I was going to do, whether he liked it or not.

"I will tell you what." Sternly I spoke, "We will have a look at it, and there is no harm in doing that." A childish, victorious smile smeared across his smug face, as he assumed that I was warming to the idea, which was far from the truth. I twitched with frustration, but I couldn't be bothered to correct Ricky. I just knew we would come across something that would make this all a bad idea, and make Ricky look like a fool.

As we then started to explore Gizmo's hard work, we tried to understand what Gizmo's fast-thinking, technical mind was plotting. It became apparent that none of our minds could compare to the intelligence of his. We slightly grasped the fact that he thought an attack on Ms Willow's vast mansion was the best bet. Her home was a maze though, and she seemed to live a life of luxury, but there was a massive dilemma confronting us.

A feeling of dread pulsed round my body violently, and sadness shortly followed, as I glanced down and noticed Gizmo's plan had included himself and Tank to be a part of this mission. How were we going to do this without Tank and Gizmo? It seemed that we would have better luck finding a pixie prancing around in the estate, than being able to carry out this plan. It was also apparent that Alana would be surrounded by her ruthless body guards. In fact I think it's safe to assume that Alana would be surrounded by them at any time, and with their fierce reputation of remaining loyal, out of fear or respect for Ms Willow, would only make the assassination much harder.

My eyes began to grow weary, as my mind started to develop a dull thudding pain. I could not concentrate any longer, and staring for endless hours at pieces of paper and discussing Gizmo's work was driving me crazy. It seemed that we were not making any progress, and I was becoming more and more frustrated; even more so when Ricky and Hazel persisted on going through everything ten times over, in a desperate attempt to make sense of the plan. To me this all seemed like a waste of valuable time.

I then declared loudly. "This is insane!" I took a couple of paces away, turning my back to the table. I took a calm steady breath to compose myself, then carried on. "We can't follow this plan, it's no good to us." Both pairs of eyes peered up at me, looking exhausted, but Ricky still had a twinkle of determination in his dark eyes. I knew he was going to fight back.

"Of course we can use this plan," he snapped.

"No we can't." My anger started to build on top of my frustration.

"Why?" Ricky began to sound like a stroppy child that couldn't get his own way. I found it incredibly repulsive. I then gave an explanation in its most simplest of forms.

"This plan includes five people, and we were supposed to use our individual strengths, so the plan became more full proof. Now, I want you to solve this simple mathematics equations for me, five people, take away two, leave us with..." Ricky ignored me; it was as if he could not see any logic anymore, and his reply proved that he seemed to be becoming more brain dead by the second, or even deaf.

"We can still use this plan, there is nothing wrong with it."

"What!?!" I stomped, "Has the poison already killed off your common sense!"

I slammed both hands hard down onto the table's surface, not feeling any pain, as I began to reach boiling point. Hazel jumped back into her chair, and then made a little shiver motion, as she grew uneasy with the raised voices.

"Don't shout at me," ordered Ricky with a disapproving frown on his face. "We will just have to adapt it, and take on more responsibilities and tasks."

"Really, you think it's that easy do you?" I shook my head, and placed my hands on my hips firmly. "None of us has Tank's strength; a bloody rhino doesn't have Tank's strength!" I spoke maliciously with a hint of sarcasm. "And as for Gizmo, we have no idea what half of these gadgets are, or how we us them. You would be a fool for thinking that we could; the chances are we'd kill ourselves trying to figure out how half of that crap works, before we even get to Alana's mansion! It's too dangerous for us to even consider using this plan. If we go with this plan, and we pretend to have the abilities that we don't have, or not to the standards that the plan has, then we risk exposure and being caught, and then we are a hundred and ten percent dead."

My hands were shaking, and sweaty, my heart raced, and my mind was dizzy. I couldn't take any more back chat, but something odd happened. I found myself pacing up towards Ricky, and squaring up to him without me even realising I was doing so. I was clearly not thinking, and all I could see was red. I began to growl.

"One thing's for sure, I want the rest of us to pull through this, and survive, without facing an ugly end. You only want to use this plan, because you think it will be quicker, and easier, a cheat if you will, but news flash for you Ricky, you've wasted hours poring over the same shit, and still have got nowhere with it, and those hours are irreplaceable. You're not only wasting your own life, you're wasting ours too." The room felt deadly silent. No one said anything. No one moved. The only sound was my huffing and puffing, from breathing furiously and heavily, whilst I coldly glared at Ricky.

"It's what Gizmo would have wanted." Ricky muttered. My eyes squinted at him, and my nostrils flared. I gritted my teeth to the point where it felt as it I was pushing them back into my gums. As I spoke, my voice shook and sounded croaky, as my throat was so tense it seemed to have closed up.

"I don't believe you said that. HOW DARE YOU PLAY THE GUILT CARD ON ME?" I spat, like a poisonous snake spitting venom. I was so infuriated I felt I could have passed out. "GIZMO LOVED

HIS GOD DAMN PLANNING, YES! BUT AT LEAST HE HAD
THE NONCE TO LISTEN TO PEOPLES CONCERNS, AND
TOOK NOTE, AND WORKED THEM INTO HIS PLANS!" At
this point I suddenly realised I was practically standing on Ricky's toes.
Then it hit me. This man that has made me so aggressive, and cross to
the point of me being sick, was my partner. I had completely forgotten
we were in a *'loving'* relationship. A part of me wanted to stand down,
but the majority of me didn't care anymore. In my eyes my life was
worth saving more than love, otherwise what would be the point of
love with no life. I couldn't get my head round the fact that was being
so dumb, hurtful, stubborn and selfish.

"You know what," I groaned. My voice was low, I was fed up and
sick of this situation. "I can't even stand the sight of you anymore." With
that I turned my back on him, and walked away. I hoped that those
words swirled around his head, and that he would immediately feel bad
and that feeling would stick with him for a long time.

I headed to the one place that truly made me feel calm, and more
human, and that would always promise to bring me back down to earth.
Within moments, walking across the estate, I found myself tucked
away in my own little piece of heaven, concealed by the large drooping
willow by the edge of the lake. I couldn't bring myself to think of my
time here, in this hellish nightmare. I had so many questions, so many
confusing thoughts, and so many emotions constantly in conflict with
one another. I realised that I had lost the real me, and had allowed the
present situation take over my mind. It was as if the poison had already
destroyed who I was.

I felt as if I had always been lost in life, living alone, not sure of who
I was or who I had become, and not really playing a part in anyone's life.
Not meaning a thing to anyone. Apart from Ricky meaning something,
and playing a role in Ricky's life, although I wasn't sure how long that
would last now. We could never agree on a single thing. People say
opposites attract, but does it honestly make for a happy, thriving, long
term relationship? I had a gut feeling that soon I would have to face
the inevitable. The sense of frustration just grew stronger, and stronger

within me. Just one more kill, and we would be cured; I would be cured! It was just a stone's throw away. It was as if Ricky was delaying everything, just so he could be in charge, and take credit. The fact of the matter was he had no idea what he was doing.

The sun began to set over the tops of tall, leafy trees in the distance. The sky had a golden tone to it, as the clouds began to change into a candy-cotton pink. The bird song slowly started to die down, and the ripples of the water were soon the only thing to keep me company along with my troubling thoughts. I took a deep breath of the crisp, fresh air, and I began to feel like I was sinking into the soft, grassy ground. Occasionally the odd, dragon fly or may fly would skim dangerously close to the slow-flowing water surface, yet they looked so elegant and graceful. I must have spent at least an hour listening to nature, and admiring it. I began to relax, and put my troublesome thoughts behind me. However the tranquillity didn't last long.

A voice gently spoke from behind me. "Hi." I shuddered in annoyance, as I knew Ricky was standing behind me. I had just begun to feel better then he had to find me, and smother me with his *'sweet-toned'* voice.

"What do you want? I told you I didn't want to see you."

"I know, and I get that." He had an apologetic sound to his smooth voice. At this point I could hear his feet take small, and carefully placed footsteps towards my direction.

"Don't come any closer to me, I'm livid with you." I made a point of not turning around, not making eye contact with him, and trying not to acknowledge that he was there. I wanted him to understand that I was hurt by him, and that I really couldn't bear to be around him so soon, after the heated row we had. Ricky though, being the hard-head he was, ignored my order. He carried on coming closer towards me. I could feel every fibre in my body tighten, to the point where it felt as if they were knotting. I had noticed that Ricky was losing his patience, and he too had had enough of this game. His voice changed to a much more stern and serious tone.

"Grace, for-god-sake, will you just look at me." I sharply spun my head round, with a cold, empty look in my eyes. I wasn't used to being spoken to in such a way. "I know you have issues since... well, since day one here." He carried on moving closer to me, with a look on his face that was like thunder. "But I have just about had enough of this." He dug both feet into the ground next to where I was sitting. He looked down on me, which made me feel extremely small and puny. "Why are you being like this, especially towards me?" I didn't reply to his question for a little while. Each word he spoke, I found hard to take in. I didn't know how to answer his abrupt question, so I gave a simple response.

"I don't know."

"Are you sure, because you seem to have a strong opinion on everything!"

"I don't know, I don't fucking know, okay?" I screamed with rage as I jumped up onto my feet. I jumped up so fast, I could feel the blood rush to my head, resulting in me feeling a little dizzy and unfocused.

"Do you know what I think?" The stare between us grew strong, to a point where it became a competition. It felt as if whoever blinked, or looked away, first was the weaker one out of the two. "I think you can't cut this crap no more. You want to stop being an assassin, because you have become too god damn soft!"

"That's bullshit!"

"Oh yeah, prove it."

"Fine." Quicker than lighting, and faster than a cat reflex, I grabbed hold of my gun, swung it around, and before Ricky could take another breathe, I had my pistol aiming between his eyes. I froze. I was sick of being walked over by the man I loved. He showed me no respect. He showed me no compassion. He showed me nothing, and made me feel like nothing. I didn't have to take this from him anymore.

"Let me tell you something Ricky." The gun was held solidly steady in my hands. I held it so tight I thought for a brief, insane second that I had crushed it, but then my hand began to shake uncontrollably. Ricky's eyes were widened with despair. "I am still the best in this field of work, and don't you forget that, but a strong woman is allowed to feel emotions!" I applied more pressure to the trigger of the gun, whilst jamming it against his forehead.

Beads of sweat trickled down his face in panic.

"It's because of you that I am now embracing my emotions. Something I have not done since I was a child. I have felt nothing since I lost my parents. The day they were burnt to death was the day that I died, but now I feel alive again, as if I have a new lease of life. So I will live with my emotions, and express them how ever I see fit, and I will not let a man like you stop me doing so! Do I make myself clear?"

"I haven't stopped you feeling your emotions Grace." His voice sounded surprisingly confident, for a man that looked like a nervous wreck. I assumed he was trying to cover up his terror. Then he said something that totally caught me off guard. His following words penetrated my ears, like someone had shot a bullet into them. "You still have a point to prove." My eyes then became fixed onto his. "Pull the trigger. You know any assassin will kill anyone, so pull the trigger!"

Once again I just froze.

"See, this is what I am talking about, your doubting me, and my capability." I viscously growled at him.

"PULL THE TRIGER!" He ruthlessly barked at me. I could feel the temptation deep inside my soul to do so. Automatically I switched off, as I felt my killer instinct erupt inside of me, shoving all my emotions, and rational thoughts to one side. A surge of power dashed through my body, as I felt myself become one with my pistol which seemed to have grown attached to my tight grasping hands. I then felt my finger clamp down on the trigger, as my hand grew steadier. The shakes miraculously vanished. I felt so alive! I could feel my own blood rushing round my veins. I went to pull the trigger. Ricky suddenly took a sharp intake of breath as he screwed up his face in anticipation and pure fear knowing that any second things would be all over for him.

BANG, BANG, BANG! Gun shots echoed, and boomed through the desolated wilderness. A fluster of frantic flapping shortly followed the shots as birds hurried away. Then all fell silent. I could hear my own heart beat in my ears, as I dropped the gun in shock at what I had done. I stood still, almost paralyzed with my actions as I stared at Ricky.

"Happy now," I managed to grunt as I could feel the adrenaline melt away, as I began to calm down, but in doing so I found myself becoming emotional. Ricky stood firm and tall, looking more threatening and stronger than ever. I could imagine vividly, Ricky lying amongst the twigs and leaves in a pool of his own blood, with his eyes open with a vague look in them. I couldn't bring myself to kill him. As soon as I heard him take in, what was supposed to be, his final breath I found it near impossible to shoot him. Although I was so certain, so sure that I was going to do so.

"You couldn't do it," Ricky muttered quietly, with an almost evil tone to his voice. His eyes were bright and wide, and his expression on his face was a mix of relief and outrage. He looked grey, but I could see his teeth grinding. I had never seen Ricky react like this. My hairs on my arms stood on end, as I suddenly felt like I was the one in danger. "You nearly killed me, but you didn't, you just simply couldn't. You are weak, and you are a failure." Words felt like they were stuck in my throat, and then Ricky suddenly began to approach me.

"I was going to," I struggle to say.

"Oh yes," as strange grin crept onto his ill looking face. "But you didn't!" He was making it quite clear that he was not impressed, and that I didn't deserve to have the title of being number one. It was as if he was rubbing it in my face that he was still alive, especially as with each step he took towards me.

"Let me ask you this," I found myself saying. "Would you have been able to kill me?" He suddenly stopped in his tracks, and calculatedly eyeballed me. Again I found myself tensing up in his presence. He didn't answer for a while, and then he opened his mouth.

"If it was an order, and I had to, I would." Involuntarily, I gasped in horror. It was then that I realised how truly fond, and attached I *was* to Ricky. I didn't expect to find myself in this situation.

"So, you don't love me! That was all talk, was it?" I felt so small, and foolish. How could I be so stupid? Why did I allow myself to fall in love? Why have I risked everything for just one man, whom it turns out would kill me instead of protect me?

"No, I care for you a lot, and what I said I mean." I frowned at him in complete confusion. How can you love someone, but be willing to kill them in a click of a finger. I truly began to wish that I had never become an assassin. I found myself briefly thinking that if my parents hadn't been burnt to death, then what would have happened to me. Would I have had a much happier, fulfilled, meaningful life? Would I have been married to a man that would risk his life for me, and not be willing to murder me? Would I have had children by now, and swear to protect them and love them, and never let any harm come to them? Would I have had friends, a social life, more fun, lived life more?

Then the penny dropped. I gazed up at Ricky, and swiftly started to approach him. I didn't have to take this crap from anyone. I had to make do with the life that I was given, even if I didn't like it, and it wasn't what I secretly strived for.

"You want my title don't you?" I fired the question directly at Ricky, which caught him off guard. "It annoys you, doesn't it? Oh, of course!" Ricky still had the half dead, but cross look on his face. "Is this what this is about? Maybe a little ego boost for you?" I now had the taste of blood, and I wanted more. My claws were out, and I was ready to tear him apart until his soul was oozing out, and he was nothing more than an empty man! I was going to give Ricky a taste of his own medicine. "This is what this is about, isn't it? You knew that I couldn't kill you, and I'm pretty damn certain you couldn't kill me. You're just all talk and nothing more, but you couldn't help yourself could you? You asked me to shoot you, because you knew I couldn't, therefore making you feel stronger and better than I am at this game. You can't handle the fact that I am the best assassin. Well let me tell you something, I will always be better than you."

Ricky than began to look pathetic, with discouraged eyes, and a sorry expression on his belittled face. I couldn't help but feel proud of myself, as if I had won a battle. I felt like the cat that got the cream, and a lot of cream too! I had hit the nail on the head. This is why he wanted to take charge. This is why he challenged me, to make himself feel and look good. To diminish me of my title, and what I have spent my life achieving!

"You might be right."

"No!" I half smiled with smugness. "I know I'm right, and you're pathetic!"

"You don't understand." He out stretched his arm, as if he was going to gently stroke mine, and try and make amends, but this was it. This was the final straw!

"Don't!" I sharply ordered, looking at his outstretched hand and extended fingers. I couldn't stand the thought of him laying a finger on me ever again. "I don't want to understand Ricky." I then looked up at him. "I don't want anything to do with you, unless I have to acknowledge that you are there."

"But Grace, I…"

"No!" I repeated, sounding even more abrupt. "Enough is enough, I'm through with you. When we complete the assassination of Ms Willows, I never want to see, hear or be around you, ever again! It's over for good. Well done!" With that I stormed past him, not making any eye contact, and headed straight to my room to clear my mind of the drama that had exploded today.

As I sat alone with my thoughts on the bench by my oversized window, I found myself grow slightly tearful. It was as if the pain and swelling of my heart began to grow worse and wouldn't ease up. The only comfort I took from all of this, was that I was the one who broke it off with Ricky, and not the other way around. If I felt this bad now, then I had a feeling that Ricky would have been feeling ten times worse. After all, a heart never breaks evenly.

My eyes then fixed onto the sight of Ricky emerging from the woods in the distance. I couldn't help but watch him through my bedroom window. In a weird and perverted way, I hoped to see him cry, and be completely distraught, but the closer he got the less satisfied I became. Yes, he looked miserable and lost, but for some reason I wanted to see him in more pain. Then the vivid image that my imagination had created, of Ricky lying dead in the undergrowth, flowed through my mind. It made me shudder. I wasn't sure what was going on in my head, but I had learned a few new things that I didn't realise before.

I had learnt that I really did love Ricky with all my heart, but he was an evil, nasty piece of work, trying to make himself look bigger and better than myself. That he was a man obsessed with power and control. I also realised that I did have some pride in the fact that I was the best at doing what I did, even if it was killing people, and snatching away lives. At least I was good at something.

CHAPTER 11

RISK TAKER

THE FOLLOWING DAY, JUST after noon, I dragged my poor, depressed, heavy heart towards the planning room. I was not looking forward to today, just like other hard-going days in the past. In the pit of my stomach I had a deep seated feeling of trepidation, as I did not wish to see Ricky any time soon. A nervous tingling sensation aggressively tickled my nerves, which made me feel extremely uncomfortable, yet sickened. The thought of having to face him, made me want to crawl up into a tight, tiny, tangled ball, and cower away in a corner somewhere far away from here. As I became dwarfed by the doors to the planning room, which seemed like the entrance to a fiery hell, I paused. I couldn't help but stare at those doors with hatred.

I knew that there was a good possibility that Ricky could be standing behind those doors. Waiting. What added more worries to my concerns, was the fact that Hazel may not have even arrived yet, and I certainly didn't want to be stuck in that room, alone with that man. God only knows what would happen otherwise. I was close to killing him once before, but now, pumped full of anxiety, and pulsating with a passionate hatred towards this man, I was not sure if I would be able to hold back, or control myself like the time before. Especially if he began to viscously challenge me again, undermine me, or push me to the very edge of my limits. Although there was nothing to say that he wasn't waiting for me, behind those closed doors, with a loaded pistol. He could have been longing to prove his point to me quite clearly. He too was more than likely feeling the same amount of rage and mixed emotions as myself, which was not a pleasant thought.

'Deep, calm, breaths' I thought to myself, trying to sooth my unnerving feelings. *'You can face him; you showed him whose boss yesterday.'* I slowly began to feel in control again, cradling the comforting thought that I did take charge yesterday. Ricky probably felt small, and pathetic after I had finished with him, which I was sure he wanted me to feel instead. I attempted to chuck my doubts out of my mind, and tried to stop winding myself up over this matter, so I would be completely in control. I made a promise to myself that I wasn't going to let any of this affect our hard, ongoing work. Also I wasn't going to sit in that room feeling sorry for myself. I didn't want him to know that I was hurting; I didn't want to give him that satisfaction.

We all had a job to do, and I was damn sure that I was going to get everyone's arses into gear before time ran out. As I fully prepared myself, and raised my own spirits, I entered the room with a big, long, powerful stride, and held my head high. If Ricky was waiting for me, or was sitting alone in that room, I wanted him to see me stand tall and proud, with no regrets. I needed him to be in my shadow of towering strength. As I gazed confidently around the room I found myself completely alone. My mood changed slightly. I let out a loud huffing sound, as I thought to myself *'all that effort to make myself look empowered was for nothing.'*

I clumsily slouched my back against the door after I closed it behind me. A part of me was slightly relieved that Ricky wasn't here. I just hoped, wished and prayed that Hazel would be the next person to turn up, before he made an entrance. I scuffled forward towards the dreaded, large, wooden table. My eyes clapped onto the pieces of paper, which were scattered hectically around the surface of the table. It looked as if someone threw all the paper work, high up into the air, and left all the pieces of paper where they fell. At least when Gizmo was in charge of the planning everything was perfectly placed, processed and precisely organised.

As I begun to sieve through and sort out the pieces of paper, I heard the door handle rattle slightly, as someone was turning it, and was about to enter the room. It made a steady clunking noise and each slight noise the handle made my heart shake in anticipation. I straightened up, and inhaled a deep lung full of air, until my lungs felt like they were at bursting point. As I gingerly looked over my shoulder, I saw Hazel standing in the distance, half filling the doorway with her petite body.

Today she was wearing a snug wine-red tank top, with tight black skinny jeans, all of which showed off her drop-dead-gorgeous figure. Even in her most casual clothing she still looked stylish, and luscious. I noticed how I began to admire Hazel, more now than I did before hand, at the start of this journey. Her fluent, flirty, foxy ways used to irritate me no end, as I had no time for it, but now, as I grew to love her as if she was a sister, and learnt much more about her, everything she did seemed to make sense to me, and I adored her for it. At this moment in time Hazel was the closest person, and only friendship I had, and I was going to cherish it as much as I could, under these difficult circumstances.

I then noticed Hazel had a peculiar look upon her face. I chose to ignore it for the time being, and looked back down at the table, and made myself busy as I shouted out,

"Hello!" in a friendly voice, but it took a while for Hazel to reply. I even recalled the fact that she hadn't shut the door behind her yet, as if she wanted to sprint back out of the room as soon as she walked into it. I stood up straight, and became slightly more formal, and turned round to face her properly. She stood very stiff and rigid, holding the side of the door, for security or comfort, I couldn't quite tell. I examined her face whilst I checked she was alright by asking her. Hazel did not reply, and just carried on gawking at me, keeping the same odd expression on her face. Not a muscle nor an eye lash moved or battered. She looked very timid, yet sad.

Then, all of a sudden, Hazel spoke and it all became apparent why she was acting strangely.

"Darling, the question is… are you ok?" She now looked concerned and sympathetic, but still kept her distance as if I was going to attack her, like I had done Ricky the day before. I felt like rolling my eyes back and screaming in annoyance. This was all I needed. I certainly was not in the mood to talk about Ricky, or the events of yesterday before he entered the room.

"I'm absolutely fine," I replied whilst turning back round again, after Hazel gently shut the door behind her.

"Are you sure?" She had a motherly sound to her voice.

"Yes…" I grunted, "I am fine."

"Ricky told me what happened yesterday."

"Good, then you don't need me to explain anything to you then," I barked bitterly. I then bit my own tongue, and looked up at Hazel as I had no right to snap at her so rudely, and I began to feel out of order. "Sorry," I sighed tiresomely. "I'm just trying to get on with this. This is my main concern right now, and time is slowly but surely running out. Personal problems don't matter to me at a time like this, because if we don't start working we will never have any personal problems again." It was a terrifying, and daunting thought that was hanging over my shoulders heavily that day.

An hour had passed, and there was still no sign of Ricky.

"Odd." Hazel frowned whilst carefully perching on the edge of the table, with her legs crossed, looking rather lady-like. "Ricky would normally be here by now."

"Yeah and…" I carelessly shrugged with my head buried in paper work, and rough plans. I then grumpily added, "If he wants to be a child, and wants to sit somewhere sulking then let him. If he's in that mood he isn't going to be much help to us anyway."

"I suppose." Hazel reluctantly agreed. She must have felt as if she was stuck in the middle. I was so blinded by my hatred for my ex, and so consumed with work that I hadn't given Hazel's thoughts much consideration, which was selfish of me, but I was desperate to crack on. Like I said to Hazel, Ricky wasn't going to be much use to us, and probably would throw me off track too.

As time went by, and Hazel and I bounced ideas between us, I had a growing suspicion that she may have been feeling guilty, about the fact that Ricky wasn't around to agree to these ideas, or be having any input into the plans, but I didn't care. I had more important things to deal with, but on the other hand, there was a part of me that was thrilled that Ricky may have been so depressed that he couldn't show his face. In fact it made my life a lot easier without him under my feet. I didn't trust that plan that Gizmo drew up, and it wouldn't have worked with the three of us. I wasn't about to ruin everything, and our chances of survival because he couldn't be bothered to work things out, and wanted an easy way to get things done quickly. I then briefly wondered, if it wasn't for that plan, would myself and Ricky still be together? Would we have been happy? The mind boggles.

Then something clicked in my mind.

"Hazel?" I said in an inquisitive voice. "You haven't mentioned anything about Gizmo's so-called-plan. Why? I thought you were for it."

"Oh darling, god no," she said rapidly shaking her head side to side, and then randomly pouting her lips outwards afterwards. "No, I agree with you now darling. At first I thought Ricky's was the right choice, but after a lot of time thinking about it, what you said made sense, and we were better making a new plan. I mean there are parts of the other plan that we could use, but like you said most of it wouldn't have worked. Well, not now any case." Hazel then stood up and started to casually strut about the room. She then added quietly, "In fact Ricky was being unbearable about the whole situation really. He was extremely angry, and he tried to have the most say about everything. It was almost like it had become his plan."

"Doesn't surprise me."

"Yes... but... it was almost like a man obsessed."

"Ricky doesn't like not being in charge or in control. He always thinks he so bloody amazing, even though most of the time he's just be an accessory through most of these missions!" In all fairness we all played a part, but I just wanted to slander him as much as I possibly could. It was interesting to hear what Hazel's thoughts were on the subject, and I felt pleased that her views, and opinions, didn't differ that much from mine.

"I thought he was jealous of you," Hazel slyly added. I didn't reply, but none the less she still carried on. "I suppose coming from a family of world renowned assassins, maybe he has always tried to be the best. In fact I think if he wasn't in love with you, he would have probably killed you for the title. He'd probably would have done it a long time ago, given the chance." I glared up at Hazel, with a stern look upon my face. Once again I didn't reply, simply because I didn't know how to react. It was an interesting and new thought she had placed inside my head, but an unwanted one. I wasn't sure whether to shout at her for saying something like that, and put her back in her place, or to just ignore her once again.

The truth was, Ricky was in love with me, and he could have killed me if he wanted to, but there again, someone who loves someone else wouldn't put them through such a horrific ordeal, yet some truth ran through Hazel's explanation, and played on my mind. If reputation was really that important to Ricky, he would have killed me, in fact he would have killed me a long time ago, but yesterday would have been the perfect chance to do so if he wanted to. Mind you if he did, it would have made the final assassination that much harder, for himself and Hazel, yet if he had succeeded, it would have only added to his glory and new found title and fame in the assassin's world. He would have been well credited, but surely he wasn't that desperate to be that well known, and fruitful? To kill me would have been killing those two as well. The final assassination would have been impossible with two killers, it's challenging enough with three.

I then simply told Hazel, "The only reason why he probably hasn't killed me, is the fact that you both need me. If we want to survive and pull through this nightmare then we need each other, we certainly can't afford to lose anyone else." With that the room fell silent once again. I tried to distract myself, and focused on the important issues at hand, and encouraged Hazel to do the same.

More time had passed as Hazel and I had made steady progress with the planning. We had decided that the best way to tackle this assassination was when Alana was on the move. She was constantly surrounded by her body guards, all day and all night; targeting her at her large mansion or any of her well hidden offices would have been suicide. Gizmo's plan was brilliant, but only if we had five people; three was too little to pull off his plan. The deciding moment that helped us choose to assassinate her, whilst she was on the move was the fact that we could plan a getaway route, which would make it extremely difficult for her men to give chase after us, and also we could have a clean, fast getaway too.

Ms Alana Willows seemed to be a creature of habit. She obviously liked to run a strict regime, and it seemed to run like clockwork, which worked in our favour. She would be in certain places, at certain times, to meet and engage with certain people. Depending on the type of person she was planning to see, influenced what area, and type of place she was willing to meet them in, such as restaurants, and bars for the more privileged clients or business partners, and for those who weren't, there were back street alley ways, underground car parks, and shady, secret places. It seemed very strange for a woman like Alana, who gave the impression that she valued her life above others, to make her whereabouts very clear and known, but there again she seemed to be the queen of her criminal empire. She'd probably expect her subjects to die for her if any danger were to occur. If anything it made a very powerful statement that she was confident, and not afraid, and the number of body guards around her at any time showed off her wealth, power, and strength. I found it disdaining.

The only problem I was having was how were we supposed to make sure she read the note? We couldn't plant it in the car, as this could raise alarms to the fact that she is wanted for assassination, which would inevitably lead to tighter security, which would make our job impossible. We couldn't shoot the message into the car, because the car would most likely be ordered to make a quick getaway, which again would make the assassination tediously harder, and the probability of us being exposed was a high risk. We certainly couldn't hide in the car to 'give' her the message, as all the cars seemed to be checked by her security. I was getting extremely frustrated. I didn't even understand what the notes were about. Why were they so important? Why should the victims have to read them? They didn't make any sense, and even Gizmo couldn't crack the code, but all the people we assassinated knew what the strange scribbles meant. Also I couldn't connect any of the people that we had been order to assassinate with one another. Yes they were all unpleasant, evil people, apart from poor Oscar Brown, but it looked like none of them knew one another. It was driving me insane!

Hazel and I had driven ourselves to work so hard and so furiously to the point of madness. I had done the majority of the planning, whilst Hazel either switched off and started to day dream, or sat there looking pretty. Occasionally something would catch her eye, or pop into her mind and she would interject with the odd fact, problem or solution. All in all she wasn't a huge amount of help. Her attention span was appalling. I glanced at the direction of the ticking clock, and I found myself feeling slightly shocked and bewildered. I hadn't realised how fast the time had flown by. Before I knew it, it was 7:30 pm. No wonder Hazel couldn't keep focused for long. I had been such a slave driver! Hours had vanished like magic, although I was under the impression that Hazel wouldn't agree with me! *'I have to hand it to Gizmo'* I thought to myself, *'how he did this for hours on end is beyond me!'*

"Wow!" I gasped whilst looking up at the clock. "I had no idea what the time was."

"No darling, neither did I!" Hazel stood up onto her dainty feet, and dramatically stretched. There was a slight tone of sarcasm in her voice. "And no sign of Ricky all day!" She suddenly added.

"Hmmm... maybe you should go and check on him Hazel." I suggested feeling a little concerned, but not hugely. There was no chance of me going on the hunt for him.

"Why don't you do it?" Hazel whinged whilst letting her body slouch lazily.

"Because I'm probably the last person he wants to see right now," I reasoned sternly. Hazel then tiresomely huffed, "Fine!" Like a typical teenager would. She begun to make her move, and as she left the room, I couldn't help but think of what she had said earlier. About Ricky not wanting to kill me, because he loved me. Maybe now, he wasn't so afraid of challenging me for my title, simply because our relationship was one hundred percent dead in the water. A sinking feeling dragged my mood down once again, as heart ache filled my mind, but I had to keep reminding myself that I shouldn't feeling like that, as he himself was no good for me.

I slouched back into the chair that I had been sitting in for hours on end to relax, and began to rub the back of my neck carefully with my hand. I forgot how unhealthy it was for the body to remain in the same position, for such a long period of time. I started to ache as I began to slightly move about and tried to get some motion back into my body. As I slowly rose from the chair, I let out a grunt as I could feel my knees and back stiffen up drastically. *I wonder if this is what it feels like to be about eighty years old!* I joked to myself in my mind.

My mind certainly felt like an eighty year old's mind. It was as if it had slowed down and wouldn't function properly. I had over used my brain! As I regained feeling, I wandered over to the large window. It was another window, of which there were many, that faced onto the large acres of land that this estate held. A wash of calm drifted over me. It was a feeling that I clung too, as it was not an emotion that occurred often.

"OH GOD!" Hazel bellowed in a horrified tone. I heard her repeat that sentence again, and again, and again as she came pounding up the corridor, "OH GOD, OH GOD, OH GOD!" Then she came screeching around the corner and burst into the room, huffing and puffing, and looking very red in the face. She looked as if she had ran a marathon.

"What now?" I groaned carelessly, not really paying any attention to the urgency to Hazel's voice. I had grown tired of the drama, and weary of tension, and fed up of Ricky's stupid behaviour.

"It's Ricky."

"And?"

"He's gone!" I frowned with a quizzical expression upon my face.

"What do you mean he's gone? Gone where?" Hazel took a deep, nervous gulp as she plucked up the courage to tell me the gut-wrenching news.

"He's gone to Alana's mansion!" My lower jaw dropped and hung; it dropped so much it felt as if it could have smacked the floor, and shattered into pieces.

I stood motionless as my whole body began to tense up once again. My heart started to pound heavily to the point where I thought I could have been sick. This was a disaster, a nightmare, hell even! How could Ricky think he was capable of completing this assassination by himself?

It hit me that this must be to do with his ego, and the fact he wanted the top spot of being the number one assassin, which surely wasn't going to happen, because he was like a lamb going to the slaughter house. My mind went into melt down mode, as I couldn't think straight, or even contemplate what would happen next.

"He has put not only himself in danger, but the mission and our lives in danger!" I shouted. "I knew he was a bloody idiot but this is taking the piss!" I stormed past Hazel in a frantic dash, and she followed me closely. We rushed through corridors, and barged through doors, like aggressive bulls charging through a red cloth. At one stage I thought I could have passed out from anger. I could see nothing but red. I wasn't sure why, but I was heading for the front door. It was as if my instinct had taken over, and my actual self was sitting back watching what was happening, and unfolding before my very eyes, like watching a movie in a cinema.

As I reached the front door, I exploded into the cold outside with my fiery temper. To my relief I could make out a black car, speeding off towards the main gates of the estate.

"We are not that far behind him!" I half rejoiced as I now knew we could stop him, but only if we acted fast. "We have to stop him before it's too late, if he gives the game away then that's it!"

I ran towards the garage, which was about 10 metres from the front door. The garage itself was detached from the house, and was the size of a small bungalow. I knew inside there lay a whole collection of cars and motorbikes. Edward was fond of his motors.

"You take a vehicle, and I will take one too. We may have a better chance of stopping him that way," I spurted. Without thinking I grabbed a set of keys off the wall, where a number of keys hung. As I peered down I noticed that I had grabbed a set of keys for a motorbike. I then dash about like crazy trying to find this motorbike, as Hazel grabbed a set of keys as well. I found the motorbike and leapt onto it.

I was in a desperate rush to go after Ricky. I didn't bother waiting for Hazel to get into her vehicle, as I zoomed off. I wondered if Ricky ever looked backed, and realised how much of a big risk he decided to take, or if he even saw us in the interior mirror in the distance. I felt some of the tiny stones flick up as I drove onto the stony driveway. I felt as if nothing could stop me now, and as if I was invisible. The motorbike started to pick up speed more and more rapidly. I soon found myself hurtling forward. *'I'm coming after you Ricky.'*

I began to feel empowered and encouraged chasing after Ricky. It was almost as if I had a point to prove to him as well, as if catching him would force him to see, that he isn't better than me, and that I am number one for a reason. I wasn't sure how I was going to stop him once I caught up with him, nor what I would do to him when I did stop him. One thing for sure though; I couldn't kill him. We were two men down from the team already. One more life down, and we would be rendered useless, and then for sure it would be game over. With this thought floating about in the forefront of my mind, I hoped that Hazel too realised the slight dilemma. I hoped she'd recognise that we couldn't put a bullet through Ricky's head to stop him destroying the assassination. In fact, I had a shuddering realisation that Ricky may try and kill us, as he was so determined to complete the final assassination by himself. There was no reason for him not to shoot us. I then started to wish that I had worn a helmet and some sort of armour or protection!

As I sped at dangerously high speeds through desolate rural lanes, I felt a buzz that I hadn't felt for a long time. The buzz that gave me a tingling sensation in the pit of my stomach, the mixture of nerves and excitement pulsed through my veins, as I felt every sense heighten to the point where I almost thought I was indestructible. This feeling of being so alive was what I missed from being an assassin. The thought that your life could end at any second was exhilarating and spurred me on even more. This rush of pure insanity was what made me love my work, but recently it had all gone and fizzled away. This amazing feeling was like welcoming an old friend into your arms and embracing it.

My ears suddenly picked up a low roaring sound of an engine. I acted as if I was an over excitable dog, about to play fetch! I bent down lower, revved the engine, and really tore up the tarmac. My hair was whooshing manically behind me, and then I suddenly saw myself emerge in a bright light. I quickly glanced into my side mirror, and saw a car behind me. I couldn't make out who was in the car, or what type of car it was, as I was blinded by their headlights. I took the liberty, when it was safe to do so, to peer over my shoulder. I could just about make you a silhouette of a woman. *'It must be Hazel.'* I thought to myself, it was the only logical assumption that I could think of, whilst my mind was impressively reacting to every sudden sharp bend in the roads. I felt at times I was going down a cork screw, or driving through a twisty maze.

Soon I had become disorientated, and had a feeling that I was lost. I couldn't figure out where I was. I knew that Ricky was heading for the Alana's mansion, but I didn't know the way off by heart, which made it more vital that I didn't lose Ricky, otherwise there would be no chance of stopping him. To my brief relief, I saw a pair of red, rear lights up ahead in the dark. *'Bulls eye.'* I smiled evilly, as I made the engine work even harder; I was pushing the motorbike to its limits, like Ricky was doing to me. At this point my face was burning, from the force of air rushing past my raw flesh. It felt as if my skin would be torn away from my skull if I went any faster. It felt as if I was driving into a brick wall, but the pain I was feeling was nothing compared to the pain of knowing that we would die a horrible death if I didn't push myself. It was torture!

When I drove behind the car I was able to slow down a little bit, as the car in front couldn't compete with the speed of my motorcycle. I could feel the muscles in my face relax a little, even though the speeds we were travelling at were still insanely and dangerously fast. I wasn't sure what to do next, as I was desperately trying to stay on my bike, but I was very aware of the vehicle in front. I wasn't sure what was going through Ricky's mind right now. He might slow down and see sense, or go into a panic frenzy, and do something stupid that could put all of us at risk.

Before I knew it, there was a gun pointing out of the driver's window. I took a sudden deep breath, and yanked out my gun, faster than you could blink. Ricky fired his gun. I swerved to a side to make sure that the bullet didn't hit me, or the bike. As I held on tight to my pistol, and the handles of the motorbike, I could hear the frightening sound of gun fire from behind me. As I quickly looked round, I could see Hazel's arms out of her driver's window firing back at Ricky, and trying to protect me. The problem was Hazel wasn't a good shot, and at one stage I thought I heard a bullet brush through my hair and whistle past my ear. It made my heart stop! *I need to do something now, before either one of them blow my head off.*

I don't know what came over me, but it felt like my instincts suddenly took over. I got ready to brake, and steer aside as I held out my gun. My hand and arm was shaking from the bike rumbling along the surface of the road. I switched my attention from everything that was going around, and focused on the back wheel of Ricky's car. It felt as if everything had slowed down, and even the sound of the guns being fired sounded distorted and distant.

Within seconds I aimed my gun, pulled the trigger, and deliberately slowed down and moved over to the edge of the road. I followed Ricky slowly as I watched the chaos unfold, right before my very eyes. Ricky's car started swaying and screeching from side to side on the road, as my bullet ripped through the rubber on his tyre, and made the tyre explode. Sparks started the fly all over the place, as the smell of burnt rubber filled my nostrils. Ricky had slammed on the brakes, but then crashed into a verge on the side of the drama filled road. As he crashed to a halt, the sound of his crash, and squeal of his shredded tyres echoed through the emptiness. I was also glad that Hazel managed to react quickly enough not to crash into the back of Ricky's car, or knock me off the road.

I pulled over cautiously behind the crashed car, and crept off the motorbike. I remained low to the ground and stealthily crawled around the car. The smell of burnt, worn down tyres was intoxicating and felt as if it was burning my nostrils. My gun was close to my body, whilst I remained alert. I wasn't sure if Ricky would pull a gun on me, that is, if he was still alive. For all I knew, experiencing a hard impact like that could have killed him. My heart was in my throat as I approached the driver's door. The window was still open and the side mirror had been shattered by bullets. I froze for a moment, trying to figure out whether I could hear any sign of movement, or breathing. Nothing. I took silent but deep breaths, as I composed myself, then shot up onto my feet and aimed the gun through the window, where I knew roughly Ricky's head would have been.

To my surprise Ricky was fully conscious and wide eyed. He then saw me, and stared. He gave me a look I had never seen a human make before. It was a cold, your-dead-to-me look, whilst being amazed that he was still alive, mixed with fear. His eyes were frozen solid, as his mouth remained shut tight, and not a muscle twitched in his face. It gave me the chills for the brief few seconds he remained like that. He then snapped out of that phase of mixed emotions, and gave me a look that was much more familiar to me, which was an expression of rage. He then sarcastically grinned, whilst shoving his middle finger up into the air, and abruptly spat.

"Fuck you."

"Come here you fucking rat-bag!" I bellowed, whilst flinging open the driver's door, nearly tearing it off its hinges in the process. Aggressively I plunged my hand into the car, roughly grabbing Ricky's black, tight fitted jumper, scrunching my hand up viscously, so I had a nice tight grip on him. Then I yanked my arm back, launching Ricky out of the car, and slammed him against the cold, hard road surface.

Before Ricky could react, I spun round on my feet, and pointed my gun at him, whilst firing out the question, "What the hell do you think you are playing at?" The excited buzz had been replaced with fury! I wanted to beat Ricky to death. He lay there on the floor, looking amused and smug with himself. "I'm not bloody playing any more Ricky," I blurted out, now not thinking straight, and saying anything that came into my head. He still just lay there smiling up at me. I wanted to stamp and jump all over his face, and see if he would be smiling after that. Instead I slammed the butt of my gun across his face at such a force it must have felt like a train hitting him. He clutched the side of his face and gritted his teeth in pain. I then had this strange guilty feeling stirring in the pits of my stomach. I covered it up and suppressed it all by reminding myself what he had done, and the risk he had put Hazel and I in.

"You don't have the guts to kill me," Ricky hissed bitterly.

"Oh trust me, I do now, but I can't... Unfortunately, we need you alive to complete the final assassination, but if I found a way of completing this last mission without you, I would have made sure that

that car didn't just crash into the verge. I would have made sure it would have blown up!"

"Such big threats for a woman that thinks she's the best."

"I am." I bit my tongue as I glared at him. Ricky the removed his hand and I saw a smear of blood across his face. I quickly glared down at the butt of my gun and also saw Ricky's blood and a little bit of skin on it. "Get up." I barked whilst turning around and looking at Hazel dashing over, in typical Hazel style.

"Don't kill him!" she whimpered, whilst her hands flapped from side to side as she ran over pathetically.

"I won't."

"Good." As Ricky scuffled to his feet, he looked over at Hazel.

"You are a shit shot Hazel; you're a disgrace!"

"Don't you start on her!" I bit back harshly. "Now answer my question Ricky. God help me after we complete this mission, you might be dead meat to me if you don't start explaining yourself very soon." Ricky stood in silence still clutching the side of his face in agony. "Come on, or I'll smack you again, but this time I will make sure it will break your cheek!"

"Whatever." He laughed. I raised my gun into the air, and was about to come down hard on Ricky.

"WAIT!" He flinched rapidly.

"Changed your mind then?" I smiled evilly, wanting to make Ricky feel small and puny.

"Fine." He composed himself for a moment and then began to tell us what was going on in his selfish little mind. "I don't believe you girls have what it takes to be able to finish this mission, and I am not pinning my future and hopes on you two. If I am going to die, I want to be the one to cause my own death, not you, not Hazel, and not Edward. ME!" His voice began to rise in volume as I could see the stress and tension show.

"Darling, we can."

"Shut up Hazel!" Ricky snapped and he started to shake. "Will you drop the whole act, the darlings, and the looks, and everything. I can't trust my life in your hands. I mean look at you!" I watched Hazel as she stood up right. She moved her shoulders back, and for once I saw her take control.

"Ricky," She said sternly like a strict school teacher, immediately grabbing hold and capturing our attentions. "I don't care much for what you have just said, and do you realise you are a bloody fool?" I waited with baited breath to hear her following words. "We have worked as a team since day one! Yes we haven't all seen eye to eye. Yes there has been drama, and heart aches, and fights, and not everything has gone to plan, but we all, including Gizmo and Tank, worked as a team!" Hazel then started to make bold hand gestures, and started to speak as if she was a world leader. "Yes, we were nearly caught and revealed in our first mission, in the casino, but we got through it, and improved. Yes, we have had personal clashes with one another, over love, status, friendships, and morals. Yes, we have lost friends on the way through terrible circumstances, but look where it has got us. This whole situation has made us stronger-minded people. This journey has enabled us to get to know ourselves more, and to feel like humans instead of cold hearted killers, and I believe that we have grown close to each other, as if we were a family."

Ricky and I stood in astonishment. I felt so inspired, and strangely upbeat. A part of me was pleased that Hazel revealed her true self. I knew she wasn't a ditsy, dippy, dumb tart, and that through the weeks she had developed into a much more detailed thinker. I was proud of her, although a part of me was awaiting her to say the word *'darling'* at some point during her wonderful speech. Ricky let out a huge sigh, and hung his head for a moment. I began to think that he was going to argue back, but then his shoulder suddenly dropped as if he was going to give up. A quiet grumbling sound came from his mouth.

"Yeah." Ricky took a deep, steady breathe inwards, and then straightened up like Hazel. Chest out, and feeling good about himself he announced "You're right Hazel." He then stretched out his hand, and placed it lightly on her delicate shoulder. "I am sorry. I didn't think about what we have all been through, and how much work each and every one of us has done, and how much we have achieved. We've done great. I guess for once in my life, I have been thinking about life. Before all this happening, all I could think about was, money, power, status and assassinations, but now I see the bigger picture of life. I guess, I was so desperate to survive to be able to live it and enjoy it. It is as if Lord Edward Hamston brained washed us all. Killing, and being cold, just like he was."

Once again, I could feel myself becoming much stronger and more powerful by the honesty, and words that were spoken between everyone. I then reassured Ricky, "You're not the only one who is scared of dying, Hazel and I are too. It's nothing to be ashamed of." He nodded as my words penetrated his ears. This was the most vulnerable, and sensitive I think I had ever seen Ricky. In fact looking at Hazel and Ricky, I could see their true selves evolving and revealing themselves. It was odd, but strangely beautiful as well. It's like watching a child grow up to become something big, and something to behold. My mind then thought about Gizmo and Tank, and I couldn't help but wonder what they might be thinking, or what they would say and do if they were still around. I was sure that Gizmo would think it was a revelation, and Tank would be happy and smiling.

I wished so much that Tank and Gizmo were still with us. I longed that Tank hadn't lost his mind, because of the stress, and him finding letters from his mother, and killing Gizmo. I then started to wonder what Edward would think. I don't think he would have meant his best assassins to turn out like this. It was as if we had all softened and grown extremely fond of one another, something that he would not approve of. It made me feel rebellious!

"Let's do this," I declared, as I too stood like the others, with my head held high full of pride. "Let's do this for Gizmo and Tank, and save ourselves right now. We owe it to ourselves." Ricky and Hazel looked at one another, and then back at me. Ricky said as whilst raising one eyebrow in uncertainty, "Are you sure?"

"More than ever. I don't think I have ever been so ready in all my life."

"What about the planning?"

"Forget it! Even with all the planning between us, there isn't a sure certainty that we would survive anyway. If this is going to be our last assassination, I want to go in there with all guns blazing, and if tonight is the night I am going to die then I want to make the most of it, and go out in style!" My chest started to heave, as I grew more and more anxious with anticipation and excitement.

"Fuck it, let's do it!" Ricky leapt, and Hazel joined.

"Let's do this!"

"We are going to have to pick up some more equipment though." Ricky added making the moment more realistic. "I dropped my gun somewhere, whilst you guys were shooting at me." I found a sideways smile creeping onto my face, as for some reason I found it slightly amusing. We agreed that there would be no harm in stocking up.

It then struck me, that was that. We had recklessly decided to do this, to really go for this, our final assassination. This could be the last few moments that I am with these two people, team mates, friends. It was all or nothing, and I didn't think the stakes had ever been higher. Our freedom was moments away. Our souls and lives would be able to break free from the maddening, dark dungeon that this poison held us in. I couldn't wait for the moment to come where I get my hands on the sweet antidote, the nectar of life, and live my life till I grow old. A thought that never crossed my mind when I was younger. I was determined to pull through this, and I was going to make sure that my two friends were about to as well. I'm not losing any more friends, at the hands of the brutal gang leader Ms Alana Willows, or the purely evil, sadistic genius Lord Edward Hamston.

CHAPTER 12

THE FINAL ASSASSINATION

FTER METICULOUSLY GATHERING THE equipment and weapons we thought we might need, we were back on the road again. The excitement and buzz hadn't died down between us three. If anything it grew stronger. We were all drunk on the thought that we would be free people within a few hours or so. Crazy! Racing down the roads towards the mansion, we were assassins not to be messed with. Assassins that were on a clear, deliberate mission. Assassins that were desperate to be able to save our own lives.

"Wait!" I shouted out suddenly, realising that we could have forgotten one of the most critical items to be able to complete the mission.

"What? What is it?" Hazel replied, whilst driving like a woman that had had one to many expressos!

"The piece of paper, the note, the coded writing, have we got it?"

"Chill." Ricky soothed, as he placed his hand into his pocket, then pulled out a white piece of paper with the scribbles on it. "I've got it, don't worry. When I was going to do the assassination by myself, I was going to do it right you know!" He half joked, whilst catching my eye.

He then stuck out the coded message, and for the final time we both examined it.

"What do you think this means? What it is?"

He frowned whilst sounding perplexed. I replied in an unsure voice, "I have no idea. I have been asking myself that for weeks now. I'm sure Gizmo was no closer to finding out what all this meant either, but I have a feeling that because of these silly coded messages it has resulted with us being in this mess in the first place. These messages hold the answer to everything."

"Must be something big, if it's worth Edward risking all his best assassins, after he died."

"I can't make any logical link between any of the people that we have killed. Why would they been involved with one another? Why would they all understand this scribbled rubbish? How do they know what it reads?" It was insane that none of us could figure out what was going on with these notes. What made it worse was I was so sure, surer that I have ever been in my life, that these inscriptions held the key to the truth, and the purpose of us being here, and why we had been brought together like this.

"The mind boggles, but I am sure we are close to finding out the answer." Ricky then made a good, genuine gesture towards me that really meant the world to me. "Here." He passed over the message and held it in front of me. Hands steady as a rock. "You have it."

"Why?"

Ricky then looked away for a second or two, as he pieced his thoughts together, then looked straight back at me, with a serious, but peaceful look upon his face.

"Because you have the right to hand over the note to Alana... to our final target." I was touched and taken aback, whilst feeling a little pleasantly shocked, as I repeated myself once again, "Why?" Ricky then smiled at me, and held onto both of my hands, whilst placing the note in the palm of my hand. He softly cupped my hands together.

"For many reasons Grace." I could feel his smooth thumb rub against the skin on my hand, but I knew it not to be in a sexual, or pestering way. It was in a sentimental way that only true friends would understand, true friends that had been through a lot together. "I believe you have suffered the most through this process Grace. We all have, but you are one heck of a woman!" I giggled and blushed slightly as friendly compliments fell on my ears, but slowly I felt tears prick my eyes after what Ricky said to me next. "You have had your heart broken by me twice, which I am deeply and truly sorry for. Also you lost two friends, but I knew how much Tank meant to you, and how confused and lost you felt after his death. Also I have to say it takes a loyal friend to do what you did for Tank that night. You managed to forgive all of us at one stage or another, whilst being poisoned by your former boss who classed you as the number one assassin." A lump formed in my throat as a mixture of feelings rushed around my body, but I was determined to remain strong. "You managed to lead us all. You were and have always been the strongest member of this group, and I know for sure, and in my heart of hearts, that you are the best assassin, and you will always be the best, no matter who comes along next. Your name will go down in history."

I sat in silence, not sure how to react, not even sure if I could speak because the lump in my throat had grown so big. I think he knew how I felt, and that I wanted to tell him how much it meant to me that he said something like that with such elegance and emotion. I was scared if I had spoken I would have started to cry, and I didn't want that to start happening to me. Even though we were running into the final mission carelessly, it didn't mean that I wasn't going to be focused. We all had come so far; it would be dreadful and unthinkable if we didn't pull through it.

Ricky then tried to lighten the mood, as he sensed that I was turning a little bit emotional. He randomly said, "I wonder what the antidote to the poison tastes like? Best not be bloody foul! I hope its tastes sweet, like honey or jam. Yes… that would be fitting, a sweet cure for a sweet victory!" Hazel and I laughed aloud, as I too started to wonder the same thing. Ricky had a point you know! Then a dark sinister thought crossed my mind. What would happen if there was no antidote? What if Edward didn't expect us to pull through this? What if he was using us like puppets to scare some people? I sure did feel like his puppet as it felt like he had been playing games with us, and making us do what he wanted even beyond the grave. Only a dark minded person could dream up something as cruel and inhuman as this. I prayed that it wouldn't be the case though, and I didn't want to air my concerns with the others, just in case it knocked them off their game.

"I'm going to drive past the mansion, so I can hide the car somewhere. It will make it less obvious that we are here," Hazel suggested wisely as we began to approach the side of the mansion. High, grey bricked walls surrounded the grounds.

"She looks like she has as much land as Edward does," Ricky gasped as the walls seemed to go on forever, and forever more. It reminded me of a prison. The walls looked sturdy and solid; not even a tank would be able to run through those walls. I began to think that if that was just the outer walls, which were amazingly secure and probably protected her quite well, then what would the rest of the place be like. I remembered from the blue prints that there would be hundreds of guards, and guard dogs, patrolling all over the place, with set routines, and regular check-ups held in certain places too.

Finally we drove past the main entrance to the grounds of the mansion. My mouth dropped in awe as I caught a glimpse of a beautiful, stunning building. It was hard to see, but what I did see of it was breath-taking. I could make out hundreds of old-styled windows covering the brick work from head to toe, whilst gorgeous greenery climbed parts of the building making it look quaint and magical. The front doors seemed to be the height of an elephant, and the security guards glimmered in the moonlight.

As the car drove casually past, so not to draw attention to ourselves, I slyly peered over my shoulder and could see something that would definitely prove that the front entrance was a no go.

"They have a guard box by the entrance gate. The gate looks like it's electronic, so if we are detected the chances of them locking the gates electronically so we would be trapped, is more than likely, like the notes said on Gizmo's plan."

"Damn it!" Hazel slammed her hands on the steering wheel.

"What?" Ricky and I jumped.

"Look up on the walls. Every so often there are security cameras mounted up on the wall."

"Damn! That wasn't on the blue prints."

"Hmmmm…" I thought to myself. "Hazel I have an idea," I told her as I peered out of the car window whilst scheming a plot and studying the surroundings. "If you slow the car down so Ricky and myself can carefully roll out of the passenger side door, and into a bush and conceal ourselves, then you make the car come to a halt, so it looks like the car has broken down or something I'm sure a couple of guards will come out to inspect the reason why you have stopped. Then, if you can get the guards round the other side of the car, me and Ricky will shoot them dead. We push them into the back of the car, and drive off. It'll mean fewer guards to deal with at the entrance"

"But won't more guards come out looking for the other guards that have gone missing? Plus, what if the cameras pick it up? Also what if a guard is watching on the camera?" Hazel questioned not feeling sure of the idea.

"It's alright. The camera shouldn't see me and Ricky exiting the car, nor the guards and us re-entering it, because of the angle of the cameras. Also it would help if you try and break down somewhere dark, and then turn off your head lights and just leave the hazard lights on. It would give us a better chance and more concealment." I took a breath and quickly thought about her other two worries.

All of a sudden I had a marvellous idea! "Do the guards wear hats?"

"What?" Ricky looked at me as if I was mad.

"Just answer me please."

"I saw some with hats on. They looked like black baseball caps sort of thing, but why?" Hazel answered.

"Because when we shoot those two guards dead, me and Ricky can slip into the guard's outfits, and get into the mansion. That way it looks like you have left by yourself, and the two guards are coming back. I asked about the hats because it would make it easier to conceal my hair."

"Good thinking."

"What am I going to do? You two will be inside, and I will be in the car outside." Once again I found myself thinking on the spot. It wasn't easy.

"Do you remember the blue prints clearly?" I asked Hazel, hoping that she wasn't getting herself in a panic and was able to think and recall clearly.

"Yeah," she bluntly replied.

"I remember that to the central west side of the building there were lots of trees, and stuff like that."

"Let me guess," Hazel butted in. "You want me to ditch the car out of sight, and sneak up to the mansion without being spotted by the cameras, using the trees?"

"Exactly!" I grinned.

"God I hate climbing trees!" Hazel shook her head, and then said, "I guess then you will want me to enter the ground from the west central side, and you will let me in disguised as guards."

"Sure thing."

"It's a brilliant idea!" Ricky clapped and rubbed his hands with glee.

"Yeah brilliant!" grunted Hazel sarcastically agreeing, but then shrugged it off as we prepared and waited for the perfect place to emerge.

Ricky and I were waiting poised and ready to roll out of the car and into the bush. My heart was pounding in my chest, my teeth were gritted, and my stomach was doing flips. I was so nervous, yet brimming with joy. I couldn't wait to start this operation and get inside the mansion and meet this Ms Alana Willows.

"I see the perfect place coming up. There are two large bushes, slightly separate from one another."

"Great start slowing down." Ricky gleamed. I could sense that he was feeling the thrill that I was.

"Good luck guys," Hazel wished us. Although I couldn't see her face I could tell she said it was a fond smile.

"See you on the inside." I told her.

Ricky slightly opened the door and rolled out straight into the bush. He did it perfectly, it couldn't have gone better. Then I quickly scooted towards the door, keeping low, and did the same. As I rolled me out of the car, I felt the hard surface bang up against me. I rolled so fast, it left myself feeling slightly dizzy, but I had done it. I was invisible. I looked to my right quickly, and saw Ricky crouching on to the ground beside of me. I saw him put his silencer on the end of his gun and decided to do the same. I was silently twisting the silencer on the gun as I watched Hazel pretend to have a break down. She did what I asked which was come to a gradual halt, and turn off her head lights and just left the hazard lights flashing. *'Great.'*

The sound of footsteps grew louder and louder. I knew that two guards, just like I thought would happen, approached Hazel and the car. I could hear the conversation that was going on between Hazel and the guards.

"You can't stay here. Move along." One of the guards sharply ordered. Then I could hear a faint sobbing sound coming from the car, and Hazel's voice stuttering as she pretending to cry.

"I...I can't sir."

"Why?" The first guard barked back at her, coming across as very rude and insensitive.

"I... I... t-t-think my car has broken d-d-down!"

"Do you know what's wrong with the car?" The second guard said sounding slightly more concerned.

"No sir," she replied in such a sweet, angelic voice.

"Well, then you're going to have to walk!" The first guard grumpily snapped. "We don't have the authority by our employer to fix your car. Now leave." As both guards started to turn around, I thought to myself, *'oh shit!'* but Hazel being a class act who was best at being a drama queen, pulled out all the stops and used her dirty little tricks to get what she wanted. I looked on in fascination. How she could change her personalities and emotions so quickly, and act them out so well, was beyond me. I then started to think she was in the wrong line of work. She would have made a brilliant actress, and heck, I would have spent every last penny to see her perform!

"Oh, but sirs." She half sighed and spoke in a down trodden way, "Please can you help me." She sounded desperate, almost as if she was begging them to help her. "I can't walk to where I'm going, and it's so late and dark, and a young, pretty lady like myself shouldn't be walking about at this time of night. Anything could happen." The men slowly stopped and looked at one another, and then looked round back at Hazel. I could tell they were both in two minds. "Oh please sirs!" She kept saying, making it sound like they had the power of choice, and giving them the impression that they were the ones in power. "I can't do this all by myself. I need two big strong men like yourselves to help me!" I found it rather amusing how she played the beautiful young damsel in distress. I could tell it made the men feel big and macho, especially the way Hazel excellently played her role. The two men approached the car again, much more closely than before. It was as if they wanted to see what she really looked like.

"Fine, pop the bonnet," the grumpy one agreed.

There was a clunking sound as the hood popped open, and then the men slowly walked around to the front of the car. In the process Hazel got out of the car, and when she did I was gob-smacked. Hazel was wearing a tightly fitted black, short, cleavage-revealing dress. When we were in the car she wasn't wearing that! I peered over at Ricky in amazement. He looked like he was wondering the same thing, and shrugged at me. It was like a magic trick. One minute she was wearing a black top, and trousers and the next, a sexy dress. I imagined it was a trick, or something she had done to her clothes as she spent many of her years seducing men to assassinate them.

"Your engine looks fine madam," one of the guards told her sounding puzzled.

"Well I did hear something go wrong with this car," she said loudly. I thought to myself this is it, get ready, get set, as she led them round to the side of the car, but unlike what I said to her, she was making an odd hand gesture towards Ricky and I, whilst blocking the targets. It was as if she was trying to signal us to move closer I wasn't sure at first, I didn't like it when things didn't go the way I planned it, but before I knew it Ricky was behind me, he was gently pushing on my back to move me forward.

"I think the problem is down there." Hazel said. When she looked round, and saw that we were right behind her I was surprised, to say the least, with what she did next. "Look down here", she said in her seductive voice, and of course the guards obliged and did what she said. When the two guards bent over, Hazel lowered herself as well. All three of them were now lower than the car windows, so they were completely unnoticeable to the cameras. I had a feeling that this would make the guards inside the mansion watch even closer, as they were out of sight, which meant that we would have to be even more carful then before.

Whack… whack! Before I could do anything, Hazel had knocked both of the guards unconscious. Ricky and I rushed to Hazel's side, as we quickly stripped the men of their black uniforms. The uniform was very bland and straight forward. It was just a plain black T-shirt, black combat trousers, with a belt, and black bullet proof vests which hid the fact that I was a woman, and made my breasts vanish. Luckily one of the guards had a cap. I tied my hair up tightly and shoved it under the cap so it was well hidden.

Whilst we were changing into the guards clothing, Hazel stood up straight.

"What are you doing?" Ricky panicked.

"It's ok. If I disappear for a long time the guards will suspect something. If I am in sight they won't think of anything, and they will just think that the guards are working on my car."

"How did you change your clothes so fast?" I couldn't resist asking, I was still impressed by it.

"Oh, that… that's nothing. I've developed my own clothing to change in and out of within seconds. I could walk into a building looking like one person, and leave it looking like another person."

"Genius!" I complimented her.

"Yeah enough with the girl talk." Ricky rolled his eyes, thinking it was typical of women to start talking about fashion in the middle of a job. "Why did you knock the guards out instead of killing them?" Ricky asked. Hazel pulled a tiny little pistol that was strapped to her fleshy, sexy, plump thigh and then fired her gun twice. Both of her bullets penetrated the skulls and entered their brains, rendering the guards dead.

"Because if I shot them with their clothes on, you'd have blood and a bullet holes on their uniform." I was highly impressed by Hazel's quick thinking.

"Great work Hazel!" I praised her, whilst Ricky and I slyly loaded the two dead bodies into the back of the car, without it looking obvious. Then we both stood up. "Now we have to make it look like we are telling you to move on," I said, whilst pretending to be the grumpy man. I had studied the grumpy man, as he was the one that caught my attention, and I started to mimic his movement. I began to move my hands as if

I was telling Hazel to shoo, and leave now. Ricky took on the role of playing the much nicer, slightly boring guard. He paced round the front of the car and shut the bonnet. Then we walked away. As we walked away, I heard the sound of the car engine starting. I looked over my shoulder and saw Hazel disappear into the distance. At least I knew she got away safely!

My palms began to sweat as we approached the main gate. I could feel my breathing becoming more erratic as nerves started to soar to dizzying heights. I felt as if I should begin to pray for strength, and luck, but on the outside I was acting cool, collected, and calm. *'Relax'* I told myself. I needed to make sure I didn't get flustered, so I was able to think clearly. *'It will all work out.'*

"Security card please," one guard asked Ricky and I as we approached the main gates. I felt like screaming in my head. *'Oh god!'* I panicked in my mind, *'Security card, where is it!'* I then remembered that this was not a good time to start acting stupid and unprofessionally. I gently searched the pockets on my dead-man's uniform and then felt something attached onto a piece of expandable plastic line. I cautiously pulled it out, and looked down. It was a security pass. It was attached to the line so obviously it couldn't get stolen or lost.

The guard examined the pass. Ricky watched closely for any immediate, or uncertain reaction. We were preparing ourselves for the worst scenario, which would have been that they realised we were fakes, and these passes did not belong to us. Then we would have been thrown into a very sticky situation. We both had to remain alert and ready.

Doubts ran through my mind. I started to think that I didn't even look like the male guard whose photo was on the security pass. My facial features were much more feminine than his. I began to look around me casually, as if I was admiring my surroundings, or just on the lookout for anything unusual in an attempt to conceal my face a little more, without raising suspicion. To my amazement, they allowed me access. They obviously didn't pay close attention to who went out or in. In fact I would say they didn't examine the security card at all. I reckoned that they assumed that we were the same people who had left the premises, as it looked like the same people came back from the car from the footage shot by the security cameras.

Ricky did the same, but looked straight at the guard, as he had no worries, as he was a male, so looking like a man was no major issue for himself. After all if the guard allowed me entry, they were bound to give him entry too. Once again the guard allowed him into the premises of Alana Willow's mansion.

The stories I had heard of the guards being so terrified of Alana's rage didn't seem so apparent with those guards. They seemed so half-hearted about their work. Although I was pretty sure if somehow Alana found out that Ricky and I were wondering around on her turf, there would be a bolt set aside for someone's heads!

Walking up the stoned, paved drive way I really felt dwarfed. The mansion was huge, much bigger than I imagined from the blue prints. There were five large garages to my left, all alongside each other, with dark green, electric doors. Hedge rows neatly lay along the sides of the drive way, with scented rose bushes, and other arras of plants and potted flowers. I smiled to myself as I was surprised to see such a welcoming entrance and a magnificent front garden. I thought it was odd that someone like Alana would take particular interest in plants and wild life. I could hear gentle rippling of water as I turned right, and saw a huge fountain.

Approaching the mansion doors, we saw guards standing stiff and still. There were four of them, standing like the queen's guardsmen. These guards seemed much more self-disciplined then the ones by the gate. They didn't ID us. Instead two guards looked at each other, then moved towards the front door. I felt on edge as I wasn't sure what they were doing. Both of them grabbed the handles to the doors of the mansion, and in sync opened them in time with one another. As the doors opened, I automatically started to walk forward into the entrance hall of the mansion. As I did, it felt as if my breath was taken away. The sight was stunning.

Two staircases ran along the left and right hand walls. They were wide enough to stand seven men standing side by side. Above me I could see the landing baluster. They surrounded the circumference of the room, making a balcony effect. In the centre, on the ceiling, a huge light swung low, and underneath a grand ancient rug but stunning sat covering the dark, polished wooden flooring. The walls were covered in paintings, and decorations; it was almost like walking into an art gallery. As I looked at Ricky, he seemed secretly impressed by Alana's home.

As the doors shut closed behind us, Ricky and I stood still in awe.

"Some pad she's got aye!" He sighed in admiration, with his hand on his hips.

"Never mind that. We need to make a move, before Hazel gets here." As we walked I found it odd how there were barely any guards about. I would have imagined that there would have been tons, scattered all over the place, standing by every door, patrolling every inch of the mansion. It seemed too quiet. Too quiet for my liking. "Do you remember the directions?" I asked Ricky, as each step we took I began to feel more and more confused.

"Yeah, follow me." We paced and weaved through a mixture of corridors and hallways, until Ricky suddenly said. "Grace, Hazel should be somewhere about here."

"Right, let's find a room to enter and see if we can spot her." I had a dark feeling rising within me. What would happen if they had found Hazel? Was that the reason why there were barely any guards about?

We made our way towards a door, and noticed that there was a card swipe machine placed on the lock of the door. I then looked at my security pass and examined it. It seemed to be the right width and size to slot into the electrical lock. I was about to swipe my card when Ricky abruptly stopped me.

"Wait," he hissed, swinging his arm out rapidly, and grabbing onto my arm to stop me. "What happens if the card registers the name of the guard that's on that card, onto a computer data base, and he's not supposed to be there?"

"Well you come up with a better idea!" I sarcastically huffed. "If you haven't noticed we have to gain access to a room along here somewhere, and I am under the impression that all these rooms probably have these locks, and it may not register our whereabouts… well… hopefully." Ricky just stared at me eagerly, but then stepped down and let go of my am. I stretched out my hand, and quickly swiped the card through the machine. A little light on the machine turned from red to green and a slight clicking noise followed as the door unlocked for us. I gently jiggled the handle and the door opened with ease.

Cautiously we entered the room, and to my horror there was a guard already standing in the darkened room gazing out the window. *'Shit!'* I panicked to myself, *'What are we going to do now?'* I was ready to pull out my gun at any moment. The guard turned round and looked at us both. At this point I was holding my breath!

"Oh, hey," The guard tiresomely grunted. "What are you guys doing here?" The guard didn't seem in the slightest bit concerned that Ricky and I were in the same room as him, although by the question that he asked, I was under the impression that we were not supposed to be here. It then hit me, he asked a question! How was I supposed to reply? What was the right thing to say?

Luckily Ricky was quick off his feet.

"Just checking up on you lot, making sure you're doing your jobs."

"That isn't your job to do that, it's Eddie Longhalls job to patrol this part of the building."

"He sent us to double check things, alright?" I growled in a low voice trying to sound like the grumpy guard we had killed.

"Oh, is that you Fred?" the guard randomly said sounding surprised. "Sorry, didn't recognise you there, you know… with the light's being tuned off and such. Pain in the arse really, wish we could turn them on, doesn't do my eyes any good." I found it surreal that this guard, who was is meant to be ruthless and tough was moaning about his eyes, and talking to us as if we were his friends. It was beyond belief.

"Turn the lights on then," Ricky suggested, as if he forgot who we were dealing with and where we were. To my surprise the guard's reaction and mine were the same,

"No!"

"Are you mad? Alana has given strict orders not to. She doesn't want all the guards noticeable in the building. She seems very paranoid and uptight at the moment. I'm under the impression that something is happening, or she has pissed someone off once again." There was a moment of silence as I felt myself fill with dread. *'She was suspecting something? I hope it's us and not someone else that would make life difficult!'*

As the guard turned towards the window again, I looked at Ricky as if to say Alana-knows-something.

"At least I have the outdoor lights to ease the eyestrain. Silly that she makes us stand about in the dark for hours." Once again another rush of horror washed over me within seconds. Hazel was still outside making her way towards us, and this guard could be looking straight at her.

"You know," I suddenly perked up, still trying to sound grumpy and miserable. "Go and have a break."

"What?" The guard said, spinning round on the balls of his feet again.

"You heard me, go have a break. Rest your eyes, we'll cover for you," I suggested in a desperate attempt for him to leave the room, or at least stop him looking out of the window.

"Oh alright Fred, thanks." The guard thanked me as he walked towards us. "Not like you to be so nice."

"Just do it before I change my mind," I then snapped in reply.

"That's more like it." He chuckled to himself as he strolled past and exited the room.

I let out a sigh of relief as I could hear his footsteps die down as he walked away.

"Smart thinking," Ricky told me.

"No thanks to you! You told him to put the lights on which would have given us away. He thought I was Fred!"

"I know!" Ricky looked astonished. "I didn't think you sounded anything like him," he playfully joked.

"Oh, shut up!"

"Well, on the bright side it sounds like Alana is rattling in her boots!"

"Is that a good thing?" I raised an eyebrow and peered through the window. All I could see was trees.

"Well, it is in a way. At least we know she might be expecting us."

"Yeah, you're not really selling this 'bright-side-idea' to me very well… never become a salesman!"

"She must know about Gabriel, Oscar, and Leo's deaths, and probably Edward's as well. If they are all tied in together then she is probably fearing for her life as well."

"Yes which makes me think about those bloody notes again," I replied whilst fiddling with the final note that sat in my pocket.

As we stood looking out of the window, waiting for Hazel to make her appearance, I knew that we had very little time before the guard returned.

"Come on, where are you Hazel?" Ricky began to pace back and forth and as time went by, his pacing became more frantic.

"Will you stop that?" I ordered, as he was making me feel anxious. "She will get here, have some faith in her."

Ricky stopped dead in his tracks and with joy he jumped and shouted out. "LOOK!"

I quickly hushed him, as I focused my eyes in the dark, and looked to where he was pointing. I could vaguely see someone moving around in the trees. "It must be her!" I grinned.

"I told you she could do this."

"Yeah, but she still has to get inside first." Ricky then told me with a slight hint of hesitation,

"Let's help her then."

With that, I carefully opened the window. The windows swung open slightly, I then double checked that no one was around on the ground, or nearby, and then began to wave my hands, attempting to attract her attention, and to signal her over to this window. I could see Hazels silhouette suddenly stop moving. It was as if she thought I was a guard or something, and seemed worried that she has been spotted.

"I think she thinks I'm a guard!" I exclaimed, worried.

"Hang on." Ricky then joined my side by the window, and we both tried to wave her over. As soon as he did, the silhouette began to move again, and slowly, but steadily started to grow clearer.

Hazel had now clambered and climbed through the obstacle course of branches, twigs, and leaves and was now perched on a branch opposite the window. She looked around her as she tried to figure a way over to us. Ricky and I did the same. Without warning, Hazel began to climb down the tree. We watched with baited breath, to see what she was up to whilst hoping she wasn't going to be spotted, or anything would happen to her. She climbed down the thick tree truck, and then hopped over onto the top of the security wall. I frowned as I wondered where she was going next.

My heart leapt through my chest when she took the massive risk of leaping down onto the ground, in the bright light of the security light, and shot across to the side of the building, back into the dark and shadows. I wiped my forehead whilst I let out a sigh of relief. Ricky then glanced at me as he listened to my heavy sigh and frowned.

"What is she up to?"

I replied with a simple shrug, and then both of our eyes were set back on Hazel. Now she was skimming along the wall, with her back flat against it. She almost looked like a vertical snake. She was shifting herself underneath our window, and I couldn't help but notice her cleavage from above. I looked at Ricky as his eyes really did seem particularly focused on her now. I accidently let out a tut, and Ricky turned his head whist I was mid eye roll.

"What!?!" he asked trying to make out he wasn't up to anything.

"Don't what me!" I threw back. "You're a man. I know what you were looking at, and anyway you have seen them before so put your tongue back in your gob!" That tiny situation triggered something off in me. I wasn't sure what, but it reminded me of the time when I had feelings for Ricky, but he slept with Hazel instead. Was it jealously? Was I still in love with Ricky after everything we had been through? A part of me hoped not, or was it the fact that I was slowly resorting back to my old ways on the job, and not allowing myself to feel emotions like that again, especially whilst working.

As soon as I said that I heard a slight rattle of metal coming from the underside of the window. It was Hazel, who had now mounted the drain pipe, and was climbing rapidly up it. I could feel Ricky's eyes staring at me, as if they were piercing a hole in the side of my face. I wasn't sure what his facial expression was, nor his reaction, as I didn't take time to absorb what I said.

Then my ears picked up another noise. It was a noise of little stones, such as the ones that were on the driveway, being scuffled and trodden on.

"Oh no!" I blurted out, "Hurry up Hazel, quick! Climb faster!"

"What?" Ricky then questioned.

"I can hear guards approaching from outside... Come Hazel!" I could now hear muffled voices of two guardsmen talking to each other. Hazel was only halfway up the drain pipe. If the guards saw her they'd shoot her down! I estimated she had about ten seconds to climb the rest of the pipe before she was spotted.

"Please hurry up! Now! Come on! Faster!" I eagerly urged, shouting at her. Hazel began to frantically move her arms and legs faster.

"A-h-h-h!" She cried out silently as her foot slipped, and her body slide down a few inches. Ricky now started egging her on to get her to climb quicker. Hazel managed to reposition herself and began to climb rapidly again. The voices of the guards grew louder. In my panicking mind it sounded like they were right on top of us.

When Hazel was an arm stretch away from the window, I tugged the sleeve to Ricky's T-shirt and told him to help me. With that I leant out of the window, reached out my hands, and tried to get Hazel to grab hold of them tightly. Ricky was anchored behind me, supporting my stance, and made sure I wasn't going to fall out of the window. His knees were slightly bent and locked, as his body slightly pressed up against my bottom as I was leaning out of the window, whilst his hands were gripping me strongly around my waist. Ricky then made an inappropriate remark.

"This reminds me of the old times, especially when we..."

"Ricky!" I shouted out in horror! I could hear him chuckling slightly behind me to himself, so I threatened him, "I will kick you in the nuts if you don't shut up. Now focus!" The childish giggling from behind me abruptly came to a halt. I was amazed that even now, he was still trying to muck around. It reminded me of the time in the casino, in the air vent. Ricky was always one for bad timing, or joking about, no matter what!

"Reach out," I said to Hazel as I leant even further out of the window. I felt as if at any moment I would be able to hang upside down like a bat. Hazel raised one hand and securely had hold of my hand. "Now the other one." I encouraged. Hazel made the mistake of looking down.

I heard the guards grow closer by the second. "If you drop me I'll,"

"Oh come!" I puffed, "We don't have time for this." With that Hazel took the leap of faith and clung onto my hand for dear life. The height was dizzying, and I could feel the strain on my fingers, arms and back as Ricky and I began to heave Hazel up, and dragged her through the open window.

After we yanked her through the window, she was lying on the floor huffing and puffing, trying to catch her breath, whilst I stood bent over, and began to slowly straighten up again. The voices of the guardsmen could almost fill the room at that moment in time.

"The window!" Ricky jumped, and pushed past me, and leaped over Hazel as he almost slammed the window shut. He flung them harshly, and before the last second of them closing he shut them gently. He watched, and I listened, as the guards walked past underneath us, totally unaware of the dramatic strenuous exercise that had just taken place. When I knew that they had gone, I could have almost collapsed with relief and exhaustion.

"What took you so bloody long?" Ricky said whilst puffing out his chest. Hazel looked at him as if she was going to smack him.

"Oh, I'm sorry!" she sarcastically moaned like a child whilst picking herself up off the floor. "I had to climb trees!" As she said that she began to pluck piece of twigs and leaves out of her hair and clothing. "Oh darlings… my hair!!!" She whimpered!

"Never mind about that," I announced, "At least you got in. Well done. But we don't have that much time left."

"What?" Hazel frowned, and Ricky began to explain everything.

"We told the guard who was guarding this room, to take a break, so he has gone, and also it seems like Alana is expecting us at some point." Hazel then made a nervous gulping sound.

"Really?"

"Yeah. If you think about it, everyone who understands these coded messages has been killed so far apart from one, which is…"

"Alana Willows," Hazel finished.

As we crept out of the room, we made sure that the coast was clear so we could smuggle Hazel through the corridors and into rooms. She stuck extremely close to Ricky and I, and we were all ready to fire our weapons just in case the worst happened. We didn't know where to look for Alana. She could have been anywhere amongst the vast building, but we couldn't afford to enter every room in the building, just in case we kept bumping into guards, and we certainly couldn't kill any, just in case another guard found the body, which would raise the alarm, and then Alana really would be terrified, and make it impossible for us to get our hands on her.

"Where's the most likely place she will be?" Hazel asked as we all began to think whilst moving around. We didn't want to get trapped in a hall way so moving around was for the best.

"How about her study?" Ricky suggested. "She may have left a clue to where she is now, like a diary, plans or something"

"She doesn't have a study." Hazel answered back.

"What!?! A massive place like this and she doesn't have a bloody study!" he remarked in shock.

"No, instead she has a conference room, adjoined to that she has a small office area. We could check there?"

"It's a better place than any! Come on."

As we whizzed in and out, and around a corner, highly aware of our surroundings, we began to make our descent to the conference room. I wondered what sort of meetings Alana would hold. More than likely she would have meetings with other well-known criminals who were not to be messed around with, or even possibly meetings with her gang members. After all Alana's world was like the business world.

'*This is it.*' I thought to myself, gearing my mind and mood up, ready to make the kill, if I was the one to make it. *'I will kill her. I will watch every drop of blood leave her twisted body. Every last breath she takes is another one I'm gaining.'* I almost began to get into a competitive mood as I wanted the glory and victory of placing a bullet between her sour, bitter, dead-for-nothing eyes.

My heart stopped, as we all stopped outside a dark, demure, double doors, with gold rounded hand-knobs on them. The three of us stood still. Very still. We didn't move, look or even breathe for a moment.

"This is it, isn't it?" Hazel's voice shook as the enormity of this all daunted on us.

"Sure is," Ricky said whilst taking a deep breath in.

"The end of our journey, if she is behind these doors." I added. There was something sad about it, as we had had some crazy times, and grown close to each other, although at some point nearly killing one another. "Good luck everyone." We all took one final look at each other, just in case this was the last time we saw each other.

"One…" Hazel counted nervously.

"Two…" Ricky joined sounding slightly shocked we got this far.

"Three!" I bellowed whilst grabbing the doors, and flicking them open and rushing in with the others by my side.

There she was. Ms Alana Willows. Just sitting peacefully, looking at us will a dull expression on her face. Immediately I felt cold, as if something wasn't right. Why wasn't she scared? Why wasn't she doing anything? Why was she just sitting at the end of her conference table without a care in the world? The doors behind us silently closed by themselves. Nothing happened for a while. There was an awkward tension that filled the air, as Ricky, Hazel and I were holding our guns in the air aiming them straight at her. She then spoke, and her voice filled the clinical room.

"I did wonder when you'd show up." Her voice was nothing like I expected it to be. It was deep, rough, and gravelly. She sounded like a heavy smoker, like she had a chimney for a throat, but I heard the undeniable power she held in each and every word. Each word lingered, intermittingly. Her face was drawn, thin, and weary as if she hadn't slept for nights, yet she still looked professional. She seemed very slim, slimmer than Hazel. Alana was almost nothing of a human, it was like she was just skin and bones. So Pale! Whiter than a lily. Her smart, expensive, well-made jacket bulked her shoulders out a little giving her some shape. I couldn't get over how dainty she was. She was as thin as a piece of paper and I was sure if she turned sideways we'd lose her!

Alana spoke again, as none of us replied to her. I think we were speechless that this was the woman we were after, someone who looked so ill, puny and who looked years beyond her age. "What took you so long?" she questioned as if she was taunting us, as if we were lower than her. As if we were scum. She ran her long fingers through her long, hip-length, black hair. Then she slowly brought her hands together, and interlocked them, whilst placing her elbows on the table. She rested her bony chin on her skeleton-like hands and stared at us. Each move she made was meticulous, and frightening. "Well, come on then, someone speak. It's rude not to speak to the host." Her comments were rude, obnoxious, and began to fire me up, and if the other two were not going to speak then I was. I wasn't going to take any more lip from someone that already looked half dead.

"I have something for you." I spoke aloud and clearly. My voice almost echoed in the emptiness. I began to march over towards her. I was not going to act like a terrified school girl, I had a job to do, and lives to save. I charged up to her, passing eight black leather chairs which were in line with the dark black table that stretched down the centre of the room. The lights shone off it, and it would have normally distracted me, but I wanted to show Alana who was boss in this room. I wasn't going to let her walk over me like a brat.

As I reached her I slammed the note onto the table, then angrily bashed my iron-like fist heavily next to the note, forcing her attention towards it.

"Read it!"

Instead of reading it, her hollow, brown, almost black eyes gazed up at me. I could see the evil in her soul. Her eyes were something from a horror film, as if she had the devil eyes. She then smiled at me smugly, as if to say you can't make me, which enraged me to bursting point. "I said fucking read it!" I screamed at her like a drill sergeant, whilst shoving the end of the barrel of my gun against the back of her head and roughly pushing her head downwards towards the note so she had no choice but to read it.

I wanted her to make her start shaking in her boots, but she had the opposite reaction. She began to laugh. A laugh that was more like a witch's cackle. Alana seemed to be completely unhinged from reality. I looked at Ricky and Hazel in the far distance and they looked just as spooked and perplexed as I was.

"I wouldn't do that if I were you," Alana reasoned. "Remove the gun from the back of my head."

"Oh yeah!" I spat, slowly digging the end of my gun harder against her skull. I had the image of blood and brains spraying and exploding out the front of her face, making her nice clean table a bloody mess, and the coded message blood-soaked. She wouldn't be so sure of herself after that! "What are you going to do?" I snarled, sounding over confident with myself.

"Look up."

"No, I don't trust you," I confronted her bitterly. Then I heard a quivering sound come from Ricky's mouth from a far.

"Erm... Grace... do what she says." His face had turned as white as Alana's, and Hazel almost looked as if she was about to faint. I now didn't want to look up for another reason. What was so bad that made those two look like ghosts?

I slowly peered up. Extremely slowly. I still kept the gun pressed closely against Alana, and was ready to pull the trigger if I felt any sudden movement. I was faced with such a horrifying sight, I nearly dropped my gun. All along the top of the conference room were guards. Not one, not five, not ten! There must have been about fifty! My mouth dropped, as I felt all my blood rush to my feet. All the guards were aiming machine guns, riffles, shot guns, hand held guns in our direction. We were trapped, caught, stuck. I looked at Hazel and Ricky and they looked like they had given up. It was as if they thought the game was over. I wasn't going to give up so easily. I just wasn't sure what to do though.

"Be a good little girl, and remove the gun from my head," Alana said. I paused for a minute, not sure what to do and desperately trying to think of a course of action to take, but nothing came to me. "Do it now, or I will give them the order to rain bullets down on you and your friends." Reluctantly I did what she had requested. Alana then sat up straight, and adjusted her hair so it sat neatly down her back again. It was as straight as steel. "Give me the gun," she ordered, and I followed through. I handed her the gun, well, more threw it at her, but I suddenly felt very useless and helpless without a weapon in my hand. I hated this woman more than ever. If anyone was going to have her blood on their hands, it was going to be me!

Alana then spun round in her luxurious leather, wheelie chair and lent back in it, examining me.

"I like a woman that has fire in her stomach. Gutsy, and dangerous," she said admiringly, "You should join me Grace."

"HA!" I disgracefully laughed, looking at her with displeasure. "You must be insane, I wouldn't… wait." I suddenly froze in horror half way through my sentence. "How the hell do you know my name?"

"Oh I know all sorts about you Grace, same for your two assassin colleagues over there. Ricky and Hazel. A rather amusing team you three make, and when Tank and Gizmo were around, now that was something." I gritted my teeth as soon as she mentioned Gizmo and Tank's name. I didn't want to hear what she had to say about those two, in fact I didn't want to hear anything that was about to roll off her snake-like tongue.

"How do you know about us? What the hell is this about? Explain to me, what are these bloody codes about?" I demanded my voice rising aggressively through the sentences. I began to circle Alana, and as soon as I did I could hear the clicking and clunking of guns ready to fire. Alana stuck her arms up in the air and waved her hands downward signalling the guards to stand down for a moment. I started to walk about, showing her I was no longer scared, she was not going to have control over me, and I was going to have freedom and answers, whether she liked it or not. "Start talking," I told her sourly. Alana smiled at me as she was still admiring my die-hard attitude.

"You've impressed me. I will tell you everything. From the very beginning including why your parents died in that house fire a long time ago."

"What!?!" I froze on the spot immediately, as my heart sank. *How id Alana know my parents?'*

"Sit, and I will explain everything. You two…" She said loudly toward Hazel and Ricky, "come closer. You should all know, as you won't be alive for much longer."

"Want a bet," Ricky argued back.

"Oh, you're a funny one!" She rolled her eyes at him, "but I think you will find I have the upper hand here."

"You rigged the deck!"

"Oh Ricky, life is rigged! Nothing is fair in life. Think of all those people you have killed through your career. I'm pretty sure they didn't find it far when you killed them!" She exclaimed. Ricky and Hazel stood by my sides, as I sat. My heart wanted to know more about my family and what happened to them. It was almost as if I was about to receive closure after all these years. I had almost forgotten where I was and the fact that I was surrounded by death. Alana began to explain.

"I assume you all have heard the story about Lord Edward Hamston's engagement party many years ago, turning into a brutal blood bath, and all his family and friends were killed, and the love of his life was kidnapped and never seen again… only half of that is true."

"We've heard the story, yes." I said frowning in disbelief. "But, we believe Edward was a heart-broken man, bent on destruction because of it, for so many years. I don't understand why you think it's only half of the truth. He wouldn't lie to us like that. That story is the basis of this assassination business. It's how it all started."

"Oh no. Yes he was heartbroken, but for the wrong reasons!" Alana then stood up and paced whilst recalling the true version of the story. "You see, I am Edward's sister."

"What!?!" Choked Ricky as his jaw hit the floor. "Impossible, all Edward's family is…"

"Dead… yes, that's what he told you!"

"Does that mean, the people we have been told to kill are related to Edward?" Hazel questioned anxiously.

"No, we are not all related, but we were the ones to survive that dreadful night. Leo Blake was my partner at the time. We were married. Actually we got married at a very young age; we were only teenagers, but I started doing one thing and another, and ended up running this enterprise that I have today, and Leo… well… he could never keep it in his pants! He loved his women too much, and I hated him for it. He made me look like a fool. I believe you know how it feels Hazel…" Hazels eyes darted up at her, as she crossed her arms tightly across her body, as Alana then aimed the following comment at her. "He could never stop shagging about could he!" Her head dropped, as if she was going to cry, then Alana snapped, "You think you feel bloody pain! I had to live with my heart being broken every day and night, and the disgrace of him cheating on me with everything that moved! I did want to kill him, but I couldn't, so divorce was so much simpler." Her voice and body language looked like she was chatting away to her next door neighbour. Her erratic mood changes were concerning. "Mind you, credit when it's due. I loved the bloody mess you left my ex-husband in. It was fantastic. It made me cry with joy seeing him all bloodied up like that. Served him right." She smiled.

"You've been following us?"

"Keeping a close eye on you more like, yes. After the killing of Gabriel I grew uneasy, and suspicious, especially the way he died. The head shot that was achieved was not done by a newbie, and getting in and out of the building without a trace, or anyone seeing you was talented, but it had an assassin's scent all over it."

"Why did you change your last name to Willows?" Ricky asked, scratching his head.

"Because I like it, no other reason. Much better than my maiden name, Hamston, and I couldn't stand the thought of keeping my married name, Blake."

Ricky then shook his head, and asked about Gabriel.

"Oh, poor Gabriel. He was my favourite you know. In fact he was Edwards's best friend years ago. Great fella!" She swooned fondly.

"He framed his friends in a bank robbery," Ricky bit back.

"HAHAHA!" she cackled. "Oh no he didn't frame his friends, Christ! Gabriel may have been a lot of things, but he was a loyal friend. He framed some people that were members of the gang that slaughtered our family and friends. The gang didn't recognise who he was, so Gabriel befriended them, arranged the whole plan, and carried it through, and then ran off with the money, so he was able to own his casino. That was his ambition in life. It just made it even better and better for him when he got to stitch up a few old enemies in the process." I was amazed. When I was hearing the truth and learning more about these people we'd killed, I felt like I had got everything wrong in my head. I didn't understand anything anymore, and felt as if my mind was about to buckle.

Hazel then plucked up the courage to enquire about poor Oscar Brown.

"A-h-h-h, yes, indeed poor Oscar. He was one of the police office's that tried to help us, and did everything in his power to arrest gang members, and the boss of the rival gang. Edward and I at the time were very grateful towards him, and really appreciated all the hard work he had done, but Oscar being the perfectionist he was wouldn't let it drop. So he became our inside man on the police force, and would update us, or pass on any information linked to the gang." I couldn't believe that Oscar Brown was a snitch in the police force. I knew he was a good man, and was trying to help Edward and Alana as much as possible in a time of need, but I didn't have him down as a rule breaker among his work force.

"The drugs that I drugged Tank with really took effect! I didn't expect them to take effect to so quickly. Was rather fantastic."

"What?" I glared visciously. I wasn't sure if I heard her right. She dropped that information so casually into the conversation, as if it was nothing that important. Then Ricky fired questions at her.

"What did you do to him? Why did you do it? Who do you think you are?"

"One, thing at a time! I will explain everything when I get to it." Alana waltz about. She was so full of herself. It was as if she was torturing us all, and there was nothing we could do to protect ourselves, and there was no way to fight back. I wished that I had put a bullet straight through her head when I had the chance to. I sat, stewing, digging my nails into her chair, and trying to suppress the urge to attack her.

"Where was I... oh yes...? Leo, Gabriel, Oscar, Edward and Myself became like a family, but like most families we had our fall outs from time to time, and we started to do our own thing, and we ended up hating one another as years went by. Also there was a slight problem with mine and Edward's parents will. Because our parents hadn't made one the estate was never divided up properly. So the five of us decided to make an *'unbreakable deal'.*" At this point Alana hung her head, and sat on the edge of the table. It was as if she regretted agreeing to this deal idea. "The idea behind it was whoever was the last one to survive got everything: the money, estate, you name it, that one person would get it." She then stretched out her skinny arm, and swiped the piece of paper off the table, and looked at it, even glared at it.

"This, right here... is my piece of the deal. If you over lapped this piece of the paper with the rest, you will see that it would read our family motto."

"Let me guess… aut suavitate aut vi… either by gentleness or by force." I hazarded a guess.

"How did you know?" Ricky looked at me stunned.

"It's our motto for assassination school." I answered him feeling down hearted.

"Yes, you are right, although the message was the Latin version, and not in English."

"That could be why Gizmo couldn't crack the code," Hazel piped up again.

"I still don't understand why this has anything linked to my family," I glared with piercing eyes.

"I'm just coming to that part." Alana stood back up once again, her body looking frail and unwell. She then looked very closely at me, and started to walk towards me very slowly, which made me uneasy. It was as if I was turning into a mutant or something alien the way she was looking at me. "I can see it," Alana said making no sense.

"See what?" I spat in reply feeling more uneasy by the second, but my heart wasn't prepared to embrace what I heard next. "The family resemblance between you, Edward and your mother."

"WHAT!!!" I shuddered bolting upright. "No… no, you have got that wrong."

"Oh really?" Alana then took a closer look at me, and then glared straight into the pupil of my eyes. I could smell Alana's warm breathe; it stank of stale smoke. "The woman who was kidnapped was your mother!" Alana's tone of voice changed once again. It became dark, and full of dismay and shame. "You are nothing but a bastard of a child. Your life has been a lie, and you… you are my niece, unfortunately."

"No!"

"Edward was going to marry your mother, because she was pregnant with you. Yes Edward loved your mother, but he became obsessive over her, and overbearing, but he gave her his world, love, money, EVERYTHING!"

"No," I muttered to myself not being able to control my thoughts nor my feelings. I felt like I was being swept away in a sea of emotions and there was nothing I could do. Drowning in the confusions and lies I had been told for so many years.

"But your mother couldn't stand it anymore… some may say she was becoming scared of Edward's love… heartless bitch… if it wasn't for her Edward probably would have remained sane, and you would have had a normal life, a happy life, a life without living in the shadows. Think of all the death you wouldn't have caused. All the blood that stains your hands!" Alana smirked to herself, knowing that each word she said was like a bullet being shot into my mind, causing me unbearable pain, and emotional scars that would never heal. "But why have you been given this life that you live now… one simple fact…" Alana turned her back towards me, as she shouted, "BECAUSE SHE RAN AWAY WITH ANOTHER MAN!"

"No…"

"She left Edward whilst pregnant with you, and ran off with what you believe was your biological father." Then Alana gave me another look, a look that would stay in my mind forever. A look that was so evil. A crooked grin, squinting eyes, and screwed up nose, as if she was now staring at me like I was dirt. "Edward wanted you back in his life… god knows why… I told him not to bother… but he craved it. It was not the search for your mother that made him turn so cold towards the world, it was the search for you. It took time to find you and when we found out where you were living, Edward had some of his assassins tie your family up and set fire to the house."

"BASTARDS…. YOU'LL FUCKING DIE FOR THIS!" I screeched whilst flying up onto my feet. I quickly slammed my hand around Alana's bony throat with such a force that we flew backwards, and I then had her pinned against the walls. I heard clicking and movements of the guards above aiming and getting ready to fire, but I didn't care anymore.

"Why am I finding this out now? Why did Edward never say anything about this? Why did he tell everyone a lie?" Questions spurted viciously out of my mouth, one after the other without me noticing, nor registering what I was saying. The rage and fury within me had broken me finally, and I felt myself becoming careless. Once again it took Alana time to answer me; it was as if she was enjoying the fact that I was being tortured in such a manner.

"Maybe he didn't want to get to close to you; maybe you reminded him too much of your mother, I don't know, that's something you'll have to ask him... if you ever get out of here alive, which you won't you brat."

"How the hell can I ask him? He's bloody dead!" Again Alana allowed herself to let out her horrific cackle.

"He's not dead you silly girl, he's pretending. Think about it," She managed to say whilst laughing loudly.

"I know who ever is the last one to survive gets all the wealth and the rest of that shit, but he died. He may have sent Ricky, Hazel, Gizmo, Tank and I out to kill all of you because I would get it all."

"Don't be dumb!" Alana blurted out. "He may be your father, but he's not a nice man, he's vengeful too. He's got you doing all his dirty work. Now, I don't know what he's got on all of you, but you should have stopped a long time ago." My head hung knowing that that could never have been an option. Then I realised that he had poisoned me, his own daughter, to do all of this for him. I hated to admit it, but Alana was right about Edward being an evil man, but I couldn't or didn't want to believe that Edward had been hiding, and was alive all this time. Then a terrifying thought flashed through my tangled mind.

"Tank..." I murmured to myself, then I asked quietly, "Tank found letters and personal effects that showed him he was taken from his parents. Did Edward think he could have been his son? Is it possible Tank was mistaken as Edwards's son, instead of me being his daughter?" Alana was struggled to remain in the position that I had forced her in. "You need to start answering these questions more quickly. I want to know, if Tank could have been mistaken for an heir, and you best answer because I'm losing it now." Once again she did her normal trick of remaining silent with a horrible smug expression. So I decided to force answers out of her. I began to squeeze my hand tightly round Alana's neck, and began to lightly choke her, just as an incentive to get her to tell me more information. It was the least I could do for the memory of my dear old friend.

"I didn't know he found those letters, maybe the mixture of drugs that I gave him and the letters together would explain why he changed so quickly... was amusing to watch."

"Tell me!" I grasped my hands together around her skinny throat. I could feel her voice box, and her windpipe. Oh, how I wanted to crush it, and watch her suffocate to death, and choke on her own vomit.

"I was impressed... by your loyalty towards him though..." She began to find it difficult to talk as my hands carried on growing increasingly tighter. "You nearly risked your life to save his!"

"How do you know all of this?" Smirking she said one simple word. "Cameras."

I just stared at her. She was watching us through cameras! Why did it not occur to me to check the rooms or halls, although thinking about it if I did find any cameras I would have just assumed that they were Edwards's security cameras. The thought that this woman knew so much about me, and my past, and my life, disturbed me deeply. The thought that I spent the majority of my life hiding away, and making sure no one could follow my tracks, or catch me out all seemed to be a pointless way of acting. My life seemed meaningless and useless. Alana, within a few minutes, had opened my eyes to what the reality and the truth, really was. I didn't like it.

I then heard a struggling sound behind me. As I spun round I found Ricky and Hazel in the clutches of a couple of guardsmen. They both had their legs spread shoulder width apart, and held in a painful lock, whilst guns were place against their heads. My heart thumped as I glared back at Alana. I stood away from her, and watched her as she corrected herself.

"You have quite a temper, just like Edward has," Alana sniped. I could feel myself about to explode in fury, the only thing that was holding me back was now my two friends were held hostage. I couldn't think of how to have the upper hand, or how to exterminate, let alone live through this. I gazed upwards and looked around at the rest of the guards. "Shame, it's time for you to die now." Alana told me with a hint of joy in her voice, and then started to walk away, so she wouldn't get hit by any bullets.

I heard Hazel let out a whimpering sound, like a frightened puppy unable to contain itself. My mind was working overtime. I wasn't prepared to die now, especially after all of we'd been through, and being so close to finishing our mission. Then I saw that Alana had left my gun on the table. The only thing I could think of in the heat of the moment was to grab the gun, fire it at Alana's back before she left, then take cover under the table, and try to defend myself as much as possible. Bleak chances, but it was better than standing there like hung meat.

I focused myself, waited for a couple of seconds, then dived towards the table, rapidly swiping the pistol, and rolled under the table for cover. I was about to shoot Alana, but as I was too busy trying to protect myself, she got away just in time. I could just see the back of her make a quick getaway, and disappear around the corner of the door.

"Shit!" I swore to myself in frustration and fear. Before I knew it I could hear gun fire all around me. Ricky slid straight under the table by me, as I saw two guards drop to their knees, but to my horror Hazel's scream filled my ears. Her high pitched wailing seemed to last forever, and everything in my mind slowed down. I felt like I could have vomited with shock and horror when I saw Hazel's knees hit the hard floor. Her hands then followed. Even though the guards could clearly see Hazel had been shot down they carried on shooting. Gun fire still filled the air as poor, helpless Hazel lay bare as a target whilst bullets ripped through her. Next her body slammed against the ground, lying motionlessly.

"Oh God!" I shivered, screeched, and shuddered. Hazel lay there with her eyes still opened, looking straight towards me. I thought I could see her mouth slightly move as if she was trying to say something, but I couldn't make it out. Then, her beautiful pain filled eyes glazed over. No more breathing. No more screaming. Nothing.

I desperately wanted to reach out and pull her under the table and hold her bloody, shot-to-pieces body. I didn't want the warmth to vanish forever. I could feel tears erupt from my eyes, as Hazel's blood began to crawl out from her body, and flow toward my direction. Ricky was frozen solid, barely being able to breathe. "That's it!" I growled, suddenly feeling my killer instinct fill me to the brim. "I'm coming after you Alana!"

"How?" shrugged Ricky. He looked as if he was ready to give up, and sacrifice himself so he could end this nightmare.

"Stay close to me, and follow my lead. We are getting out of here!" I told him firmly. Ricky may have wanted to stop playing games, but I had only just begun. This kill now stood for much more than my own life and freedom. It stood for my parents who were killed by these monsters, my friends who had suffered a horrible fate thanks to them, and legacy.

The room fell silent as the firing of guns finally calmed down.

"Get down there now… you lot, find Alana and protect her." I heard a male guard's voice order above, shortly following vague sounds of feet scuffling, and mindless guards following orders. Ricky just looked at me. I saw fright in his eyes that filled his soul. I needed to get us out of this room and fast. It was hard to tell where the guards were standing, as I was not prepared to stick my head out, and have a quick look around. Then I noticed in Hazel's pale, dead hand closest to me, that she had held of a tiny mirror. It was slim and narrow, and was balanced on the palm of her hand. It was as if she was going to give it to us, to help us get out from under the table. It also made me realise that it was clear Hazel didn't think she was going to survive, or be able to move as fast enough.

I snatched the mirror as fast as I would praying that no one saw my hand quickly jerk out from underneath the table. I gave a final last look at Hazel's pain-ridden face. Her mouth was slightly apart, and eyes still wide and bare with an eerie look. I nodded my head towards her direction as if to say thank you, I wasn't sure why I did it, but it would have felt wrong if I didn't repay my gratitude. Ricky watched, intent on finding out what I was up to, but then the penny dropped, as I began to angle the mirror at different positions. To my delight I could see and figure out where the guards were placed around the top part of the room. They were all leering down, waiting in anticipation, as if they were on a hunt for helpless deer or rabbits. I started to whisper very quietly to Ricky the positions of where the guards were standing, and tried to paint a picture in his mind so he could visualise what I could see,

"There are two men on the right side of the room, two at the front, and one on the other two sides."

"Do you want me to take out the guard that's standing at the door which Alana got through?" Ricky suggested. It was as if his interested had picked up.

"Yeah, but first help me flip this table over onto its side." I told him. "We can use it as a shield. As soon as the table is over I want to take out that guard immediately, then we will try and pick the rest of the guards off one by one, or make a run for it when we get a break to do so." Ricky nodded in agreement.

I stilly looked at him, and calmed myself for a moment. Then I gave the signal to begin and to unleash the chaos. I nodded and as soon as I had done that Ricky and I with all our strength pushed as hard as we could, forcing the table to turn over. True to his word, and his reputation, Ricky shot one bullet, and before the guard had time to react the bullet ripped through his chest. Ricky then took out the other single guard to the right hand side with another single shot, this time to the head. I was impressed by his skills as a gunman. I then joined in with the killing feast.

I remembered roughly where the guards were. I managed to take one guard out, but the other guard had scattered about, and was now ducking behind the half wall. As Ricky started to take out the other two guardsmen, I took my time with this one. He was playing silly buggers, popping up and down and shifting about. I listened extremely carefully, which became easier to do when Ricky had killed the other two guards. I was waiting for the slightest sound, such as a foot scuff, or heavy breathing or anything. Ricky had not clicked onto the fact that there was still someone out there trying to kill us both. He began to kneel upwards to a standing position whilst starting to say, "We have…" I slapped my hand on his shoulder, and shoved him back onto the ground with a lot of force. With that, I saw the guard appear, and was about to take a shot at Ricky whilst he thought the coast was clear. I fired my gun twice or three times, one shot after another. The first shot missed, the second shot hit his shoulder, making him drop his weapon, and then the third was the killer shot as, the bullet tore through his stomach. I heard him groan, and then shortly after heard a thudding sound as he hit the floor.

I looked at Ricky and shook my head at him.

"Now we are done in this room." We both rose to our feet, cautiously. At any point of time another guard could appear from anywhere.

I carefully examined the room, to make sure it was empty, then took one last look at Hazel, so did Ricky. I could feel an anger, and a deep passion to finish this job burning in the pit of my stomach. Looking at Hazel's hole-ridden body made me feel sick, as her blood surrounded her. She looked like an island in the middle of the sea.

"I tried to drag her under the table," Ricky explained in a very quiet and soft voice. His bottom lip began to shake, as his face turned pale with guilt. "I just didn't manage to move her fast enough."

"It's not your fault," I told him placing a hand on his shoulder, comforting him. "But we can't stick around here for much longer. We have to leave her behind." The last sentence was incredibly hard to say and face. It didn't feel right to leave her lying there alone. There was nothing more we could do though. With the bullets tearing her body apart within seconds she didn't have much of a chance to survive. I looked at the mirror which I still had clutched in my hand. I held onto it tightly and hugged it, as if I was hugging Hazel herself. I then placed it into my pocket, turned, and walked away. It felt cruel and awful as I started to take paces away from Hazel's body, leaving her behind, but we had no choice. If I could have I would have taken her with me to the very end, but I was sure that now she was with Tank and Gizmo looking down upon us and wishing us the best, and maybe give us a godly helping hand here and there.

I heard Ricky move away from Hazel as well, as he closely followed. I shuddered suddenly as if I could feel Hazel's soul rush through me. My hair stood on end, and a daunting feeling washed over me, like a giant wave smashing on the shore line of a battered beach.

"We are coming after you Alana," I swore to myself. This had become such a personal mission; it was always dangerous to mix business with the matters of the heart, but now I couldn't help it. It seemed as if this whole deal was extraordinary person to me. As I approached the door that Alana fled out of I peered round the corner making sure the coast was clear, and was about to step out, when a heavy hand grasped my forearm. As I stared at my arm I saw Ricky's hand holding onto me, my eyes darted up rapidly as I glared at him. I was so eager to get going, and I wanted nothing to stop me.

"Think clearly Grace!" he ordered sternly. "You found out a lot of information right now. Just, fight with your head and not your heart."

"The bastards have killed my friends, and have killed my family."

"Do you think Edward is your biological father?" I didn't reply for a little while, and took a moment to answer, and then shook my head side to side.

"If Edward is, and he is alive, he won't be my father for long! I will kill him!" I threatened and made a promise to myself. This nightmare had to stop, and it wasn't going to stop after this final mission and retrieving the antidote. This mission for me will carry on afterwards.

I then turned my back towards Ricky once again, and began to make the brave journey forwards. I could feel my heart beginning to race, yet my hands remained steady, and my mind stayed focused on the job in hand. Ricky and I began the hunt for Alana covering one another's backs. Guards were dotted about randomly in corridors, and some guards were hidden in rooms and would jump out all guns blazing into the corridor. The halls began to flow with blood, and as I turn round another corner a guard was standing right up top of me. He went to fire his gun, but I kicked the back of his knee, and swiped him to the floor, making his gun fire upwards missing me. As he lay on the floor I shot him in the forehead, and watched his brains blow out of his head. I then stepped over the dead body, but the problem was that other guards heard the gun shot, and now another three guards were firing bullets down the dark, unlit corridor. Ricky, with his remarkable fast reactions, pushed me behind the giant base of a huge marble statue, and leaped to the other side of the corridor hiding behind an old fashioned bench that looked like it belonged in a church.

I caught my breath from the shock of being thrown to one side, but I was grateful. If Ricky hadn't done that, then my eyes may have not have been open any more at that moment in time. As I composed myself, I tried to picture where the gun fire was coming from in the dark down the other end of the corridor. The gun fire from the guards suddenly stopped, and everything fell deadly silent. I didn't even want to breathe just in case it gave away where I was hiding. I remained very still, with my back pushed against the giant, heavy base, and my knees close to my chest as I held my gun close to my body.

I suddenly saw an image flash through my mind, where I could make out where the gun fire was coming from. There was one man hiding behind a corner, another lying on the dark carpet to left, and another guard must have been hiding behind an object for cover. The flash of the gun fire gave their positions away. I decided to kill the guard who was lying on the floor; he seemed to be the easiest to take out first. I hoped Ricky would cover me, and if need be fire some bullets towards the guard's directions just on the off chance that he hit one of the guards to kill or at least injure. I braced myself, and then forced myself to suddenly bend round the base of the statue.

Suddenly I felt very open and vulnerable, but I didn't have time to acknowledge it. As I fired three shots, I could feel myself wince with anxiety and desperation, longing for one of the bullets to hit the guard that I was aiming for. In fact I would have been relieved if those three bullets hit anything. As soon as I fired my first shot the guards began to fire back at us, naturally, but on the third gunshot I fired I noticed that I had managed to kill the guard on the floor just by pure luck. I was hoping that the death of one guard, and the fact that they were under fire, would bring the other two guards out of cover.

Then I noticed Ricky had popped his head out beside the end of the bench that he was hiding behind, and he too joined me in the fire frenzy. I quickly looked round the base again, and I could see the guard who was using the wall as cover, was fairly open and was an easier target as he had to step out from around the corner to be able to fire his gun. As he fired a shot, I could figure out exactly where he was standing. I then took the shot, and fired a bullet in his direction. It was hard to tell where it hit him, but it definitely hit him, and killed him.

Then the gun fire suddenly stopped. I was under the impression that Alana had to be close by, because of the number of guards clustered together. I think Alana thought we wouldn't make it this far through her manor. I hoped with all my heart that she could hear the gun fire, and each gunshot made her shiver in fear for her life. I wanted her to feel the tension of the silence as well, in the hope that she would be lulled into a false sense of hope that it was all over. I could only imagine her heart ripping through her chest when the gun fire started up again. The thought of Alana hiding away somewhere desperately trying to survive, like a rat in a sewer, cowering and shaking in horror put a smile back on my face. I suddenly, once again, began to love my line of work.

Then suddenly I could hear an odd noise that wasn't gun fire. It was the sound of somebody running. As I looked round I could make out a faded silhouette of a guard trying to escape, and make a run for it across the corridor. I fired my gun, and amazingly I shot him in the leg. I watched him fall, and heard a thudding sound as he collapsed, howling groaning followed next. I then observed to my surprise that Ricky suddenly darted up onto his feet, and sprinted towards the man who was wriggling in pain on the floor. I watched for a couple of seconds in shock, then chased after him. I didn't know what he was up to. Ricky told me to use my head, and not act on the feelings, and yet he was charging up to this man, who still could have been armed. As we grew closer to the guard I could see his outline shuffling about on the ground. I couldn't tell what he was up to, until we got a little, and then noticed he was shuffling about trying to find his gun. Ricky spotted the gun straight away and kicked it to one side, well out of the reach of the guard.

"Where is she?" Ricky growled in a tough voice.

"Who?" the guard grunted, and spat out, as if we were pigs.

"Don't fuck me about any more buddy!" Ricky spat back, whilst booting this man onto his back. The guard let out another yelp of pain, followed by heavy breathing.

"I don't know!" he then replied, so I aimed my gun at his head, applying pressure on him to give us the answer, and once again Ricky asked the question.

"Where is she?" The guard remained silent. "Where is she or my friend will blow your bloody head off?" he coldly bargained. At that point the guard broke, and the tough exterior vanished like smoke in the wind.

"She's in her bedroom. Just through there." he said whilst covering his face with one hand, and pointing nervously down another corridor. My heart leapt with joy that Alana must have been able to hear everything. Then I frowned and thought it was odd of someone to hide in their bedroom. I didn't trust this guardsman but it was the only thing we had to go on to find Alana before she escaped, or we'd be playing hide n seek all night long!

"Thanks," Ricky hissed, as he walked past the man and me. The guard looked up and seemed to begin to relax slightly,

"My friend may show mercy, but I don't." With that I fired my gun, and shot another guard through the head without a second thought. I didn't regret it. Yes they were fellow humans, but we had no choice in the matter, and I wasn't going to be a push over with these evil men who worked for Alana. I was going to make sure I wiped out her whole work force so she was completely without protection and loyal fellow followers!

This was it. This was the big moment. I was going to make sure I killed her, and watched the life drain bit by bit from her eyes, as her soulless heart slowly came to a stop. I'd make her watch me whilst dying, so I would be the last memory and face she ever saw. I and Ricky snuck up to the door, quieter than a feather landing on a surface. I stuck my index finger up at Ricky to tell him to go no further. In front of us were two huge, dramatic door like the doors that led into the conference room. I noticed everything in Alana's mansion dwarfed me. I couldn't tell whether she had all these big, expensive, impressive items to show off her power and wealth, or whether it was to compensate for her puny, pathetic size.

I wanted to double check that Alana was in the room, and what I and Ricky may have to face in a few seconds. I crouched down, and peeped through a key hole in Alana's door. I could see Alana pacing back and forth nervously; clearly she was slowly admitting defeat and was unnerved. I couldn't blame her. It looked as if she had a mobile phone tightly grasped in her hand, which made me wonder who she had contacted, and if she had called for help or something along those lines. I was surprised that Alana didn't do much more to try and save herself. It just seemed too bizarre to hide away in a bedroom. I also saw two guards both standing up right, with barrelling, gorilla chests, and arms that were so muscly the veins seemed stick out a mile! I gently tapped Ricky on his shoulder and indicated that he needed to have a sneaky peek through the key hole. I wanted him to know what we'd be facing. That way we could be as prepared.

I signed to Ricky telling him that I'd take the guard on the left hand side, and Ricky should take the other. He nodded showing me that he understood what I meant. We both stood back from the bedroom door ready to kick the life out of the door, and go in all guns blazing. I began to count,

"One, two, three." On the count of three we both charged forward at such a powerful rate, whilst flicking our legs up, and hammered our feet into the door. The strength of my kick felt as if I could have dragged my body through the door, but it worked. They flung open faster than the guards could react. Ricky and I fired our guns at our chosen victims. Thud, thud… the guards fell and were no more. Alana looked horrified, wide eyes, mouth dropped open and began to move about frantically, not knowing what to do next.

"Was this really the best you could do?" I huffed placing my hands on my hips, showing her that I was no longer scared or intimidated by her, and that I was a woman set on killing her and nothing was going to stop me. "You're going to die Alana," I told her point blank. Alana's eyes busily looked at the guard's blood that had splattered up the walls and on some of her furniture. Their blood had started to dribble and drip onto the floor. The sense of satisfaction was overwhelming. Seeing the great Alana Willows struggle and panic like a mouse cornered by a cat was a beautiful sight to behold, and one I would cherish forever.

"Fine," Alana huffed, and finally gave up. "What has Edward got on you guys? You have killed about thirty of my men to get to me. This would have been a suicide mission for any normal assassin, like your friend, but you two managed it. You make a good team." There was something odd in her voice, she almost sounded sincere, which wasn't going to sway me, or make me take my eyes off her, but I could feel Ricky's eyes looking at me. It was that same look that he had given me a number of times, with his love struck eyes gazing and admiring, plus reminiscing about me and him. I then spoke loudly in a way that would snap Ricky back into the room.

"I don't care what you have to say Alana." All eyes were back on her now. "You are evil, and you deserve to die."

"Tell me this then, as I'm about to die," she said whilst slowly wandering about and sitting gently, perching herself at the end of her four poster bed, which had pastel pink and white swirled drapes hanging down either side of the bed. "Would you really kill someone you're related to?"

"I'm not related to you, and I never will be. I won't believe it ever. The good people that are my true family, will always remain my family. Nothing will change that."

"But surely there must be a part of you that craves to have a family now."

"I would rather die than have you as a member of my family."

"Well, what about lover boy standing right next to you." She winked in a perverted manner.

"Fuck you!" I screeched, whilst raising my gun and my voice.

"Grace, she's winding you up. She's playing with you, calm down." Ricky tried to reason with me, and I too didn't want to kill because she had angered me and got under my skin. I didn't want to give her the gratitude of knowing it too, but Alana kept prodding me for a more violent reaction.

"What will you do when you see Edward again?"

"He's dead," Ricky replied on my behalf, allowing me to calm down.

"You really think that, don't you? No, this is all his doing. He's just using you, and what will he do to you both after all your hard work, aye?"

I had, had enough of all of this now.

"Enough now Alana! You have had your fun and games, and said what you needed to say in a last ditch attempt to save yourself." I placed my finger on the trigger and aimed.

Without warning Alana moved, she pulled out a gun from under her bed and fired it at me. A body hit my body knocking me to the ground to safety. Ricky save me. He had thrown himself on top of me to protect me. I didn't move for a moment and just lay on the floor, completely confused and disorientated as to what had happened. Everything in the room remained extremely still for a moment. When I came to, I noticed Ricky and I had landed behind a sofa.

I carefully wriggled free from under Ricky, and then looked at him. He was injured. I saw his face reveal pain as he bit his lip intensely. I couldn't quite figure out what had happened to him, nor the extent of the damage he had been caused. My heart wobbled, and my nerves rattled to see Ricky in this state. It was not a sight I thought I'd ever see in reality. *'That's it'* I bitterly growled in my head. I heard Alana let out her horrible witchy cackle, as if she thought it was fun. I could see her feet approaching us both from under the sofa. I waited, and lay still, whilst having my gun lying on my chest, as I saw her feet stop moving. I was looking up at the ceiling, with my finger on the trigger, ready to fire, and kill!

The next thing that came into sight was the end of the barrel of Alana's gun. I held my breath and made sure I didn't mess this up, and tried to remain focused, and put my worries to one side for the time being. More of the gun slowly appeared, and then Alana's, long thin hair started to dangle over the side of the sofa; I saw Alana's face, peering down. Everything afterwards happened in slow motion, as my mind went into over drive and adrenaline took over.

I remember Alana's face looking amused at first and then seeing in horror that I was lying with a gun pointing straight up at her face. Alana struggled and tried to aim her gun at me and was about to fire it, but she was too slow. My gun already had sight of her and all I had to do was pull the trigger. A loud bang echoed through the room and seemed to ring in my ears forever. I watched carefully and eagerly, as I saw the bullet hit her face, and made an impact through her skull. I could almost hear the shattering sound as the bullet tore through her. As the bullet ripped through Alana's brain, I saw her eyes open incredibly wide, to such a point that I thought her eyes looked like they were going to fall out of her head. She let out a scream so high pitched it made my blood curdle. She began to move out of sight as the force of the shot sent her flying backwards.

The next thing I knew and saw was her feet and legs hitting the floor and then shortly after the rest of her body collapsed, which brought flash backs to Hazel's death. When I saw Alana's face from the other side of the sofa, I felt a great sense of achievement. I watched her life ooze from her body, her blood drain from her mouth and head, and I was the last thing she ever saw!

I stood up slowly, legs and hands shaking uncontrollably. I peered over the sofa and there she was. Alana. Her tiny body, lying as a bloody pile on the ground. I couldn't believe it. I had done it. I was the one that killed the fierce psychotic Alana. I kept staring in disbelief. It was as if I was expecting her to come back to life. I had gone numb, not knowing what to feel or do with myself.

"I...I...I'm free," I stuttered to myself feeling gob-smacked that at last the final assassination had been completed. I could imagine Hazel's, Gizmo's and Tank's faces, with delight and pleasure watching from above! I was rooted to the ground, not able to move or take my eyes off Alana still. It was certainly a moment in life that I would ever forget, no matter what.

Then I heard Ricky groan and moan in agony. I quickly snapped out of my daydream like trance and appeared by Ricky's side. I crouched down next to him.

"Ricky I'm here," I whispered softly into his ears. I held onto his hand tightly, which was hot and sweaty. He clutched onto my hand, with immense strength as his pain seemed to worsen.

"I've been shot," Ricky said forcefully, not really wanting to admit that this had happened to him. I suddenly panicked. It took a while for the words he had spoken to process through my mind. Ricky had been shot! I must have been so caught up in the moment that I hadn't realised the series of events that took place. Ricky must have taken the bullet that was intended for me. He had sacrificed himself.

"What... where?"

Ricky painstakingly moved my hand, which he still held, then lowered it to a part of his chest on his right hand side. I could feel his warm blood gush onto my hand where he had attentively placed it. As I removed our hands I saw the bullet wound; it wasn't good. The bullet had pierced him just under his lower rib. I felt myself suddenly turn white, as if all my blood had rushed out of my body. I felt slightly faint from the shock of Ricky being so badly hurt. I knew there when times were I wanted to hurt him, but now he was seriously in danger. I found myself wanting to cling onto him and not let go. At that moment in time I realised how much Ricky really meant to me. It was then that I learnt that my hatred for him might grow, but my love would never lessen. The heart-breaking thing was I could lose him any time soon, but I wasn't going to let that happen, not without a fight.

"Hang on Ricky, keep your hand here, and try and apply some pressure. I will be back."

"Where are you going?" he asked, sounding scared weak.

"Just over there, I'm going to find some stuff to help you, okay... I won't be far away from you I promise." Ricky gave me a slight nod, and did what I told him to do. I dashed around the room like a mad person. I stumbled across some of Alana's clothing and tore them up, so I could make bandages, to try and stop the blood flowing out of him. Then I saw a glass vase with flowers in it. I chucked the flowers to one side, and kept the water. I ran back over, and to my horror more blood had escaped is body. "Hold on," I told Ricky, then tried to distract Ricky by making him smile, as I joked, "This is the first thing you have ever done that I have asked you to do." I saw his familiar, comforting, cheeky grin appear on his face.

"Yeah, don't think I'll be doing it again anytime soon," he joked back. I was glad that he was still able to react with me in his usual manner.

I ripped open Ricky's top, and saw his chest pounding up and down as Ricky tried to breath. He saw I was in shock by how hard he was trying to breath, but Ricky being Ricky just gave me a naughty wink.

"Bet you miss this... bet you never wanted to give me up secretly because of my body!" he playful said whilst straining.

"Not the time!" I chuckled lightly. "Now try to breathe more slowly Ricky," I softly ordered him. It was important for him to have a steady breathing pattern.

"Never a good time with you!"

"Stop it Mr!" I tried to keep a calm and collected exterior, but inside my mind was going crazy as my emotions just wanted to make me cry. Eventually I managed to get him to slow down his breathing slightly, to make sure he was getting enough oxygen into his body, and to try and calm him down. I quickly rinsed the bullet wound, with the water from the vase.

"Grace," Ricky hesitantly muttered. I looked into his eyes. "You might have to pull the bullet out." My stomach turned, as I knew that removing a bullet would have no effect on him for the time being. He wasn't going to worsen with the bullet still lodged in his body. I didn't reply to Ricky's statement, and I carried on trying to wash the wound and stop the blood flow. "Let me say something," Ricky began to say as I tried to examine the bullet wound closely. "If I don't survive I really do love you with all my heart. I know you hate me at times, and I've been an arse, but we were made for one another Grace," he pleaded at me. At that point I could feel hot tears prick my eyes.

"I know," I told him. He out stretched one of his hands and gently touched the side of my face. At this point I felt a tear tickle down my cheek. Before the tear fell, Ricky wiped it away with his thumb. He slowly pulled my head closer to his, and placed his lips upon mine. It was the softest and sweetest kiss I had ever felt or experience, yet tragic and sorrow filled. I didn't want the kiss to break, but he pulled his head back, and smiled up at me.

"Come on then, carry on!" He laughed, but then began to wince and squirm in pain. He began to rapidly look paler and his eyes didn't seem so bright and full of life. He was growing weaker, as death approached him.

"I need to bandage you up now," I told him clearly, although I wanted to be sick. He just looked at me aimlessly. "It means I'm going to have to move you." I knew this was going to cause him great pain, and to possibly lose more blood in the process, but it had to be done. I felt as if I was going to put Ricky through the seven rings of hell! I gently wrapped my arms around him, and began to shift him towards the wall, to slouch him upright against it. Ricky tried to help me move himself with the very last little bit of strength he had left.

I began to cover his wound with the torn up pieces of Alana's clothes. I tried to do it as fast and effectively as I could. I then started to wrap long pieces of clothing around Ricky's body to hold the other pieces onto the wound with pressure. When I was done I examined my work to make sure it was good enough to try and keep Ricky alive for the time being.

"Let's get back to the estate," I told Ricky. He didn't reply and looked at me. His eyes began to grow wearier, and were slowly shutting as if he was going to go to sleep, but there was no chance I was going to let him shut his eyes. I wanted to keep him conscious for as long as possible. I was terrified that as soon as he shut his eyes, he may never open them again. I feared the thought of losing him. "There are more medical supplies back at the estate. I will be able to help you more then, but we need to get out of here." Each word I spoke was slow and piercingly sharp, as I wasn't sure at this point if he was taking in any information. He just looked at me, with half shut eyes, and with a drained, drawn face. "I'm not letting you go Ricky." I sternly told him, as I than began to put his arm around my shoulders.

I picked us both up onto our feet, and with the last bit of remaining energy Ricky tried to support himself, whilst clinging onto me, and tried to walk as fast as he could. As we made our way out of the manor, I saw the car hidden up the road. I wasn't sure whether to leave Ricky behind, run to the car, drive back and get him, or make him walk all the way to it. If I left him I was worried that he would slip into an unconscious state, but if I made him move about even more it would be burning more energy, which he needed to retain to try and keep his strength up as much as possible. I rapidly made the decision to leave Ricky behind for a few moments and go and fetch the car. I told him in very precise terms what I was doing, and ordered him to keep his eyes open, and remain as focused as possible, but as I looked at him I wasn't sure if he was going to be able to do it or not.

Reluctantly I placed Ricky on the floor, and was just about to run off when he whispered.

"I love you."

"I love you too," I replied, a hard lump forming in my throat. "Just hang on, I will be back in a second." I could imagine a second to Ricky right now, felt like a lifetime. I began to run as fast as I could. My legs pumped hard, launching me forward with power. Before I knew it I could feel my lungs beginning to burn, with the amount of air I was sucking up in one go, but I shoved the pain to the back of my mind and continued to soldier on. The thought that Ricky may not last long, sent a spin-breaking shudder through me, and spurred me on to run even faster than before. The car grew closer and clearer in my sight. As I approached it, I flung open the door, and was relieved to find the car keys still in the ignition! If they weren't, we really would have been in big trouble.

I rapidly started the engine, spun the car round, and drove towards where I left Ricky. I could see Ricky as he appeared in the headlights of the car. He looked as if he was nearly dead. I flung open the passenger door, jumped out, flung my arms round his body, and carefully put him into the car. I then sped off into the dark distance.

CHAPTER 13

A NEW ASSASSINATION

CRASHING THROUGH THE FRONT door to the mansion, I was amazed that Ricky was still alive. He was frail and limp, but I admired his courage to hang on in there. I'd like to think my presence gave him that extra little bit of strength to keep on fighting for his life, plus his stubborn attitude and determination would have a lot to do with that. I gently laid Ricky on the floor, as my body continuously, and mind-numbingly ached from the strain of carrying his heavy body around. I thought it would be best to retrieve the medical supplies, instead of forcefully dragging Ricky around the mansion. I wasn't even sure if I had the strength to lift him anymore, plus I didn't want to put him through any more pain. I think deep down, I had major doubts whether he would survive, and be alive by the end of this dreadful night.

I began to sprint off until I heard a strange noise. A slight sound of footsteps made me prick up my ears. I stopped dead in my tracks, only a few metres away from Ricky. I could hear Ricky tiresomely breathing and panting. As I peered round, examining every inch of the room I grew troubled. Something wasn't right. I could sense it. Someone else was here with us. '*Maybe it is the person with the antidote*', I hopefully thought to myself. I remained still and silent, but nothing. '*Maybe I'm going mad!*' I started to move away from Ricky again, then the footstep sound appeared again, but this time much clearer. It was as if someone was looking for us. This time I stopped and listened harder than before. The footstep sound grew clearer. My breathing was heavy with nerves, and I felt like my stomach had twisted with anxiety. Then the footsteps stopped. I held my breath, not moving an inch. Suddenly, a voice filled the horrible silence, nearly making me jump ten feet off the ground.

"Grace." A deep voice boomed and echoed in the entrance hall. "I'm pleased you're here." There was a cynical tone to the voice. As I peered up, I saw a bold silhouette in the darkness, standing at the top of the staircase. I squinted my eyes, trying to figure out who had approached me. The outline portrayed a body that looked slightly hunched. An average-looking build. Then my heart sunk in the realisation of who this man could be.

"No."

"Oh yes Grace." The frightening, fearful, familiar voice filled my ears, like water filling a glass and I froze on the spot in disbelief.

"No, you... you're... no!" I found myself gasping for air, and struggling to speak a word. I was sure at any moment I was going to faint, as I grew light headed and sick.

"You made it." The voice sounded cheerful, which was completely the opposite of how I felt by far. "I thought you would be pleased Grace. You have survived all this." I wanted to speak but found myself choking on words. The silhouette moved down the steps until he was standing in the moonlight which shone through a glass window.

Edward. Lord Edward Hamston. He was standing in front of me. I could see him as clear as day. From Edwards point of view I must have looked so startled, or as if I had seen a dead person, but in my mind I had! I didn't know what to do or think, or even how to react. I found myself completely helpless and lost. Was everything Alana said true? Bile rose within me, as I stared in horror.

"Say something then," He then heartlessly ordered. Nothing. It was as if I forgot how to speak. No words formed in my mind. I had drawn a blank. "I gather you're shocked... understandable." Something about his careless nature sparked something within me that brought me back to life.

"Shocked... understandable!" I found myself shouting out aloud, as rage took over. "You're supposed to be dead!"

"Ah, yes... well, I had to pretend to be dead."

"Because of you my life has been turned upside down. Nothing in my life is real, and those who were closest to me, and gave me some sense of reality have been taken away from me because of you!"

"I know that." Again, his voice was so relaxed, yet he still had a sense of vicious power.

"You have played your top assassins against your own family and friends. Your assassins where like your own children. You spent so much time and effort with each of us, and for what? So you can lay claim to all this..." I waved my hands aimlessly around in the air. "You did all this because of greed and power!"

"It's more than that Grace."

"How?" I spat. If words could punch, I would have knocked him out by now with the fury I was firing these words. "Alana told me everything. She said not to trust you. I didn't want to believe anything she had said, but all along that bitch was speaking the truth, and it's sickening."

"I did this all for you."

"Why?"

"You're my daughter."

I looked at him, and shock my head angrily.

"No, no I'm not." I wasn't going to accept the fact that this evil, horrid, wicked man was my biological father.

"Accept it Grace, you are my own flesh and blood."

"Why did you keep it a secret?"

"I wasn't sure at first. When you ran away we had a job tracking you down, but when I found you I knew it was you."

"Just shut up!" I couldn't handle it any more. None of this could have been real.

"I loved your mother you know... I gave her everything. I didn't want to kill her." I tingled with aggression. I wanted to kill Edward right here, and now.

"Not another word Edward! You have told me lies after, lies after, after lies. You have made us kill so many people for your glorification, and I have lost friends because of you."

"I did it for you," he repeated.

"What? How the hell can all of this benefit me?"

"This will all become yours someday." I saw his croaked lips form a smile, as his glassy cold eyes looked on. I had no idea how he expected me to react to this news, but I wasn't going to react in a happy way.

"I don't care, I don't want any of this," I sternly told him strongly standing my ground. "I want a normal life Edward. I don't want to kill any more. I want a life where I can have fun, friends, and love, all of which you have stolen from me for years. You have never given me a life, and me killing all these people so I can have money, and a big house, and whatever is insane!"

"Here," Edward muttered, not sounding pleased at all. "You've earned this." I was surprised he didn't make any remark to what I had just said. He threw down a small plastic bottle about the size of my thumb. I looked at it as it slid across the floor to me. "The antidote." My eyes lit up, and for a brief moment I forgot about everything. I swiftly swiped it off the ground, and downed the whole lot in one go. It had a bizarre taste, almost an aniseed taste that made me cringe. After swallowing it I caustionsly spoke,

"That's it… the poison has gone? I'm cured." Edward nodded and didn't say another word. I wasn't sure whether to trust him or not, but whatever was in the bottle gave me a moment of relief and hope. "What about Ricky?" I had almost forgotten about Ricky, as I was majorly distracted with everything else that had occurred. He lay motionless. Anyone would have thought he was dead, but I could just make out his chest moving up and down where he struggled to breathe. Edward didn't reply, so I repeat myself with urgency, "What about Ricky Edward?"

"There's nothing for him."

"What!?!" I then saw Edward reach into his pocket and pull something out. It was a gun.

"NO-O-O-O!" I screeched in terror, and started to run towards Ricky. BANG! By the time I was by Ricky he had stopped breathing.

"Oh god, no, please no… RICKY!" I cried out heartbreakingly, and threw myself on top of his body pleading that somehow he would come back to life. My head lay resting on Ricky's chest, as I wept uncontrollably. Tears poured from my eyes and onto his body. I had tried so hard to keep him alive, and Edward had undone all of my hard work. Edward had taken away the one thing I truly loved. "YOU BASTARD EDWRAD, YOU FUCKING BASTARD" I exploded, as I looked at Ricky's face, he looked so peaceful as if he was sleeping. Then in a softer tone, "Oh god, please help!" I kept whimpering, as my face grew hot with emotion, and my eyes let out my deepest of sorrows.

"There is no such thing as god Grace. We are gods. We decide who lives and dies. We control the life." I slowly lifted my head away from Ricky, still leaving my hands on his body, as his blood and soul trickled out of him. I didn't want to leave his side, and I didn't care if Edward shot me, because he was displeased with my behaviour.

"You're fucking mad Edward."

"No, not mad. I have a different way of viewing the world compared with other people." The fact that Edward had shot Ricky without a second thought proved his ruthlessness.

"I thought Ricky was like a son to you, in fact you both were so close. He told me that."

"Yes, well times change. I can't have my top assassin and daughter falling in love with some cocky idiot who can fire a gun."

"He's not a cocky idiot. This man that lies here is more of a man than you will ever be," I stated boldly with venom. "Ricky was a bloody amazing assassin, with strength, determination, a good heart and soul, and he was such a wonderful character too, and if you think I'm going to be your assassin or daughter you have another think coming Edward." I pulled out my gun, and then suddenly remembered Edward still had his gun aimed in this direction.

Bang! Another shot had been fired. A searing pain washed over my body, as I fell backwards and dropped my gun beside Ricky's body. A burning sensation pulsed through my arm as I yelped in agony. Edward had shot me! As I looked down to see what the damage was, I saw he had only shot my arm, causing me to drop my gun so I couldn't shoot him. As I peered back up, Edward had vanished like magic. I forced myself onto my feet, roughly grabbing the gun from the ground, and headed towards the stairs. Nothing. He had run off and escaped.

"I'M GOING TO GET YOU EDWARD!" I threatened, hating the fact he had escaped. "I WILL HUNT YOU DOWN, MARK MY WORDS!" My voice carried through the manor with hatred and meaning.

I lowered my gun, and hung my head, hoping that Edward heard what I had said, and wished he knew that they were not empty words. I had no more energy to run after him, and was in need of rest and to come to term with events, and accept what had happened. I wearily turned round to face Ricky again. My eyes once again filled up. I sat next to Ricky, and lovingly cupped his hand in both of mine, and held his hand close to my face. I tenderly kissed his hand and softly but pointedly spoke whilst tears fell from my eyes.

"I'll get him Ricky I promise. I swear I will get revenge. Not just for you and I, but for Hazel, Gizmo, and Tank too. He won't get away with this, I'll make sure of it. I will kill him, even if it's the last thing I do." I promised soulfully with an aching heart.

So here I stand now, alone, and with my own personal mission. I've told you my story, and what happens now… well… I'm not sure. I'm a free woman, but freedom is not much when you don't have a lot to live for. The only thing that will keep me going now is hunting down Edward. His days are numbered trust me! Each breath I take will only make me stronger, each step I take will only bring me closer to Edward, and each person I kill to get to him will help me get my own back for the lives he has snatched from me. Edward is running out of time.